Simply
Sexual

Books by Kate Pearce

The House of Pleasure Series

SIMPLY SEXUAL
SIMPLY SINFUL
SIMPLY SHAMELESS
SIMPLY WICKED
SIMPLY INSATIABLE
SIMPLY FORBIDDEN
SIMPLY CARNAL
SIMPLY VORACIOUS
SIMPLY SCANDALOUS

The Sinners Club Series

THE SINNERS CLUB
TEMPTING A SINNER

Single Titles

RAW DESIRE

Anthologies

SOME LIKE IT ROUGH
LORDS OF PASSION

Published by Kensington Publishing Corporation

Simply Sexual

KATE PEARCE

APHRODISIA

KENSINGTON PUBLISHING CORP.
www.kensingtonbooks.com

APHRODISIA BOOKS are published by

Kensington Publishing Corp.
119 West 40th Street
New York, NY 10018

All Kensington titles, imprints, and distributed lines are available at special quantity discounts for bulk purchases for sales promotion, premiums, fund-raising, educational, or institutional use.

Special book excerpts or customized printings can also be created to fit specific needs. For details, write or phone the office of the Kensington Special Sales Manager: Kensington Publishing Corp., 119 West 40th Street, New York, NY 10018. Attn. Special Sales Department. Phone: 1-800-221-2647.

Aphrodisia and the A logo Reg. U.S. Pat. & TM Off.

ISBN-13: 978-1-61773-417-5
ISBN-10: 1-61773-417-9
First Kensington Trade Paperback Printing: February 2008

eISBN-13: 978-1-61773-504-2
eISBN-10: 1-61773-504-3
First Kensington Electronic Edition: February 2008

10 9 8 7 6

Printed in the United States of America

1

Southampton, England 1815

Sara pressed her fingers to her mouth to stop from gasping as she watched the man and woman writhe together on the tangled bedsheets. Daisy's plump thighs were locked around the hips of the man who pushed relentlessly inside her. The violent rhythm of his thrusts made the iron bedstead creak as Daisy moaned and cried out his name.

Sara knew she should move away from the half-opened door. But she couldn't take her gaze away from the frenzied activity on the bed. Her skin prickled, and her heart thumped hard against her breasts.

When Daisy screeched and convulsed as if she were suffering a fit, a small sound escaped Sara's lips. To her horror, the man on top of Daisy reared back as though he'd heard something. He turned his head, and his eyes locked with hers. Sara spun away, gathered her shawl around her shoulders, and stumbled back along the corridor. She had her hand on the landing door when footsteps behind her made her pause.

"Did you enjoy that?"

Lord Valentin Sokorvsky's amused voice halted Sara's hurried retreat. Reluctantly she turned to face him. He strolled toward her, tucking his white shirt into his unfastened breeches. His discarded coat, waistcoat, and cravat hung over his arm. A thin glow of perspiration covered his tanned skin, a testament to his recent exertions.

Sara drew herself up to her full height. "The question of enjoyment did not arise, my lord. I merely confirmed my suspicions that you are not a fit mate for my youngest sister."

Lord Valentin was close enough now for Sara to stare into his violet eyes. He was the most beautiful man she had ever seen. His body was as graceful as a Greek sculpture, and he moved like a trained dancer. Although she mistrusted him, she yearned to reach out and stroke his lush lower lip just to see if he was real. His hair was a rich chestnut brown, held back from his face with a black silk ribbon. An unfashionable style, but it suited him.

He arched one eyebrow. Every movement he made was so polished, she suspected he practiced each one in the mirror until he perfected it. His open-necked shirt revealed half a bronzed coin strung on a strand of leather and hinted at the thickness of the hair on his chest.

"Men have . . . needs, Miss Harrison. I'm sure your sister is aware of that."

As he moved closer, Sara tried to take shallow breaths. His citrus scent was underscored by another more powerful and elusive smell that she realized must be sex. She'd never imagined lovemaking had a particular scent. She'd always thought procreation would be a quiet orderly affair in the privacy of a marriage bed, not the primitive, noisy, exuberant mating she'd just witnessed.

"My sister is a lady, Lord Sokorvsky. What would she know of men's desires?"

"Enough to know that a man looks for heirs and obedience from his wife and pleasure from his mistress."

She felt a rush of anger on her sister's behalf. "Perhaps she deserves more. Personally, I cannot think of anything worse than being trapped in a marriage like that."

His extraordinary eyes sparked with interest as he appeared to notice her nightclothes and bare feet for the first time. Sara edged back toward the door. He angled his body to block her exit.

"Is that why you frequent the servants' wing in the dead of night? Have you decided to risk all for the love of a common man?"

Sara blushed and clutched her shawl tightly to her breasts. "I came to see if what my maid told me was true."

"Ah." He glanced back down the corridor. "Daisy is your maid?" He swept her an elegant bow. "Consider me well and truly compromised. What do you intend to do? Insist I marry her? Go and tell tales to your father?"

She glared at him. How could she tell her father that the man he regarded as a protégé was a licentious rake? And then there was the matter of Lord Sokorvsky's immense wealth. Her father's seafaring enterprises had not faired well in recent years.

She licked her lips. His interested gaze followed the movement of her tongue. "My father thinks very highly of you. He was delighted when you offered to marry one of his daughters."

He leaned his shoulder against the wall and considered her, his expression serious. "I owe your father my life. I would marry all three of you if such a thing were allowed in this country."

"Fortunately for you, it is not," Sara snapped. His face resumed the lazy, taunting expression she had come to dread. "As to my purpose, I thought to appeal to your better nature. I wanted to ask you not to dishonor my sister by taking a mistress after you wed and to remain true to your vows."

He stared at her for a long moment and then began to laugh. "You expect me to remain faithful to your sister forever?" His eyes darkened to reveal a hint of steel. "In return for what?"

"I won't tell my father about your dishonorable behavior tonight. He would be so disappointed in you."

His smile disappeared. He stepped so close his booted feet nudged Sara's bare toes. "That's blackmail. And there's no way in hell you would ever know whether I kept my word or not."

Sara managed a small triumphant smile. "You do not keep your promises then? You are a man without honor?"

He put his fingers under her chin and jerked her head up to meet his gaze. She found it difficult to breathe as she gazed into his amazing eyes. Why hadn't she realized that beneath his exquisite exterior lay a deadly iron will?

"I can assure you, I keep my promises."

Sara found her voice. "Charlotte is only seventeen. She knows little of the world. I am only trying to protect her."

He released her chin and slid his fingers down the side of her throat to her shoulder. To her relief, his air of contained violence dissipated.

"Why didn't your parents put you forward to marry me? You are the oldest, are you not?"

She glanced pointedly at his hand, which still rested on her shoulder. "I'm twenty-six. I had my chance to catch a husband. I had a Season in London and failed to capitalize on it."

He curled a lock of her black hair around his finger. She shivered. His rapt expression intensified.

"Charlotte is the most beautiful and biddable of my sisters. She deserves a chance to become a rich man's wife."

His soft laugh startled her, and his warm breath fanned her neck. "Like me, you mean?"

Sara stared boldly into his eyes. "Yes, although . . ." She

frowned, distracted by his nearness. "Emily might be a better match for you. She is more impressed by wealth and status than Charlotte."

"You possess something neither of your sisters has."

Sara bit her lip. "You don't need to remind me. Apparently I am impulsive and too direct for most men's taste."

He tugged lightly on the curl of her hair. "Not all men. I have been known to admire a woman with drive and determination."

She lifted her gaze and met his eyes. Something urgent sparked between them. She fought a desire to lean closer and rub her cheek against his muscular chest. "I think I will make a far better spinster aunt than a wife. At least I will be able to be myself."

His lazy smile was as intimate as a caress. "But what about the joys of the marriage bed? Might you not regret sampling those?"

She gave a disdainful sniff. "If what I have just seen is an example of those 'joys,' perhaps I am well rid of them."

His fingers tightened in her hair. "You didn't enjoy watching me fuck your maid?"

Sara gaped at him.

His smile widened. He extended his index finger and gently closed her mouth. "Not only are you a prude, Miss Harrison, but you are also a liar."

Heat flooded her cheeks. Sara wanted to cross her arms over her breasts. She trembled when he stepped back and studied her.

"Your skin is flushed, and I can see your nipples through your nightgown. If I slid my hand between your legs, I wager you'd be wet and ready for me."

Sara's fingers twitched in an instinctive impulse to slap his handsome face. She waited for a rush of anger to fuel her courage, but nothing happened. Only a strange sense of waiting, of tension, of need—as if her body knew something her mind hadn't yet understood. She let him look at her, tempted to take his hand and press it to her breast. Somehow she knew he would assuage the pulsing ache that flooded her senses.

As if he'd read her thoughts, he reached out and circled the tight bud of her nipple. Sara closed her eyes as a pang of need shot straight to her womb.

"Sara. . . ."

His low voice broke the spell. She covered herself with her shawl and backed away. As soon as she managed to wrench the door open, she ran. His laughter pursued her down the stairwell.

Valentin stared after Sara Harrison as his shaft thickened and grew against his unbuttoned breeches. He absentmindedly set himself to rights and considered her reaction to him. She needed a man inside her whether she realized it or not. Perhaps he should reconsider his plan to marry the young and oh-so-biddable Charlotte.

His smile faded as he followed Sara down the stairs. John Harrison had a special bond with his eldest daughter. Knowing Valentin's sordid history, would John allow him to marry his favorite child? It was interesting that she hadn't been offered to him as a potential bride to begin with.

He strolled down one flight of stairs and made his way back along the darkened corridor to his bedroom. There was no sign of Sara.

Valentin surveyed his empty bed and imagined Sara lying naked in the center, her long black hair spread on the pillows, her arms open wide to welcome him. He frowned as his cock throbbed with need. Sara Harrison would not be a complacent wife. To lay the ghosts of his past, he needed to settle down with a conventional woman who would present him with children and leave him to his own devices.

Before leaving town, he'd spent an uproarious evening with his friends and current mistress, composing a list of the qualities a man required in a society wife. One of her sisters would definitely be a better choice. He suspected Sara would be a challenge.

Her frank curiosity stirred his senses. He'd wanted to part her lips and take her mouth to see how she tasted. He'd forgotten how erotic a first kiss could be, having moved onto more interesting territory a long time ago. Her innocence and underlying sensuality deserved to be explored. Wasn't that what he truly craved?

He stripped off his clothes and let them drop to the floor. The meager fire had gone out, and coldness crept through the ill-fitting windows and door. At least he had a few days' grace before he needed to make his decision. John Harrison was not due to return to his family until Friday night. Valentin climbed into bed. His brief, interrupted tryst with the enthusiastic Daisy had done little to slake his desire.

Valentin tried to ignore the unpleasant smell of damp and mildewed sheets as he closed his fist around his erection and stroked himself toward a climax. Imagining it was Sara who touched him made him want to come quickly. He didn't allow her image to destroy the sensual buildup of sexual anticipation that burned through his aroused body.

He pictured her startled face as she'd watched him fuck Daisy. Had she wanted to touch him herself? The thought made him shudder. His body jerked as he climaxed. He closed his eyes, and a vision of Sara's passionate face flooded his senses.

His last thought as sleep claimed him was of her coming under him as he took his release deep inside her again and again.

2

Sara glanced over her shoulder as Charlotte's girlish giggle rang out again. Whatever Lord Sokorvsky had said was obviously highly amusing. She resisted an urge to frown at the engrossed couple. She'd asked him to pay more attention to Charlotte and had no right to feel disappointed because he'd heeded her words. In truth, she should be delighted. She took a savage swipe at a buttercup in the grass with her parasol and decapitated it.

Daisy, her maid, had been ecstatic about Lord Sokorvsky's prowess in bed. Apparently he was the best lover Daisy had ever had. She'd gone on and on about the size of his cock and exactly what he could do with it until Sara begged her to stop.

Surely a true gentleman would make love to a woman with more gentleness and civility? Lord Sokorvsky reminded her of a swaggering pirate. Even his skin was tanned like a commoner. And the way he'd rutted with Daisy . . . She ignored the subtle throb of desire she experienced low in her stomach every time she pictured that rude coupling.

She sighed as she reckoned the distance to the ruins of the medieval castle on the hilltop above them. Her mother had arranged the outing in the hopes of furthering Charlotte's acquaintance with Lord Sokorvsky. To Sara's surprise, her plan appeared to have worked.

She lifted the hem of her olive-green calico skirt and set off up the last part of the hill. Someone touched her elbow. She turned to find Lord Sokorvsky at her side.

"Good afternoon, Miss Harrison. Are you enjoying the view?"

Sara favored him with a cool smile, aware of the heat of his gloved fingers on her bare skin. "Good afternoon, my lord. The view was delightful until you obscured it. Please feel free to find another, less able lady to assist up the hill."

His fingers tightened on her arm. "But I wish to walk with you. You left me in a devil of a quandary last night."

She shot him a suspicious glance. "I am glad you have reconsidered your options and that I was able to guide you."

He looked politely confused and then gave her a slow smile that screamed danger. "I'm not talking about your little moral lecture but something far more important that kept me up," he glanced down at his breeches, "and awake for most of the night."

Sara kept her gaze on the ragged yellow grass in front of her. Did he think she was naive enough to ask him to explain himself?

"You are far too modest, my dear. Would you not like to know what I am referring to?"

Sara counted each torturous step and tried to control her ragged breathing. Her temper smoldered as the slope grew steeper.

"No."

"I was thinking about your breasts." He glanced at her

averted profile. "If I might be even more specific, I spent several hours wondering what color your nipples are. Some women's nipples match the color of their lips, others are a surprise. Now, your lips are a deep rose pink. Are your nipples the same shade?"

To her annoyance, her nipples hardened into two tight buds as if they enjoyed being discussed. She continued to slog up the hill, refusing to join in such an insulting conversation. An urge to shove her outrageous companion in the chest and watch him roll merrily down the hill threatened to overcome her.

Lord Sokorvsky laughed softly as they reached the outer ring of fallen stones. "Silent, my dear Miss Harrison? That seems so unlike you. Perhaps you are breathless after our steep climb."

She stepped back and planted the tip of her parasol in the center of his chest. She met his amused violet eyes, a challenge in her gaze. Before she could apply any real force, Lord Sokorvsky brought his hand up and yanked the parasol from her grasp.

"Oh, no, you don't."

Deprived of her weapon, Sara cried out as she lost her footing and fell forward. He caught her in his arms and deliberately pulled her flush to his chest. The strength of his muscled grip surprised her. His heart thumped against her cheek as she struggled to right herself.

"Are you all right, Sara?"

Charlotte's anxious question made Sara jerk herself free. Lord Sokorvsky's triumphant grin disappeared as he turned to speak to her sister.

"All is well, Miss Charlotte. Your dear sister felt unwell after her exertions." He bowed to Sara, a picture of concern, and placed his hand over his heart. "I am simply glad that I was available to help a beautiful damsel in distress."

Sara straightened her bonnet. "You, sir, are no knight," she hissed as soon as her sister's back was turned.

His eyebrow rose in a slow arc. "I never said I was. And if you choose to challenge me, don't expect to be treated like a lady."

She swung on her heel and stomped off across the grassy mound of the ruined bailey to find better company. This was the second time Lord Sokorvsky had bested her in a fight. Should she ignore him for the duration of his visit and hope he made the right decision about Charlotte or continue to try to influence him? She couldn't decide.

She glanced sideways at him and found he was still watching her. His gaze settled on her breasts. Blast the man, all she could think about was him coupling with Daisy. He winked. Sara resisted an urge to button her pelisse.

A dense heat shuddered through her belly. He unsettled her in ways she didn't quite understand. Part of her, the wild, dangerous part she tried to suppress, was drawn to him; the rest wanted to run back to the safety of her boring life and hide. With all the determination she could muster, she began to talk to her sister Emily.

Sara spared a smile for her dinner companion as she rose from the table at her mother's signal. Sir Rodney Foster was an entertaining and clever man. He treated her like an intelligent woman. It was a shame he was already married. She stifled a yawn as her mother shepherded the ladies into the drawing room. Thick red velvet curtains blotted out all the natural light and created shadows in the overfurnished, fussy room.

Tea awaited them, with the prospect of a little musical entertainment and a lot of idle gossip. Sara often wondered what it would be like to stay with the men and discuss matters of real importance over a glass of port. As she matured, she'd begun to understand why men avoided coming in to see the ladies until they were foxed.

Sometimes she felt so trapped she wanted to run out of the

stuffy drawing room and never return. She often dreamed that her mother and sisters stood over her, their faces full of love as they slowly suffocated her beneath a growing pile of petticoats. Despite her considerable abilities, she had begun to understand that her choices had narrowed to spinsterhood or marriage.

She glanced across at Charlotte. Her sister had appeared in her room again last night, her face flooded with tears. Charlotte claimed Lord Sokorvsky frightened her and that he made her feel stupid. If it wasn't for her mother's objections, Sara knew Charlotte would already be married to her childhood sweetheart, the local curate, rather than chasing a man of Lord Sokorvsky's exalted rank.

Charlotte gave her a watery smile. Sara felt a familiar surge of exasperated affection. Why couldn't she simply say no to their mother and do what she wanted instead? Surely Lord Sokorvsky wouldn't want a wife who'd been forced into marrying him?

After an hour of insufferable boredom, Sara was even glad to see Lord Sokorvsky enter the drawing room. He was dressed in a simple blue coat and white breeches that clung to his muscled thighs. His thick, dark hair was confined at the nape of his neck with a narrow black ribbon.

Exactly how long was his hair? Sara's fingers twitched to untie the ribbon and touch his luxuriant locks. She imagined it unbound, curling onto those broad shoulders. She folded her hands in her lap and stared down at them as Lord Sokorvsky came closer.

"May I get you some tea, Miss Harrison?"

Sara looked up, which gave her a perfect view of the bulging front panel of Lord Sokorvsky's tight-fitting pantaloons and his flat stomach above.

"No, thank you, my lord."

He continued to study her. "You look well in that gown,

Miss Harrison. With your strong coloring, you are wise to avoid the pale colors debutantes often prefer."

She glanced down at her rose-red gown and suddenly felt naked. "I'm no debutante, but thank you, my lord. I didn't realize you were an expert on fashion, as well."

Without asking for permission, he sat beside her. "When you've helped as many women as I have out of their clothes and back into them, you form some opinions."

Sarah opened her fan with a snap. She must stop baiting him. Every time she tried, he trumped her efforts with the skill of a professional card shark. The sound of a harp being tuned saved her the necessity of replying.

To her consternation, Lord Sokorvsky continued to sit by her side as several young ladies performed with varying success on the harpsichord and harp. He stretched out his legs, and his long thigh touched hers. There was no space for her to move away, so she suffered the intimacy in silence.

Sara applauded Charlotte's dutiful if uninspired performance and glanced over at her mother. Surely it was time to end the dreadful evening? Lord Sokorvsky caught her hand as she attempted to rise.

"Miss Harrison, are you going to perform for us? How delightful." He linked his arm through hers and towed her inexorably toward the harpsichord. Sara's mother frowned and shook her head.

He sorted through the music and placed a double sheet in front of her. "If you are unsure of the notes, Miss Harrison, I'll sing along and try to drown you out."

Her mother sat down again, a false smile pinned to her lips. Sara began to play and immediately lost herself in the music. To her delight, Lord Sokorvsky had a pleasing baritone voice that blended well with her husky contralto.

A smattering of applause brought her back to the present

and the realization that Lord Sokorvsky was smiling at her. Well, not exactly at her—his gaze had dropped to the low lace-edged bodice of her gown.

"Damnation," he murmured, "pink or red? I'm still not sure. . . ."

Sara tried to stand, but he handed her another piece of music. "Play this for me. I'm sure it's well within your capabilities."

She glanced at the Mozart concerto and began to play. The storm of applause that greeted her performance made her blush and hurry to her feet. She avoided her mother's eye as she gathered up the music. The chattering guests drifted out of the drawing room, leaving her alone with Lord Sokorvsky.

He took the pile of music away from her and stacked it neatly on the table. "You play like an angel. Why does your mother disapprove?"

Sara covered the harpsichord and blew out the candles. "Because she believes I play too well, and that is not ladylike."

"She's a fool. With your talent you might perform professionally."

She gave him a guarded smile, aware that they were the last people in the room. "Ladies do not do that. I was quite disappointed when my mother told me I couldn't continue my studies abroad. Even when I begged my father, he refused to agree with me."

He laid her hand on his sleeve and led her toward the double doors into the hall. "I should imagine you were more than a little disappointed. You probably made your displeasure known for weeks and drove your father to distraction. You strike me as a little spoiled."

Sara laughed to disguise her annoyance. "I really can't remember how I felt, my lord. It seems so long ago." She attempted to disengage her arm as they approached the doorway.

Before she could manage it, he pulled her behind the door. He pressed her against the wall; his body covered hers completely.

She bit back a scream as he stared down at her, his vibrant eyes full of heat. Every inch of his lithe, hard body was pressed firmly against hers. His mouth feathered her lips, and his tongue sought admittance. He kissed her slowly until she learned to kiss him back. When he drew away, Sara opened her mouth to speak.

"Shhh." He stroked his index finger across her full lower lip and continued the movement down her throat. She swallowed hard as his finger came to rest on her ruffled bodice.

She closed her eyes as he delved beneath the warm silk and exposed the tip of her breast. The rush of cold air on her heated flesh felt like ice on fire. His finger circled the tight bud of her nipple, and she shivered.

"Ah . . . deep rose pink. Like raspberries and cream." His approving murmur made her want to touch him, to beg him to touch her. In the hallway behind them she could hear her mother exchanging pleasantries with one of the departing guests. He leaned closer, and she opened her eyes to find herself viewing the top of his head.

He cupped her breast through her bodice, forcing her rounded flesh to overflow her corset, and licked her exposed nipple. Sara bit down hard on her lip. Who would have known that such a small thing could bring such pleasure? He did it again, more strongly, and then sucked her nipple into his mouth.

Instinctively Sara arched her back and tried to give him more. She kept her hands fisted at her sides in a desperate attempt not to grab hold of his head and hold him there forever. His teeth grazed her, and she couldn't hold back a whimper of pure need. This wasn't right, but it felt so good. From the moment she'd watched him with Daisy she'd wanted him like this.

He brought his head up and stared at her. He dragged down

the other side of her bodice to reveal her other breast. "Spoiled and possibly shameless. If you were mine, I'd sit you on my lap every morning. I'd fondle and suck your breasts until you begged me to stop, until they were swollen and sensitive with need."

He returned to torment her until it felt as if she would explode. When he lifted his head, his breathing was ragged.

He studied her taut nipples. "Imagine how they'd feel against the lace of your gown and your corset. All day long, every time you took a breath, you'd remember my mouth on you." He slid his knee between her legs and pressed against the silk of her dress. "By the time I came to your bed, you'd be desperate for me to finish what I'd started. You'd be begging me to fill you with my cock."

Sara forgot about her mother and the servants. She could barely remember her own name. She shamelessly rubbed herself against the firm pressure of Lord Sokorvsky's knee wedged between her thighs. Somehow it seemed to relieve the ache that had built there since she'd caught him with Daisy. As she moved, another, more frantic sensation grew instead. Her body was poised on the edge of something, but she didn't know what.

Lord Sokorvsky rolled her nipples between his fingers and thumbs. "If you looked at me like that, Miss Harrison, I might have to visit you during the day and fuck you on the dining table. Would you enjoy that? Would you like my cock filling every inch of you?"

His casual crudity made her stare intently at his face. Was he punishing her for interfering in his courtship of her sister? He ground his hips against hers, and she forgot all about her family. Her body warmed to his touch; her nipples ached from his attentions. She wanted to climb inside his clothes and lick his skin.

He dragged her hand down to his groin. "Can you feel what you do to me?"

The thick rod of his erection stirred under her hand. She

wanted to unbutton his breeches. She wanted him to stop tormenting her and give her whatever it was she needed. He spread his hand over her buttocks and lifted her until she fitted against him. His mouth returned to plunder hers. Then he abruptly stopped.

Sara pushed him away and scrambled to pull up her bodice. She'd completely forgotten Lord Sokorvsky was expected to propose to her sister tomorrow. How could she have behaved so brazenly? He was her sister's intended. She still wasn't even sure if she really liked him!

"My father is due back tonight. Do you intend to inform him of your decision then?"

Lord Sokorvsky helped rearrange her bodice. His knuckles constantly brushed her sensitive flesh. "My decision?"

Considering her tumultuous state, Sara was amazed she sounded so calm. She drew in a deep, steadying breath. Damnit, he was right about the delicious friction of her aroused flesh against the fabric of her gown. "About marrying Charlotte. I'm sure he will be delighted."

He drew back and offered her his arm as they moved out from behind the door. "As to that, Miss Harrison, I haven't quite made up my mind about Miss Charlotte."

A familiar dry voice rang out from the hall and startled Sara. "I'm glad to hear it, Lord Sokorvsky, because if that is the case, you seem to be displaying an interest in the wrong sister."

She ran forward to hug her father, who waited at the bottom of the stairs in the deserted hall. He looked tired, and his greeting to her was distracted. Sara resisted the temptation to pat her flushed cheeks and check her bodice. Did her father know what she and Lord Sokorvsky had been doing?

"Sir, it is good to see you again." Lord Sokorvsky strode forward and offered his hand to Sara's father.

"Valentin, my boy, come into my study and share a glass of brandy with me." He turned to Sara. "Go to bed, my dear. And a word of advice: try to avoid being left alone with young men until you are suitably married."

Sara smiled at her father and kissed his cheek. He understood her so much better than her mother did. She curtsied to Lord Sokorvsky, who bowed. Her last sight of them was as her father firmly closed the study door.

Valentin took the glass of brandy from John Harrison and cradled it in his hands. Thank goodness he'd heard the carriage approach or he might have been discovered doing something far too intimate with his host's eldest daughter. There was no denying that Sara stirred his blood. He glanced down and hoped John hadn't seen the extent of his arousal as he approached him in the hall.

He waited until John took the chair opposite him. His old friend looked tired and drained. His once abundant hair was thinning, his eyes sunken.

Valentin raised his glass to his host. "Thank you for inviting me to your home."

John grimaced as if the brandy tasted spoiled. "You know why I asked you here."

Valentin hid his hurt beneath another smile. He'd never been invited to meet John's family before. He was considered too dangerous. "Of course. You want me to marry one of your daughters. Preferably the youngest, if I recall."

"You've done well for yourself, Valentin. Your shipping business prospers."

"With Peter's help."

John drained his brandy glass. "You should rid yourself of Peter Howard, my boy. He does nothing to help your reputation."

Valentin smiled again, although the effort this time was greater. It was an old argument, one he grew weary of discussing. "I owe Peter the same debt of gratitude I owe you. Without him I wouldn't have survived." Images of the lush, repellant brothel he and Peter had escaped threatened to flood his mind. With the ease of long practice he pushed them aside.

"I did not offer Sara to you as a bride, yet you seem taken with her." John hesitated. "Sara is exceptional. Yet I fear she wants too much from the world."

"Because she is a woman?" It irritated him to hear John belittle his daughter. It was not surprising Sara felt stifled. Needing something to do, Valentin got up and added more brandy to both glasses.

John nodded. "She would've made a fine boy. All that intelligence and drive, wasted on a female. I admit I am to blame for her lack of docility. I allowed her too much freedom as a child. I encouraged her to pursue her studies in both music and arithmetic." He drank from his glass. "My wife insists I have made Sara discontented and unwilling to behave like a proper young lady."

"She seemed perfectly ladylike to me, sir."

"Sara will require careful handling. I see her marrying a much older man who is willing to tolerate her eccentricities."

Valentin drew in a breath. "Am I too young and repulsive for Sara, then? Or do you fear my 'interesting' past will taint her innocence and make her worse?"

John flinched and avoided Valentin's gaze. "You are a good man, Valentin, but . . ."

"After what you know of me, you don't want me to marry your favorite daughter." Valentin shot to his feet. "Well, I regret to inform you that she is the only one who interests me. If I can't have her, I'll pay off my debt to you in another way."

He left the study before he said something he might regret. The brandy burned a hole in his stomach. John Harrison had rescued him and Peter from a life of erotic slavery in a distant barbaric country. To his credit, John had never revealed to another soul exactly where he had found the two young Englishmen. His being enslaved for seven years was enough for most people to consider Valentin an oddity. Twelve years had passed since his rescue, and yet he felt as sick and vulnerable as his eighteen-year-old self.

It was obvious that the man he'd admired for over a decade didn't consider him fit to mate with his favorite daughter. He knew just how desperate John's financial state must be if he'd even considered him suitable for the other girls. The man hadn't quite masked his disgust at the thought of Valentin touching one of his precious children, although, to his credit, he had tried.

Valentin loosened the knot of his cravat. Christ, he wanted a bath, but it was far too late to disturb the servants. He paused at the bottom of the stairs and considered saddling his horse and disappearing into the night forever.

Turning, he walked back through the deserted kitchen and let himself out into the back garden. He fumbled in his pocket for a cigar and lit it. Should he abandon his visit? The cloying scent of honeysuckle invaded his nostrils and clashed with the smell of brandy and cigar smoke on his breath. He'd always hated strong fragrances. They reminded him of the lush per-fumed bodies of the customers he'd serviced, willingly and un-willingly.

In the distance, the lap of the sea against the shore stirred his overwrought senses. He moved sharply away from the long brick wall that bordered the garden. Would he ever be able to shrug off the rumors and innuendo about his life with Peter in a Turkish bordello?

For a brief while after his rescue by John Harrison, he and Peter had become reluctant celebrities. The release of two Eng-lish boys after years of captivity had fascinated the nation. To his annoyance, the newspapers still found it necessary to allude to his scandalous past whenever they mentioned his commer-cial success. Thank God they didn't know the full story or he and Peter would be considered social pariahs.

After finishing his cigar, he turned back to the crumbling stone manor house. Perhaps John was right. Sara deserved a better husband. He pictured her slender figure in her rose-pink gown, her black hair braided high on her head in a shining coronet. He'd sensed her frustration, her desire to be free, and had deliberately offered her one way to relieve some of that tension.

Her eager response to his touch had unmanned him. Even now, a wave of lust shuddered through him. She didn't have the sexual experience to realize how strongly he was attracted to her.

Perhaps it was just as well.

A single tallow candle illuminated the somber grandeur of his bedchamber. Valentin strode to the window and drew the thick brocade curtains. A moth flew out of the fabric, drawn by the flickering candlelight. From the ramshackle state of the house, it was obvious that John needed money. The family lacked sufficient servants, and he'd noticed Sara and her sisters wore unfashionable, well-mended gowns. He was also convinced that Charlotte had no desire to marry him at all. Was she being forced into considering him by her rather overbearing mother?

He frowned. Was it possible that John was in danger of losing everything? If so, his desire to protect Sara from Valentin might cost him dearly.

Valentin caught the circling moth between his finger and thumb and pinched hard. Damnation, he'd leave a draft from his bank that should see John through the worst of his debts. He'd also try and forget his ridiculous notion that he was capable of sustaining a marriage.

3

As soon as she reappeared downstairs after breakfast, Sara was summoned to her father's study. Her mother's anxious air and the nonappearance of Lord Sokorvsky at the breakfast table had made her nervous. Had her father dismissed him after witnessing their far-from-casual embrace on the previous evening?

She smoothed down the skirt of her best blue muslin day dress and patted her braided hair. When her father bade her enter, she half expected to see Lord Sokorvsky, but he was absent. Her smile disappeared. Had he left without saying goodbye? Her mother followed her into the room and shut the door. She nodded at her father, but he didn't respond.

"Sit down, Sara, there is something we wish to discuss with you."

After a wary glance at her mother, Sara sat.

"Lord Sokorvsky has asked for your hand in marriage."

She stared at her father, uncertain she'd heard him correctly. Why did he look so grim, and why did her mother appear triumphant?

"I, of course, declined his offer. I consider him a far more suitable partner for Emily or Charlotte."

Why? What was wrong with her? Her heart beat an unsteady rhythm. "And did Lord Sokorvsky agree with your decision?" She had to ask. She couldn't decide whether to feel affronted by his offer or delighted that he'd chosen her over her sisters. At least Charlotte would be pleased.

"No," her father muttered. "He declined that honor."

Sara half rose from her chair. "I assume he is leaving us then?"

"Unfortunately, my dear, the situation is not quite that simple." Her father rubbed his eyes and put on his spectacles. "Your mother has very properly reminded me that I have little choice in this matter."

Sara glanced at her mother.

"What your father is trying to say, my dear, is that he desperately needs money. He can't afford to let Lord Sokorvsky walk away."

Sara didn't need to ask her father if this was correct; she could see the truth of it in his anguished face. She studied her clasped hands, which had started to tremble. Valentin wanted her? A mixture of joy and trepidation rushed through her veins. She was being asked to ensure her father's financial survival by marrying a man who both intrigued and excited her. Heat flooded her senses even as she tried to look grave and composed. At last she had the chance to experience life beyond the stifling world defined by her mother.

"Lord Sokorvsky's family is very well connected." Sara's mother was still talking. "He has ties to both the Russian and British nobility. His mother was actually a real princess, can you imagine it! You would be in line for a very exalted position in society. I should hope you wouldn't forget your sisters when you are in a position to help them marry well. . . ."

Sara shot to her feet. "Of course I'll marry him, Father. I consider it my duty."

She wanted to laugh as her body rejoiced at the mere thought of being bedded on a regular basis by Valentin. During his short but exciting visit, he had forced her to see herself as a woman who needed to be touched by a man.

Her father's shoulders sagged, and he covered his face with his hands. "Perhaps you would like to find Lord Sokorvsky and tell him of your decision. I believe he is breakfasting in his bedchamber."

In the deserted hallway, Sara picked up her skirts and twirled around until she felt dizzy. When she'd regained some composure she headed up the stairs. At the door to Lord Sokorvsky's room, she hesitated. She'd never gone into a man's bedroom before. It was not at all proper. Why had her father sent her up here alone? It was almost as if he were too ashamed to face Lord Sokorvsky himself. Shouldn't her marriage be a joyous occasion?

She tapped on the door and opened it. Lord Sokorvsky sat on the side of his bed pulling on long black leather boots. His blue waistcoat was unbuttoned and his cravat untied. Her hands curled into fists.

When he saw her, he rose to his feet and bowed.

"Miss Harrison."

"Lord Sokorvsky."

Sara advanced into the room. Sunlight patterned the faded carpet and made the dust motes dance. He didn't seem particularly pleased to see her. In the bright morning light he looked older, harder, and less amenable. Doubt flooded her bright certainty. How could she broach the subject? She opened her mouth to speak.

He turned his back on her and strode to the mirror to tie his cravat. She watched his deft fingers assemble the intricate folds and knots and secure them with a diamond pin. He caught her gaze in the mirror and held it.

"Miss Harrison, if your father sent you here to beg money from me, you can tell him—"

"Sir, he did not!" Sara interrupted him. It was suddenly imperative that she had her say. "He sent me to accept your proposal of marriage."

His fingers stilled on his cravat, and he turned to face her. "He did what?" His smile returned, the one that always seemed to mock her. "Damnation, he must be more desperate than I thought."

Sara stiffened. How dare he assume that about her father? "You are mistaken, my lord. He succumbed to my pleas to marry you. I was the one who begged."

"And what about your loyalty to your sister, Charlotte? Is she laid down weeping on her bed because you have poached her potential husband?"

She found herself glaring at him. "Despite your inflated idea of your own importance, Charlotte is in love with someone else."

He strode toward her, and she resisted the temptation to step back. He placed his fingers under her chin and tilted her face up until he could see into her eyes.

"You begged for me?"

"Why would I not? You have shown me the delights of being a woman." Sara stared back at him. Her bold words were not entirely a lie to protect her father's reputation.

"By God, I'll make you beg."

He lowered his mouth to hers. She whimpered as he thrust his tongue inside her mouth. Overwhelmed by the rough texture of his tongue and teeth, she grabbed hold of his shoulders to anchor herself against the raging storm of his assault. He dragged her closer until they touched from mouth to toe. His erection pressed hard against her stomach. She fought a mad impulse to wrap her leg high over his hip, push against him, and echo the pulsing rhythm of his tongue with her entire body.

He drew his mouth away from hers and held her at arm's length. "Miss Harrison, will you do me the honor of marrying me?"

She gazed at him and imagined spending the rest of her life in his bed.

"Yes, Lord Sokorvsky, I will."

4

"Drat this gown!"

Sara reached behind her and attempted to untangle the laces of her wedding dress. Through the bow window that overlooked the tranquil park of the old country house, darkness crept toward her. Her new husband had every right to expect her to be undressed and waiting for him in bed by now. Close to tears, she tugged at the pearl-trimmed bodice and tried to pull her arm clear.

"May I help you?"

She clutched the silk fabric to her breasts. In the mirror she saw Lord Sokorvsky's reflection. He still wore his navy-blue wedding finery, which deepened his eyes to a darker violet and provided a perfect contrast to his tied-back hair and handsome features.

To her mother's immense disappointment, and Sara's relief, the wedding had been a quiet affair at the local church attended only by her family and two of Valentin's business associates.

Sara attempted a shrug. "I sent my maid away. I wanted to undress myself."

A frown creased Lord Sokorvsky's brow and then cleared. "Of course, I should have realized. Your mother must have sent Daisy with you." He came toward her, his shadow darkening the carpet between them.

"Well, I could hardly ask my mother for a different maid without offering an explanation." It had been a long day. Her tone was sharper than usual, her patience nonexistent.

"Did you fear Daisy might offer you some unwanted advice?" He stepped closer and studied the back of her lavender silk gown.

Sara shivered as he traced the curve of her bare shoulder with his fingertips. "I have received enough advice from my mother and my aunts to send me screaming from you in horror."

He caught her tangled laces and tugged hard enough to bring her back against his chest. The lace of his cravat itched between her shoulder blades. His knuckles brushed her skin as he worked to free her. "And what exactly did your mother tell you?"

"That I should lie still, hope you finished quickly, and pray for many children so that you would keep away from me."

His soft laughter stirred the hair at the exposed nape of her neck. "And is that what you want?"

He turned her to face him, his eyes steady on hers. She felt breathless. "No, it's not. I have this strange desire to lick your skin and crawl all over you."

His eyebrow went up as he lowered his gaze to her partially exposed bosom. "That is very enterprising of you. Are you sure you are still a virgin?"

She went to cover herself, but he caught her wrists. "And if I wasn't? Would I disgust you?" She stared at the front of his tight white satin pantaloons. "I would wager you aren't a virgin."

He followed her gaze and lowered her right hand until her

palm was flattened against his erection. "That's the reason I ask, my dear. I am reputed to have a very large cock. You could never disgust me. But if you are a virgin, your sheath will be tight."

His frankness about carnal matters no longer surprised her. In truth, she found it reassuring and curiously liberating. On the rare occasion she'd seen him in the four weeks since their betrothal, he'd kissed her repeatedly and murmured a litany of the sensual delights that awaited her in his bed.

Even after he let go of her wrist, she kept her hand pressed to his groin. A steady, hot pulse thrummed under her fingers as she caressed the cool satin.

"Surely there are ways . . . to help my body accept you?" His cock throbbed and grew again. She widened her fingers, desperate to capture every inch of him.

"There are many ways, and I intend to use them all. By the time I enter you properly, you'll be so desperate to have me inside you you'll hardly notice any pain." He stepped back and studied her, his expression intent. "When you play the harpsichord, what do you think about?"

His abrupt change of subject confused her. "I think about the music, the way it flows through me." She half smiled. "Sometimes I forget who I am."

He nodded and took her hand. He turned it palm upward and kissed it. "Then do something for me tonight. Forget you are a well-brought-up young lady and pretend you are the instrument I will play upon. Allow me to use your body as a conduit for the beautiful music we shall create together."

She smiled at his confidence and withdrew her hand. "Show me, then, for I am eager to learn."

He helped her to step out of her gown and petticoats, leaving her dressed in her loosened corset, thin muslin shift, and gartered stockings. Under his gentle guidance, she seated herself at her vanity table. He removed his coat and waistcoat and stood behind her. She felt his fingers in her hair, gently teasing apart the curled and braided strands of her elaborate hairstyle. She sighed as the last pin was removed and stretched her neck.

He took up her brush and started to comb out her hair. "I didn't realize your hair was so long. It's almost to your waist."

Sara leaned back into the long, steady strokes of the brush. "The hairstylist you sent from London wanted to cut most of it off this morning. He insisted it was most unfashionable."

"I'm glad you didn't listen to him. I can't wait to see it fanned on the pillow beneath you." He stopped brushing, and his fingers worked on her loosened corset laces. "If you take this off, I'll be able to continue more easily."

She let him slip the corset from her body and then resume his brushing. Her eyes threatened to close as she luxuriated in the soft sounds of the bristles moving through her hair. After four frantic weeks dominated with wedding plans, dealing with her mother, and an elusive bridegroom, she was ready to drop with exhaustion. She jerked awake when Valentin drew her hair over her shoulders and passed the brush over her nipples. He continued the stroke from collarbone to hip until she wanted to purr.

Her nipples poked out through the thin muslin like unripe berries. Valentin caught her gaze in the mirror. He circled the tip of her right breast with the handle of the brush, making her shiver.

"Do you like that?"

She nodded as he increased the pressure and then transferred his attentions to her other breast. Her breathing quickened. Valentin put the brush down.

"Then you'll like this even more."

Still standing behind her, he slid his hands down from her shoulders and cupped her breasts. Sara licked her lips as he rolled her nipples between his fingers and thumbs. Heat seared straight to her womb. She resisted the urge to squeeze her legs together.

Her head fell back against his torso, and she encountered the thickness of his shaft against her cheek. She turned and nuzzled the satin. His fingers stopped moving over her breasts and then pinched hard. She nudged him again, tried to bite. His whole body shuddered.

"Not yet, my dear." He stepped away from her. "We've a long way to go before you're ready to take my cock in your mouth."

She studied him carefully, but he didn't appear to be joking. Why on earth would any woman agree to do that?

He knelt in front of her and picked up the hairbrush again. She frowned and caught his wrist.

"You have hair here, too, Sara," he said, smiling. "I need to attend to all of you."

Cool air glided over her thighs as he inched her shift up to her waist. She locked her knees together in an unconscious barrier.

"Let me in. I swear I will not hurt you. And if I do anything you don't like, just tell me and I'll stop."

She forced her knees to relax, felt the cool linen of his shirt against her inner thighs as he moved between her legs. He touched the brush to the curls covering her mound. Sara closed her eyes and listened to the soft scratch of the bristles. Lord Sokorvsky's warm scent rose up to engulf her senses.

His finger replaced the brush, flicking lightly at the swollen bud that guarded the entrance to her woman's secrets. She resisted a sudden urge to grab his hand but whether to stop him or make him to move faster, she didn't know. When she touched herself like this, it never felt so intense.

As the pad of his thumb continued to circle, his middle finger slipped inside her. She suppressed a gasp as pleasure rolled over her.

"You are wet. Your body is preparing to welcome me despite your fears."

Sara opened her eyes and looked down. Her mother always said her unladylike curiosity would be the death of her. Lord Sokorvsky's attention was fixed on the slow inward glide of his finger. A soft sucking sound punctuated the silence as he probed her sheath.

"Is it normal to be so wet down there?"

"Of course. Your pussy wants my cock. Your cream will ease my way and make it more pleasurable for you."

His frank, matter-of-fact answers about sex made Sara relax. She suspected she could ask him anything and he'd answer her. He eased a second finger alongside the first. She tensed but found her body eager to accept him, willing to stretch.

He knelt up, his fingers still working her, and brought his mouth to her breasts. He licked one nipple through the filmy muslin and then drew it into his mouth, suckling in time to his thrusting fingers.

Sara's hips pushed up from the chair as she fought to increase the pressure of his hand against her. She knew something dangerously pleasurable awaited her, but she wasn't sure whether she wanted to embrace it or run from it.

Lord Sokorvsky added a third finger. All sense of self-preservation fled as Sara's attention centered on the luscious sensations he provoked. She strained to meet his thrusts, grinding her mound into the welcoming, waiting palm of his hand. Her hands crept up to his broad shoulders, and she dug her nails into his muscled flesh. She gave a frustrated cry as the sensations she could only imagine refused to flower.

He raised his head, his smile teasing. "This isn't a race, Sara, we have all night." He rubbed his thumb against her lower lip. "In truth, we have the rest of our lives to learn how to pleasure each other."

He winced as she dug her nails in harder. "But I want to know, my lord, I want to know why some women fear this and others dream of it."

He smiled then and looked down to where his fingers disappeared inside her. "My name is Valentin; you of all people have the right to use it. And don't be so impatient. By the time I've finished with you, you'll not be afraid." He got to his feet and pulled her up with him. "Help me take off my shirt."

Sara grasped the heavy linen at his waist. It refused to budge. She considered the fastenings of his pantaloons and tugged at the buttons. He trapped her hand against the bulging front panel.

"Do you feel my cock, Sara? Does it please you?"

She studied the impressive thick rod outlined in his pantaloons. "I'm not sure, my lord, I mean, Valentin." She bit her lip. "It seems rather large to fit inside me."

He brought her hand up to his mouth and kissed her fingertips. "I'll fit. You'll make room for me."

His confidence inspired hers. She tackled the buttons of his pantaloons and allowed the front flap to fall. To her disappointment, his full shirt covered his torso. He worked on his diamond cuff links and dropped them onto the dressing table with a careless clatter.

"Come." He took her hand and led her toward the large canopied four-poster bed that stood in the center of the magnificent room. He bent his head. "Pull my shirt off."

In the light summer darkness, his skin was bronzed and rippled with muscle. Curling brown hair covered his upper chest and narrowed over his flat stomach. Unable to stop herself, Sara reached forward and traced a small crescent-shaped scar under his right nipple.

He shuddered and leaned forward, trapping her between his hands, the bed, and his large hot body. Sara kept her mouth closed as he kissed her until his teeth nipped at her lower lip. Her palm was pressed to his chest, and she could feel the thump of his heart.

Without speaking, his hands closed around her waist, and he lifted her to sit on the high bed. Sara tried to balance herself as he pushed her thighs wide with his broad shoulders. The feel of his hard, muscled flesh against her inner thighs made her want to groan.

She shivered as his tongue traced her navel and headed south. He spared her an intent glance. "Take off your shift. I want you naked." She struggled out of the garment and braced her hands on the bed. He made a soft sound of approval against her most intimate flesh.

"You're very wet now. I like that. I'll make you wetter, though."

Sara felt the first gliding pass of his tongue over her sex and almost fell off the bed. Her already aroused flesh felt as hot and vulnerable as an open wound. It was nothing like the fleeting warmth she felt when she touched herself. How could he give such pleasure with just his mouth? She gripped the embroidered bedcover in her fists as he continued to lap at her.

When he sucked her swollen bud into his mouth, she forgot all about being a lady and groaned and thrust her hips forward in time to his urgent pressure. His fingers joined his mouth, pressed upward into her tight sheath, and widened her for his entry, making her wet and ready.

Sara managed to unclench one of her hands from the bedclothes and wrap it in Valentin's long hair. Her left foot crept up to his shoulder as she strained against him, keeping him close, craving the tight, hard slam of his fingers and mouth.

He moved faster now, the wet sound of his fingers and mouth in rhythm with her moans. He groaned against her clit, sending delicious shivers to her womb, dragged his unshaven chin up and down her pussy.

"Come for me, Sara, take your pleasure." His voice sounded hoarse as he set his teeth gently on her inner thigh. She could hardly hear him, so intent on gaining her release, so desperate to explode with the unknown feelings he created in her.

"Come for me." Harsher now, his fingers ramming into her as she strained desperately against him. And then, even his voice faded as a roar of excitement flooded her and sent great pulsing waves of pleasure from her womb to her breasts and back down to her toes in an endless circle of delight.

When she opened her eyes, she lay on the bed. Valentin lounged next to her, his face still wet with her cream. He buried his head between her breasts. She inhaled the scent of her own arousal as it warmed her skin.

He gazed down at her. "I told you you would enjoy it, and we haven't finished yet."

Sara sat up, already realizing that he still had more clothes on than she did. "Shall I help you with your pantaloons?"

Valentin's boots fell to the floor with a thump. "Yes, but be careful. My cock is primed and ready to come."

She was careful as she pulled his pantaloons down and tossed them onto the carpet. She crawled back up the bed to study Valentin's monstrous erection. His cock had to be at least eight inches long and was very thick at the base. At the tip, Sara noticed a bubble of clear liquid. She touched it, rubbing the moistness between her fingers.

"You are wet, too. Does this help ease your way?"

He nodded as another pearl of liquid formed and slid down to coat his already glistening cock. "Touch me again."

Sara gulped and wrapped her fingers around the base of his shaft.

Valentin sucked in a breath and laid his hand over Sara's. He was both amused and intensely stimulated by her innocent sensuality. Despite her inexperience, she seemed unafraid.

"Have you seen an aroused man before?"

He asked the question before he considered the implications of her answer. The thought of her appreciating another man's cock was too infuriating to be contemplated.

Sara slowly shook her head. Soft hair trailed across his groin, adding to the urgent thrust of his need.

"Only you with Daisy." She half smiled at him. "And even then I didn't see," she squeezed his shaft, "this."

Valentin showed her how to slide her fingers up and down his shaft. She pushed herself into a kneeling position. He admired the sway of her breasts and the curve of her narrow waist as she unconsciously rocked against him.

As his excitement built, he took her other hand and cupped it around his balls. She was breathing faster now, her grip on his cock exquisitely tight, almost to the point of pain. The rhythm was irregular, and her nails dug into his most tender flesh. It didn't matter. He always enjoyed finding the extreme edge of passion.

He disengaged his fingers and allowed her to work his shaft alone. Sliding one arm around her buttocks, he urged her closer until her breast swung against his cheek. He drew her nipple into his mouth and suckled hard.

Sara moaned as he slid two long fingers inside her sheath and thrust in time to his mouth and her pumping fingers. He felt his balls tighten and his come travel up his shaft. With a groan, he managed to release Sara's nipple before he bit too hard. He came in hard, pulsing waves, his hot, thick seed flooding out over her fingers.

When he sat back on his pillows, Sara still had her hand wrapped around his now flaccid cock. He raised an eyebrow.

"Have I shocked you?"

She released his cock and stared at her soaked fingers. "I didn't know that would happen." She brought her index finger to her mouth and gave it a tentative lick. Valentin's shaft jumped in an instinctive response.

"You taste like the sea." A smile curved her luscious mouth. "At first I thought I'd done something wrong. Then I realized you were groaning with pleasure, not pain."

His shaft thickened at the sight of her pointed red tongue licking his seed. He imagined how her mouth would feel sucking his cock.

"You are a very unusual virgin."

She glanced at him, her expression uncertain. She pressed her hand into the sheets and wiped her fingers.

"Have I displeased you? I forgot, I am supposed to be an innocent maiden who couldn't possibly be interested in such matters."

"Why should you think that? Do you imagine I looked forward to bedding a woman who couldn't understand that sex is enticing and exciting and irresistible?"

He wrapped his hand around her neck and brought her face-down to his level. "I want you to enjoy our marriage bed. I want to know that the thought of it makes you wet and aroused. I want you to want me."

His newly erect cock jabbed at her stomach. He pulled her down and rolled her onto her back. She stared at him as he fanned her hair on the pillow. When he touched her knees, she obligingly opened her legs. He pushed them wide, eager to see her aroused pussy.

Jesu, he was hard again just looking at her swollen clit and puffed-up labia. She was ready for him. Cream poured from her channel, making him want to rub his face in her juices until she screamed his name. He crawled toward her until his balls pressed against her pussy. The underside of his cock nudged her swollen clit, and she shuddered. Bracing his hands on either side of her head, he looked down at her.

"I'm going to lick your sex now, and you're going to love it. When you're screaming and begging to come, I'll slide my cock inside you and you'll love that even more."

Sara couldn't speak. His words destroyed the last of her resistance. His long hair, barely contained now by the loose blue ribbon, hung over one shoulder. She reached up and pulled the ribbon out. He shook his head, and his hair settled around his shoulders in dark, glorious waves.

He kissed his way down her throat and latched onto one of her breasts. She sighed at the silken feel of his hair against her skin and the insistent tug of his mouth. When both her nipples were hard and wet from his attentions, he moved lower, brushing his lips over her navel before pausing at her mound.

"Raise your hips."

Sara reacted to his gentle command, and he slid a pillow underneath her buttocks, opening her further to his gaze. The first silken glide of his tongue over her sex made her jump. He curved a firm hand over her hip and kept her pinned to the bed.

She strained against him, ignoring his laughter at her ineffectual attempts to tame his excesses. His tongue probed her sheath, accompanied by four of his long fingers. He worked her toward a climax, his mouth rougher on her soft flesh, his teeth nipping and holding her clit until she writhed with the need to come.

She screamed and tried to pull his hair when he drew back, his pirate face ablaze with lust. He knelt between her thighs, one hand massaging his thick cock.

"You'll take me now."

Sara shuddered as he worked the first couple of inches of his shaft inside her. He watched her face, stopping when he met the barrier of her maidenhead. Still holding her gaze, he drew her index finger into his mouth, licked it, and then pressed it against her clit.

She almost bucked off the bed, driving him deeper, and tried to ignore the heavy surge of pain that followed. He grunted and kept up his inexorable slide inward. For the first time, Sara considered the possibility that she might break in two. She glanced down at his groin and stifled a moan. He was only halfway in.

"I don't think I can take any more." Her voice sounded high-pitched and most unlike herself.

"You will." Valentin remained braced over her, his expression intent. "You just need to relax." He bent his head and slowly licked her nipple. "Come now, don't turn all maidenly on me. Remember, you are my instrument of pleasure. Let me play a while longer." She watched his tongue flick back and forth over her breast. He moved his hips in the same subtle rhythm; his cock slid deeper inside her with every gentle flex of his pelvis.

Enthralled, she gave herself up to the erotic dance he led her into. The slide and glide of his shaft and the soft lick of his tongue became the focus of her being. She let her pleasure build with his until her fingernails dug into his shoulders and she screamed her release. His body jerked as he released a hot stream of seed deep within her womb. He collapsed over her, his mouth close to her ear.

"You're mine now. I'm the only man you'll ever let between your thighs. I'm the only man who will ever bring you pleasure."

When dawn broke through the still open curtains, Sara turned on her side to observe her sleeping husband. He no longer wore the coin medallion she had glimpsed during his encounter with Daisy. In the soft light, she could see the fine silver lines she'd felt etched on his back during the night. She reached out to touch the nape of his neck. Her fingers brushed a raised patch of skin, and she tried to trace the pattern.

She stifled a shriek as Valentin erupted from the bed and pinned her beneath him.

"What the hell are you doing?" He rolled her onto her back and glared down at her.

Sara swallowed and tried to meet his ferocious gaze.

"I didn't mean to startle you."

Valentin ran a hand though his tousled hair. "I'm not used to sleeping with anyone."

Sarah frowned. "So you fear to be attacked in your own bed?"

After a long moment, Valentin laughed. "In other people's beds, certainly. Husbands do have a tendency to arrive home unexpectedly."

She struggled to conceal her hurt. "I touched the scars on your back. That is probably what awakened you." She took in a breath for courage. "You've been beaten, haven't you? Just before our marriage, my father told me you were a Turkish slave for seven years of your life."

He moved away and sat on the edge of the bed, presenting her with his scarred back. He smoothed the linen sheets with his long fingers. "And what else did he tell you?"

"Only that he happened upon you and another English boy and insisted on buying you. He brought you both back to England."

"He saved our lives. I will always be grateful to him."

She sensed a lack of emotion in his carefully spoken words. Would he have preferred to be left to die?

"I'm glad he saved you, too."

Valentin swung around to stare at her, one eyebrow raised. "Because of this?" he glanced down at his growing erection. "Any man could give you this."

Sara smiled. "Actually I was thinking of my father. It makes me proud to be his daughter."

"Touché, madam." He crawled toward her, his cock grasped in one hand. "And now since we are both awake, perhaps you'll let me inside you again?"

5

So much for the perfect honeymoon. Sara stormed into her bedroom and slammed the door. Valentin's polite excuses about having to work sounded forced to her ears. She contemplated her disconsolate reflection in the shadowed gilt mirror over her dressing table. He noticed her only when she was in his bed. Was he determined to keep their lives separate? She wasn't used to being ignored. Her last two days at the secluded Essex manor house had settled into a pattern she could no longer ignore.

Every attempt she made to appear interested in Valentin's work or to offer her help was politely dismissed or ignored. Even her request to visit the local gentry was put off with a smile. With no one to talk to for most of the day, she'd taken to wandering around the grounds and paddling her feet in the lake.

She expected better of him. He had seemed to like her boldness and curiosity. Had it all been a sham to persuade her to marry him? Was she going to be ignored and patronized by her husband like most of the wives of her acquaintance?

She rang for her new maid to unlace her and then put on her

nightgown. The faded elegance of her bedchamber no longer held any appeal. She even missed her mother's complaints and her sisters arguing. A small china clock on the mantelpiece chimed eleven times, startling her. She threw the brush down and stomped toward the bed. A headache threatened behind her eyes. If Valentin's work was so important, perhaps he wouldn't even bother to join her tonight.

Sara scolded herself for being so childish. Maybe Valentin was right to call her spoiled. Marriage wasn't a game, and she wasn't one of those women who couldn't exist without a man to order her world. Her father had often worked long hours to secure his various business interests. Why should she be surprised that Valentin was the same?

And he had given her so much. . . . Determined to be more charitable, she drew back the bedcovers and found a package on the pillow. She pulled off the gold string and unfolded the crackling brown paper to reveal a silk-covered book. There was no name on the vibrant scarlet cover. Intrigued, she opened the first page and began to read. The flamboyant handwriting was unfamiliar.

This book is for us. Share your dreams and sexual fantasies until you grow bold enough to ask for them out loud. I will endeavor to fulfill any desires you have.
Don't be afraid to imagine.
Valentin.

Sara ran her fingers over the finely written script. How astute of Valentin to realize that her courage didn't always live up to her recently discovered needs. She turned the page and found he had written more. Softly she read the words out loud.

"I sit at my desk in the study. It is late and I am thinking of you lying in bed alone. Does my beautiful bride believe I have abandoned her? Perhaps she needs to understand that I am no pampered aristocrat but a man who chooses to work for his living, despite the contempt of his peers.

"I shift in my seat as my cock swells within my breeches, wishing I could be inside you driving you to a climax. My ledger draws me back; the columns of figures blur and dance before my eyes.

"A sound draws my attention to the door. You are there, your hair loose around your face, a solitary candle in your hand. Before I can get up, you walk toward me and ease yourself into the space between my chair and the desk. I spread my legs, and you move between my thighs. Without speaking you untie your robe. You are naked beneath it."

Sara stopped reading, hand to her throat and headache forgotten. Was Valentin inviting her to come and make love in his study, or was it merely a pleasant fantasy meant to amuse her? She dropped the book on the bed as if it burned and paced the carpet. Common sense and prudence dictated she should be offended by his suggestion. He shouldn't assume she would feel comfortable appearing naked and willing in any place other than her bed, especially after his recent neglect of her.

As she walked, her body stirred to life and a heaviness grew in her breasts and between her legs.

She paused to stare in the mirror. Her eyes looked wild. Tentatively she squeezed her nipples through the silk of her nightgown. Despite her mental struggle, her body was readying itself for sex.

The book lay faceup on the bed where she had dropped it. Sara reread Valentin's provocative words and then closed the book and slipped it under her pillow.

Valentin leaned back in his chair and stretched his tired shoulder muscles. A single candle illuminated the shadowy rows of books surrounding him. The scent of old leather, smoke and brandy permeated the oak-paneled walls. As a child, he'd often run away from his nurse and sneaked in here. His father's steward had given him sugar lumps and showed him some of the enormous leather-bound record books. His father had rarely visited the place, which was perhaps another reason Val felt so comfortable.

Despite his ability to relax here, he was glad they were due to return to the city in two days. Unlike most aristocrats, his business interests demanded a significant amount of his time. A week without giving them his full attention had resulted in several problems only he could solve.

He let out a slow breath. And then there was Sara. Because of the emergencies, he'd left her to her own devices for the past two days. Despite her attempts to appear unaffected by his neglect, he knew she wasn't pleased. In truth, he regretted it himself. He would much rather spend a day in bed with her than sit behind a desk. He glanced at the clock. Had she discovered his present yet? And, more importantly, would his fantasy intrigue or horrify her?

He pressed his fingers to his brow. His secretary's recent correspondence had also drawn his attention to another troubling matter. Someone was attempting to blackmail his business partner, Peter Howard, and Peter hadn't bothered to mention it to him.

A slight noise made him look up. Sara stood in front of his desk, a challenging expression on her face. She wore a long crimson dressing gown, and her hair was loose around her shoulders. Her cheeks were suffused with matching color. His cock stiffened in one painful jolt and threatened to burst out of his breeches.

She slid between him and the desk to stand between his thighs. The soft silk of her dressing gown brushed his clenched fists. He stared mesmerized as she undid the sash and exposed her nakedness.

Valentin gazed at her luscious body. Her skin gleamed in the soft candlelight like the finest porcelain. He licked his lips and imagined sucking her nipple into his mouth. Without conscious thought, he leaned forward and touched the tip of his tongue to her navel. The scent of her arousal tugged at his senses. He resisted an urge to lick his way down to her sex and thrust his tongue deep into her channel. To his astonishment, she made him harder than any of the more accomplished women he'd taken as lovers.

With exquisite control—she was his wife, damnit, not some voracious foreign slut—he pulled her onto his lap so that she straddled him. He kissed her lightly on the mouth.

"I was in need of a diversion. Whatever gave you the idea to come and visit me?"

She smiled then, her generous mouth curving with unconscious invitation. "I was bored. I'm not used to being left alone. If you don't require my help with your business, perhaps I can relieve you in other ways." She hesitated. "Your note interested me."

He loved that about her, the way she met his questions head-on with clear-eyed honesty. She had no idea how refreshing that was to a jaded cynic like himself. Her innocence made him feel clean, gave him faint hope that all human life wasn't corrupt.

"You are spoiled, my lady. You expect too much of my attention." She frowned. "Now you look like a little girl about to stamp her foot."

Her chin came up. "I'm not a child."

He leaned forward and licked her taut nipple. "I can see that." She shivered delicately in his arms. "But I'm still tempted to put you over my knee and spank you."

He watched for her reaction to his half taunt. She didn't know how much he'd enjoy spanking her, or that she would enjoy it, too. He found the sudden awakening of her sexual awareness intriguing. She'd already left a damp patch on his buckskin breeches.

She worried her lip. "I'm not used to being idle. When I agreed to marry you, I expected my life to change for the better, not become even more boring."

Valentin bit back a smile. "I bore you?" He cupped her mound in his palm. "This bores you?"

Sara wiggled against his questing fingers and looked disapproving. "There is more to life than that."

"On our honeymoon? Surely 'that' is all we are expected to do?" Valentin slipped a finger inside her. "In two days we leave for the city. No doubt in a few weeks, you'll be complaining that you are too busy to lie abed with me."

She opened her mouth. Valentin laid a finger over her lips.

"My fantasy didn't include arguing with you. If you recall, it was about fucking you." He encircled her waist and sat her on the edge of his desk, her legs spread wide. Pushing back his chair he opened his breeches one careful button at a time, bringing some relief to his aching cock.

He took his erection in one hand and stood up. She drew in a sharp breath as he rubbed the tip of his shaft against her creamy sex. "I'm going to drive into you hard and fast. You'll take it all. Even if one of the servants comes in and sees you here naked on my desk, you'll not want me to stop, you'll beg me to finish."

Valentin studied Sara's dazed expression as he continued to circle her clit with the crown of his cock. He doubted she would notice if anyone interrupted them. She had the same intensity about sex as he did. His notion of the Red Book seemed to have been successful. His thoughts spiraled to other public places, other secret trysts where he would enjoy fucking her.

With a grunt, he slid inside, enjoying the tightness of her sheath and the buildup of exquisite pressure. He pressed on until his shaft was completely enclosed and then slowly withdrew. "Watch my cock, Sara. Watch me drive you wild."

I am walking in the gardens. You come and find me.
To my secret delight, you make love to me out in the open.
I imagine the cold air on my exposed skin, the thrill of
being half clothed and the fear of discovery.

Sara stepped back to view her watercolor and collided with a broad chest. Flustered, she turned and found herself in Valentin's arms. Had he read her first entry in the Red Book already? Had he come to fulfill her fantasy? Yesterday she spent hours thinking what to write. After she finished, she felt her dream lacked something. A man as experienced as Valentin would probably laugh at her girlish fantasy.

He smiled down at her, his severe brown coat and waistcoat at odds with the lustful glint in his eyes. "Good afternoon, my lady." He gestured at the easel. "Am I allowed to look at this masterpiece, or must I wait like the rest of your adoring public?"

Sara shrugged. "I am not very good at this. You are welcome to look." She stepped back and allowed him to study her watercolor of the house and lake. He perused it for several minutes, his head angled to one side.

"You are right. It's not very good."

Sara stopped smiling and put her chin up. "You think my painting is inferior?"

Valentin failed to suppress a grin. "No, you paint well enough, but you play the harpsichord better."

Reluctantly Sara placed her brush back on the easel. Valentin's honesty, after her father's flattery, would take some getting used to.

"I fear you are right. I've had some of the best teachers available, but all my efforts seem mediocre." She glanced at him over her shoulder. "I think my parents hoped a passion for art would discourage my passion for music."

He placed her hand on his sleeve. "I would prefer you to play for me than to paint any day. In truth, I'd prefer you to be naked and covered in rose petals as you played, but perhaps that's a fantasy we can discuss in our book."

Sara's heart rate increased as he smiled down at her. A soft, urgent pulse drummed between her legs. He patted her ungloved fingers. "Do you have time for a stroll in the gardens? There are some matters I wish to discuss with you."

He took her toward a path that led away from the house and through a wild bluebell glade. A team of gardeners, stationed along the walk, trimmed and weeded the trees and bushes. Valentin paused to talk to one of the men as Sara admired the flowers.

"I haven't been down this path before. It's such a beautiful house." On her daily expeditions, Sara had discovered that the house was at least two hundred years old. Three wings protruded from it, making the shape of the letter *E*. A walled herb garden and a maze protected the west side of the house. The lake and elm-lined driveway seemed of later date.

"I thought you might enjoy visiting the Roman temple over this hill."

Sara cast Valentin an interested glance. "You seem to know this place well. Did you visit here as a boy?"

"I lived here until the age of eleven. The house belonged to my mother, who was a real Russian princess. She left it to me in her will."

"What happened when you were eleven? Did you leave to attend school?"

The humor drained from his face. "No, I left on a journey to Russia with my father and ended up receiving an education of a highly irregular kind as a Turkish slave."

Sara felt herself blush. "You were only eleven?" She squeezed his arm. "I'm so sorry."

His most charming smile flashed out, the one that pushed her away and set her at a distance. "You can hardly consider yourself responsible for something that happened when you were a child in the nursery."

"That's not what I meant."

"Don't waste your pity on me, Sara. I've all but forgotten about it." He nodded at the last of the gardeners and continued up the gentle slope. "Perhaps we might change the subject and discuss our forthcoming arrival in London."

Sara nodded, furious with herself for stirring up such unpleasant memories. She fixed an agreeable expression on her face. "Of course, my lord, I'm looking forward to it. Do you own a house in London as well?"

"I thought we might rent one." He hesitated as they reached the brow of the hill. "But if you would prefer it, my father, the Marquess of Stratham, owns a house on Portland Square. He has a suite of rooms we could use there."

Sara glanced up at him. "But you don't wish to?"

A muscle flickered in Valentin's cheek. "My father has difficulty dealing with my ungentlemanly choice of profession and my somewhat checkered past."

"I should imagine he feels some guilt over losing you, as well."

Valentin laughed. "I've never noticed it. When I returned to England, he was almost embarrassed. He'd already started another family, and along I came to ruin all my half brother's hopes and dreams of a title."

Sara paused and pretended to admire the gleaming white stone structure atop the hill. "Still, it must have been a shock for him. Your mother died before you returned?"

He turned away from her, his hands clasped behind his back.

"Yes, apparently of a broken heart. I was informed she never forgave my father for leaving me in the hands of the Turks."

A blackbird swooped low over Sara's head and landed on one of the overturned columns. It sang a shrill challenge over the faint sounds of the gardeners working below. She walked across the grass to the stones, her skirts held up in one hand. The marble felt cool under her fingers. It was spotted with moss and the grimy veneer of the ages.

She stroked the narrow column of stone. "Did one of your ancestors travel to Greece?"

Valentin followed at a more leisurely pace, his gaze fixed on her fingers. "I believe my maternal grandfather completed his grand tour there. By all accounts, he had this temple crated up and brought back with him."

Sara studied the small circular building. It had a domed roof and eight supporting columns that rested on a waist-high wall. She stepped carefully through the fallen stones. "Is it safe to go inside?"

"Of course. I have the building checked once a year. The stones on the ground around it are merely there for effect. It seems my grandfather simply cleared the entire lot."

Inside it was cool and shadowy, and the floor was mosaic. Sara knelt to study the faded images. She traced the rough outline of a woman's face. "Is this Aphrodite?" A beautiful naked woman surrounded by a handful of lesser maidens frolicked in a field of flowers.

"From my grandfather's diaries, I would assume so." Valentin's boots echoed in the confined space as he came to stand beside her. He helped Sara to her feet.

"Thank you for showing me this, Valentin. It is beautiful." Sara spun around with a mischievous smile. "I might even attempt to paint it."

He caught her hand. "Come and look at the view. You can see the rooftops of the main house from here."

He led her toward one of the pillars and stood behind her. He slid his arm around her waist and drew her back against him. "You must be wondering why my father didn't attend our wedding."

His fingers expertly worked at her laces, loosening her bodice and corset. Sara let out her breath. Only the pressure of his arm under her breasts kept her dress in place. She stared down the hill, where a few of the gardeners continued to tend to the path and bushes.

"I didn't realize until now that your father was still alive. You haven't mentioned him before." Her voice sounded breathy and loud in the small enclosed space.

"I try not to think about him unless I have to. He made it plain that whilst I will inherit his title, he'll not leave me a penny of his money." He bit down on her neck, and she shuddered. "He'll scarcely rejoice at my marriage. I think he hoped I'd have the decency to die a bachelor so that his new favorite son could inherit everything."

Trust Valentin to bring up his problems with his family during lovemaking. Perhaps he thought to distract her. Sara fixed her gaze on the nearest of the men working below. Valentin gathered her light muslin skirt at the back and brought the frothy layers to her waist. Cold air met her heated flesh and was quickly replaced by the sensuous feel of his buckskin breeches against her skin. It was like being caressed by rough velvet from her buttocks to her ankles.

"Do you wish me to call upon your father and his new wife?"

Valentin kissed his way up her neck before he replied. "If you think you can stand it. I have already decided to hold a dinner party in your honor within a short time of our arrival." His teeth grazed her earlobe, and her nipples hardened in a sudden aching rush. "I will invite both my friends and my competitors. Like most successful businessmen, I have enemies,

Sara. I would like you to meet them and draw your own conclusions."

He rocked his hips, pressing his erection against her buttocks. She dug her fingernails into the stone. "Are you ready for me yet? Does the thought of being taken like this, in broad daylight, still excite you?"

He spanned her buttocks with his left hand and slid one long finger past her anus to probe her sheath. He let out his breath. "Ah, yes, wet and open, slippery with longing."

A movement below them caught Sara's attention. Valentin began to circle her already swollen sex with his fingertip.

"My lord, I think one of the gardeners has noticed us."

Valentin tugged at her earlobe with his teeth. "You are embarrassed? He can't actually tell what I am doing to you. He can only guess."

Sara swallowed hard as Valentin withdrew his fingers and undid the buttons of his breeches. His hard, wet shaft nudged the small of her back. He slid his cock between her legs and angled the tip until it pressed against her clitoris. Her heart pounded against her bodice, and need pulsed between her thighs. When she dared open her eyes again, the man still watched her. He winked.

"Do you want me to stop?" Valentin murmured. "I can leave you unsatisfied if you wish."

Sara bit down on her lip. "But what if he sees us?"

"What if he does?" Valentin spread out the fingers on his right hand that held up her bodice and grazed both her nipples. "Watch him enjoy you. See if he becomes aroused. Imagine how much he would like to be in my place."

Without waiting for her reply, he thrust inside her with one smooth push, lifting her onto her tiptoes.

Sara gripped the top of the wall harder as he drove deeper and allowed him to guide her into a strong, fast pace. Her body was still unaccustomed to his lovemaking, and he felt very large at this angle. She focused on the young man below who stared at her. His tanned face curved into an appreciative smile as he noticed her appraisal. Valentin pounded into her, and the gardener's hand slid to cover his groin. The swell of his cock was clearly visible beneath his muddy breeches.

"See, Sara?" Valentin whispered. "He wants you. You've made him hard. He wants you, and yet he can't have you because you're mine. He'll never get to fuck you, ever."

Valentin picked up the tempo, his thrusts pressing her into the wall. Sara felt the first stirring of her orgasm. She concentrated her attention on the man below her and allowed the pleasure Valentin gave her to show in her face. He was right. Seeing another man's desire made her feel powerfully female.

"Come now, Sara, and watch us come with you." Her body rushed to obey Valentin's command, and her climax shuddered through her. He groaned as his seed flooded her channel. Then his body sagged against hers. The gardener below them sank to his knees, his blond head bowed, his hands locked at his groin.

When Sara found the nerve to look again, she realized the other gardeners had already disappeared. Had Valentin arranged the whole scene for her benefit? She wouldn't be surprised if he had. He helped her straighten her gown and stepped away, leaving her feeling cold. He smiled as he refastened his breeches, all traces of passion instantly repressed. His expression as calm as if they had been discussing the weather.

"Tomorrow we leave for London. I suggest we have an early night. We have a long way to travel and a whole new life to lead together."

6

London

Sara smoothed the front of her corset and allowed her maid to help her into her petticoat. Valentin appeared in the doorway that connected their suites. He was dressed in a dark blue wool frock coat, and his gray waistcoat was embroidered with silver thread. His evening clothes made an interesting contrast to the rose silk hangings of her bedchamber.

"Are you nervous, my dear?"

"A little, my lord," Sara said as she dismissed her maid. She turned to look more fully at him. "But I am also excited." After her miserable first Season in London, she'd avoided coming up to town as much as possible. Arriving in the city cushioned by Valentin's wealth and family name was a completely different experience.

Valentin paused by the bed and lifted up her dress. He smiled into her eyes. "Crimson is my favorite color. It reminds me of your nipples after I've suckled them."

He brought the gown to her and tossed it over her head. Silk flowed around her body with the soft whisper of a shower of rose petals. She sucked in a breath as Valentin tied the laces at the back. Her breasts rose from a ruffle of white lace that brought out the creamy tone of her skin. Sara smiled at her reflection.

After three weeks of viewing houses, hiring staff, and meeting with modistes, she was exhausted. It was a relief to finally start her new life in London with her enigmatic husband. Every time she believed she had finally started to know him, he showed her yet another side of his multifaceted personality. He reminded her of the densely lacquered Japanese chest in her chamber. So many layers to produce that deep, rich shine. So many years to cover the base wood beneath.

"I have something for you."

Valentin drew a box from his coat pocket and handed it to Sara. Inside the velvet box nestled a multitiered necklace of rubies and pearls. While Sara gaped at the jewels, Valentin placed the necklace around her throat.

"I had this made for you as a bride gift. There are other pieces that go with it, but we will share them together later tonight."

Sara stroked the central ruby, which was as big as her thumb. "It is beautiful, Valentin. I don't know how to thank you."

He dropped a kiss on her shoulder. "Write something for me in the Red Book. I have missed hearing from you these past few weeks." He turned to the door. "I will await you in the drawing room."

As soon as Valentin disappeared, Sara ran to the bed and slipped her hand under her pillow. Her hands shook as she turned the pages. She smiled as Valentin's new message was revealed.

Tonight, I wish to adore you. Be prepared to become my jeweled goddess.

Sara stroked her new necklace. What on earth did Valentin mean? A shiver of anticipation worked its way through her body. His lovemaking was always a surprise. Surviving the imminent arrival of their guests suddenly seemed less frightening with the promise of pleasure to follow. After a final glance at her reflection, Sara went down the stairs.

The elegant town house they had hired for the Season was situated in Half Moon Street. It contained five floors, from basement to attic, and a highly efficient staff to oversee the smallest domestic crisis. Valentin had intimated that if she liked the house, he would consider buying it and setting up a permanent residence.

One of the guests had arrived early. At the bottom of the stairs, Sara could see a blond-haired man talking animatedly to Valentin. Both men looked up as she reached the black-and-white marbled hallway. Valentin held out his hand.

"Sara, this is Mr. Peter Howard, my business partner and my best friend."

Sara curtsied as Mr. Howard bowed. He was of a similar height to Valentin, his skin too tanned to be fashionable. She studied him cautiously. Her father had warned her to stay away from this man. He had also asked her to use her influence with Valentin to break the connection. She hoped none of her confusion showed on her face. Why did her father consider Peter Howard a threat to her and Valentin's future happiness?

Peter Howard's eyes were light blue, his face lined yet finely drawn like an ethereal angel. Beside Valentin's dark splendor, he should have lacked substance but, instead, provided a perfect foil for his friend. He wore a beige coat and brown breeches that were cut with elegant precision.

"Lady Sokorvsky, it is a pleasure to meet you." He glanced

at Valentin. "If my friend hadn't been in such a hurry to wed, I would've made your acquaintance at the ceremony. I was supposed to be Valentin's best man."

"Peter's ship was delayed across the Channel." Valentin smiled lazily at Peter. "I was as disappointed as you were when I realized you wouldn't make it back in time."

Sara studied the two men. Despite their banter, she sensed some tension between them. It occurred to her that Valentin had married her without any of his family present or his best friend. Had he known her father disliked Peter and made sure not to include him in the wedding party?

"Please call me Peter." The object of her thoughts brought her hand to his lips and kissed it. "I'm sure Val won't mind."

Sara remembered her manners and smiled. "I'm sure Valentin won't mind if you call me Sara. From what he has told me, you are part of his family."

Valentin shrugged. "At times he has been my only family."

"You were the other boy my father rescued from Turkey, weren't you?"

"Yes, indeed I was, although your father has never held me in the same esteem as he does your new husband." Peter smiled slightly. "I fear I disappointed him on too many occasions, and he quite rightly washed his hands of me." He bowed. "I hope you won't hold that against me. I believe I have settled down now."

Valentin frowned and touched Peter's arm. "That reminds me, can you stay behind after dinner? I have a business matter to discuss with you."

Peter's mouth tightened. "You are supposed to be on your honeymoon, Val. Can't it wait?"

Valentin smiled, and Sara resisted an urge to flinch. "Unfortunately it can't." He kissed her fingers. "I'm sure my dear wife will understand."

The butler announced another couple. Valentin bowed to

Peter and led Sara into the drawing room. An older man and his female companion came to greet them.

Valentin turned to Sara. "My dear, may I introduce one of my biggest shipping competitors, Sir Richard Pettifer and his dear wife, Evangeline?"

Sir Richard's booming laugh crashed over her. He was an elderly man with a round face and a round body to match. His yellow waistcoat was decorated with large gold buttons that resembled sovereigns, and the points of his cravat were so high he appeared to have no neck.

"Trust Valentin to get to the point!" He bowed to Sara. "It is a pleasure to meet you, my lady, and felicitations on your marriage to this rogue." He poked Valentin with his walking stick.

Lady Pettifer, who looked much younger than her husband, took Sara's hand and dropped a scented kiss near her ear. She wore an elegant puce satin gown and three matching feathers in her upswept hair. Her brown eyes looked kind. "Indeed, all the ladies in London will want to know how you caught the elusive Lord Sokorvsky." Her gaze rested on Sara's stomach and then returned to her face. "He is such a prize."

Sara smiled and resisted the urge to place her hand on her belly. Lady Pettifer's pointed comment wasn't totally unexpected. She had few illusions as to her beauty and social standing. Lady Pettifer wouldn't be the first person to wonder how a mere tradesman's daughter had snared the son of a marquess.

Valentin patted her hand. "My wife is the prize. I was honored when she accepted me." Sara looked up at him, but his face bore no sign of humor.

Lady Pettifer sighed. "I see it is a love match." She tapped her husband's cheek with her closed fan. "My dear, you can only hope that Valentin becomes so engrossed in his wife that he forgets to run his business properly."

Sara almost laughed at Sir Richard's hopeful expression. Lady Pettifer leaned closer. "If I can help you navigate the trials and tribulations of the Season, please let me know. It cannot be easy for you, what with Valentin's unusual social position."

Startled by the warmth of Lady Pettifer's words, Sara impulsively took the other woman's hand. "Thank you for the offer. I am a little concerned. It is good to know that there are people to whom I can turn for advice."

The butler announced another couple, and the Pettifers turned away. Valentin's grip on her hand intensified as he saw who was behind them.

"Father."

Valentin inclined his head an inch to the gray-haired man. Sara noticed he and his father were a similar height and build. "May I present my wife, Sara, Lady Sokorvsky?"

The Marquess of Stratham bowed to Sara. "It is a pleasure to meet you. I only wish I had been informed of the wedding." A muscle twitched in his cheek. "I never expected to find out about my eldest son's nuptials in my morning newspaper."

Sara glanced uncertainly up at Valentin, who looked amused. "You didn't get the invitation? I could have sworn I sent one. Perhaps your secretary didn't pass it on."

The marquess stepped forward, his mouth tightening. The much smaller lady by his side laid her hand on his arm. "Anton, perhaps you might introduce me to my new daughter-in-law."

"Of course, my dear. I apologize." Sara was relieved to see the marquess visibly relax. "Lady Sokorvsky, may I present my wife to you?"

Sara found herself swept into a scented lavender embrace. The marchioness gave her a dazzling smile. "May I call you Sara? Please call me Isabelle. I am so pleased to meet you. You must promise to take tea with me as soon as possible." She glanced up at the marquess. "We would very much like to hold a reception in honor of your marriage at Stratham House."

Valentin reclaimed Sara's hand. "I don't think that will be necessary. But thank you for the offer."

Sara blushed as Isabelle struggled to conceal the hurt in her eyes. "But I would like to do this for you, Valentin."

"You might, my dear stepmama, but my father can scarcely be happy about it."

The marquess snorted. "I told you, my dear. Valentin doesn't wish to be included in our family. He even refuses to use his proper title."

Valentin laughed. "What good would it do me to call myself a viscount?" He pretended to consider. "Although it might look well on my business stationery and persuade a few more Cits to toadeat me."

"Don't attempt to make a mockery of your birthright." The marquess kept his voice low, but anger resonated through it. "You are my eldest son. The title is yours whether you want it or not."

"What a shame you can't change that, Father. Anthony would fill the role so much more gracefully, wouldn't he?"

The marquess stared at his son and then abruptly turned away. The marchioness followed, whispering urgently in his ear.

Sara sighed. "Did you have to be so rude?"

Valentin shrugged. "It's the only way my father and I communicate. In truth, thanks to my stepmother, he was on his best behavior this evening." He studied her. "Don't worry; you won't have to see him very often."

Sara decided to hold her tongue. Valentin's dealings with his father were obviously far more complicated than she realized. When she visited Lady Isabelle, she would hopefully learn more. To her relief, two more couples were announced, and Valentin's pleasant social mask slipped back into place as he made the introductions.

She glanced around the drawing room with a feeling of pride. Ten couples milled around conversing, laughing, and apparently enjoying themselves. Despite her misgivings, she'd played her part as hostess without embarrassing herself or Valentin. When the butler announced dinner, she was more than ready to place her hand on the marquess's arm, smile brightly, and allow him to lead her in.

As Valentin handed out cups of tea to the assembled guests, Sara turned to find Peter Howard sitting beside her. Her teacup rattled in its saucer. He took it away from her and placed it on the small table beside him. His eyebrows rose as he studied her.

"Now what exactly did your father say about me that makes you so wary of my company?"

Sara bit her lip. There was nothing but gentle good humor in Peter's gaze. Her instincts told her that here was a man who could be trusted. If only her father had been more specific as to exactly what Peter was supposed to have done to earn his disapproval.

Cautiously she smiled back at him. Unlike Valentin, she wasn't a great dissembler. Perhaps honesty would reveal more than honeyed deceit. "My father believes you have some kind of unhealthy hold over Valentin."

She was rewarded by a smile of great beauty. "If by that your father means Val and I have a deep, unbreakable bond, then he is right. You cannot share seven horrific years of your life with a man and not end up caring about him."

Sara studied him. "Yet you are still together more than ten years later? Perhaps that is what he thinks strange."

"Now, that is my fault. For several years after our return, I clung on to Val like a pitiful child." His gaze shifted from her to Valentin, who was talking to his stepmother while still managing to ignore his father. "God knows why, but Val put up with me. Now I'm trying to repay him by being the best damned business manager I can."

Valentin turned and caught them staring at him. His eyebrow rose in a question. Peter winked at him, and he turned back to resume his conversation. For a heartbeat, Sara resented their closeness.

"Do you object to Val and I being friends?"

Peter's low-voiced question made Sara feel childish. After how much the two men had suffered, was it really surprising they remained close?

"Of course not." Sara deliberately looked right into Peter's eyes. "Do you object to Valentin marrying me?"

"No. I'm glad he's found someone so special." He paused as though unsure whether to continue. "I believe he'd reached a place in his life where the role of a rake was beginning to pale."

"Are you talking about me?"

Sara looked up to see Valentin looming over them. She smiled at him and held out her hand. "We've agreed not to fight over you. Are you pleased?"

He drew her to her feet. Peter stood as well. "I would've been surprised if you hadn't been in agreement." He glanced from Sara to Peter. "You are very similar in some ways. I know that both of you are great believers in telling me where I have erred."

Peter bowed. "Someone has to do it, Val, or else your head would be swollen fit to burst by now."

"Point taken, my friend. Now perhaps you would like to exercise your considerable charms on Sir Richard and Lady Pettifer. I'm always interested in my business competitors' plans."

Peter walked away. Valentin retained his grip on Sara's hand. "Thank you for that."

"For what, my lord?"

"For accepting Peter when your father must have warned you against him."

Sara found herself blushing. "I'm old enough to make my own decisions about people."

"Peter took a few years to find his feet after our return."
Valentin sighed. "Your father never fully trusted him after that,
but I can assure you Peter has changed. I would never expect
you to tolerate him otherwise."

Sara's gaze followed Peter, who had stopped to talk to the
Pettifers. "He has suffered a great deal, hasn't he?"

Valentin went still. "You can see that?"

Sara opened her fan and looked away. Peter's golden hair
caught the candlelight as he nodded at something Sir Richard
said. "Of course." How could she tell Valentin she saw the faint
echo of that suffering on his face every day?

Valentin kissed her fingers. "Peter will be a loyal friend to
you, I can promise you that." His attention was caught by a
flurry of movement by the fireplace. "I think my father is about
to leave. Perhaps we should go and make ourselves pleasant for
a few moments."

Sara allowed him to escort her across the room. What had
Valentin seen in her expression that had made him as eager to
end the conversation as she had been?

7

Valentin offered Peter a glass of brandy and then studied his friend across the desk. Peter looked tired, his blue eyes shadowed. Had he taken up his old habits whilst Valentin was distracted by his marriage and his business worries?

Peter finished his brandy and lit a cigar. "So what is so important that it keeps you from your marriage bed?"

Valentin extracted his secretary's note from the pile on his desk and passed it across to Peter. He waited until Peter finished reading.

"And you believed this?" Peter crumpled the sheet of parchment in his fist. "Why would I risk my reputation publicly molesting a footman at a society ball?"

"The man apparently believes that you did."

Peter swallowed hard. "And if I say it's a damned lie, will you believe me?"

Valentin locked gazes with his oldest friend—judged the fine trembling in his fingers, and the pallor of his skin. "Of course I will, but . . ."

Peter looked disgusted. "There's always a 'but.' Keep going, Val. I'm sure there's more."

Valentin let out an exasperated breath. "In the past, when you took too much opium, you sometimes forgot what you had done."

Peter got slowly to his feet. "I haven't touched opium for the last three years. Do you really think I would risk throwing myself back into that hellhole after barely climbing out of it alive?"

"No." Valentin chastised himself for automatically assuming Peter had broken his word. It was time for him to stop behaving like Peter's keeper and start trusting him as a friend. "If you will sit down again, perhaps we can work out why this ugly accusation surfaced at precisely the same time our business is under threat."

Peter sat, his expression troubled. "I hadn't thought of that."

Valentin rubbed his forehead. "I have. It seems as though someone wants to blacken our reputations and destroy our livelihood."

A faint smile crossed Peter's lined face. "Someone? I'm sure we have made more than one enemy between us."

"But I suspect that this person wants to drag up our past and use it against us as well. Someone who knows the truth about Turkey."

"And is not content just to ruin us financially but socially, too." Peter stubbed out his cigar. "I promise I'll keep all my private perversions within the discreet boundaries of Madame Helene's House of Pleasure. In fact, I'll ask Madame herself to vet all my partners and her clientele, if that makes you feel any easier."

Valentin finished off his brandy. "I'll do the same."

Peter gave him a peculiar look. "And why would you need Madame's facilities? Haven't you just got married?"

Valentin pictured Sara waiting for him in her bed. His cock stirred with anticipation. "My wife is . . . special."

"What's the matter, Val?" Peter said gently. "Are you worried she won't be able to satisfy all your needs?"

"That's none of your damned business," Valentin snarled. "My wife is not a topic of conversation."

Peter got up and headed for the door. "You're always handing out advice to me. Perhaps you might care to listen to some. Your wife is an interesting woman. Give her a chance to find out who you really are or your marriage will be a very lonely place for both of you."

Valentin stared at the closed door and slowly relaxed his taut muscles. Peter had no right to tell him how to manage his relationships. The man had enough problems with his own. Sara was his wife. She didn't need to wallow in the sexual excesses Valentin sometimes craved. She would remain pure, if it was the last thing he ever did.

He shifted restlessly in his seat. Sara would never have to experience sex the way he had, forced to provide and prolong pleasure for anyone who paid for his time. He glanced down at his growing erection. Had his initiation into the fleshpots as soon as he'd managed an erection distorted his sexual desires? If they had, he hoped Sara would never know it.

He lit a candle and climbed the stairs to his bedroom. The house was silent around him. A lingering scent of wood smoke, perfume, and red wine rose with him like an echo of the dinner party up the stairwell. A faint light shone under Sara's door. Valentin picked up the jewel case he'd left on his dressing table and headed for her room. Tonight he intended to worship her, as was her right.

Sara turned away from her mirror as Valentin came through the door that connected their suites. She'd taken off her clothes and left the beautiful ruby and pearl necklace around her throat. Valentin was still fully dressed. A sapphire glinted in the intricate folds of his white cravat. He carried another jewel case similar to the one he had already given her.

He dropped to one knee in front of her. She caught the scent of brandy and cigar smoke on his breath. He smiled.

"Did you enjoy the evening?"

"It was interesting." She decided to be honest. "I liked your stepmother. Would you object if I called on her?"

Valentin laid the velvet box on the carpet. "If you must, but promise me you'll be discreet. I don't want my father knowing every piddling detail of my life."

Sara smiled as he kissed the hem of her crimson silk robe. "I doubt we'll talk about you. It might surprise you to learn that women don't always discuss their menfolk. Sometimes they prefer to discuss other things."

He looked up at her through his long eyelashes. "Other men, perhaps?" He closed his teeth on the arch of her foot. "I would hope I am man enough to satisfy you without resorting to that."

Sara squirmed from the sharp nip of his teeth. "If only you knew."

"What?" Again that commanding slide of his teeth on her sensitive skin.

"I spent most of the dinner party imagining what you were going to do to me afterward and admiring your splendid body. It made it quite hard to concentrate sometimes." She touched his cheek. "In truth, it still astonishes me that I am able to touch you and that you say I can arouse you."

Her honesty always seemed to excite him. "Are you already wet for me then?"

Sara's nipples tightened at his husky question.

Valentin raised an eyebrow. "Show me."

Holding his gaze, Sara reached down and stroked her index finger between her legs. She revealed the thick covering of cream. He grasped her wrist and slid her finger into his warm mouth, slowly sucking away the evidence of her desire.

"I'm glad you are wet for me. I like the thought of you watching me and wanting me." He released her hand and opened the jewelry case. "Will you stand? I wish to adorn you."

Willingly Sara got to her feet and undid the sash of her robe. Valentin pulled it from her shoulders and threw it onto the shadowy bed. He kissed her navel, his unshaven chin rough against her soft skin. "The first piece goes around your waist and attaches to the necklace above."

He reached up and clasped the thick gold chain around her waist. Four strings of pearls and rubies were attached to it. The necklace she already wore reached the upper curve of her breasts. Valentin took the two strands of pearls and rubies and attached them to each side of her necklace. Sara risked a glance in the mirror. The strands passed on either side of her breasts, framing her nipples.

Valentin met her eyes in the mirror. He touched her nipples, let them harden between his finger and thumb. "When I've finished dressing you, I'm going to suck your breasts until you beg me to stop. Tomorrow I want you to imagine my mouth is still on you until you're wet and wanting me again."

Sara watched his circling fingers and grew wetter and needier. She craved his fingers elsewhere. How quickly she had learned to long for his cock and his lovemaking. He smiled as he ran his fingers down the chains to her waist. "Perhaps I'll come home early during your visiting hours. Perhaps I'll check how wet you are and make love to you and then send you back to your guests."

He traced the curve of her hip, and she moaned. "Do you think they'd know you'd been fucked hard? Do you think they'd care that your nipples were sore against your corset and your sex was dripping with my seed?"

Her knees threatened to buckle as he brushed a finger over

her curls. "I think they'd know. You can't disguise the look of a well-satisfied woman. Perhaps I'll simply walk into your sitting room and slide you down onto my cock. You'd forget all about pleasing the ladies of the *ton* and only think about pleasing me."

Sara whimpered as he slid one finger between her legs. She was so wet her cream overflowed and trickled down her thigh. Valentin urged her legs apart and stared at her exposed pussy. He turned back to the jewelry case and extracted another part of the necklace. It was a rope of large pearls. He attached it to the waist piece. The necklace was so long it reached the floor.

Valentin gathered the pearl necklace in his hand and rubbed it against Sara's clitoris. "This piece goes inside you. You must try to keep it all in for me."

She watched in the mirror as Valentin slid the rope of pearls inside her. She clenched her internal muscle around the heavy mass. He stood back and allowed her to see her whole reflection in the mirror. Sara touched the pearls that pressed into her sex and shivered.

Without speaking, she moved toward Valentin and started undressing him. After a surprised glance, he made no move to stop her. As she unwound his cravat, he plucked lazily at her nipples and caressed her buttocks. She pulled off his waistcoat and shirt. He bent his head and latched onto her nipple and sucked hard. When she removed his breeches, his stiff cock thrust against the gold chain around her waist. He groaned.

Smiling, Sara slid down to her knees and gripped his shaft. He was already wet and engorged. She carefully rubbed the crown of his cock against her puckered nipple, coating herself in his pre-cum.

"Sara. . . ." Valentin thrust a hand into Sara's unbound hair and forced her to look up at him. His surprise, as she'd taken control of their lovemaking, knew no bounds. Perhaps she was not prepared to remain such an innocent after all. She licked her lips, and his shaft thickened painfully. With an intimate smile she pushed him in the direction of the bed. He let her, intrigued by the sensual demand in her eyes, aroused by the possibilities. Keeping his gaze on her, he sat on the bed, his back against the headboard.

She knelt over him, her knees on either side of his thighs. Valentin held his breath as she hooked her finger into the string of pearls and pulled them slowly out of her pussy. He kept his hands behind his head, inviting her to continue, secretly delighted by her boldness. When she coiled them on his stomach, the pearls were coated with her cream and warm against his skin. His stomach muscle contracted as her hand circled lower.

Valentin's heart sped up when she began to wrap the pearls around his straining cock. Her head bent to the task, her long hair pooled over his groin. When he was covered to her satisfaction, she looked at him. He growled his pleasure as she licked the pearls; each gentle lick rotated the spheres against his shaft like a thousand intimate vibrations.

He reached down and rolled her nipples between his fingers and thumbs and then moved his hand lower to her soaking sex. He plunged four fingers inside her, felt her clench around him. He grabbed her around the waist, straightening her back, pulling her mouth away from his cock. He flexed his arms, held her poised above him, and brought her sex into contact with the crown of his penis.

Her eyes widened as she realized what he meant to do. He lowered her down one slow inch and watched her expression as the tip of his pearl-covered cock disappeared inside her. He held her there until he felt her body accept him.

"Did you think I'd let you get away with tormenting me and not make you take me inside you?"

"Yes, no, I . . ."

He lowered her down another inch; her heels dug into the mattress, her back arched, pushing her breasts into his face.

"Did you think I'd be too big?"

He made her take two more inches, wished he could gauge how wide he'd gotten her, glorying in the exquisite sensation of the pearls clenching around his cock and the slick wet heat surrounding him.

"You might be sore tomorrow, but you'll take me now." He lowered her the rest of the way in one smooth rush and went still. When she finished shuddering, he touched her shoulder.

"Squeeze my cock."

For a moment she looked puzzled until he leaned down to brush her clit. "With your body."

His breath caught in his throat as she clenched her inner muscles around his shaft. The pearls tightened and tightened until he could feel the press of each individual sphere against his engorged cock.

She gasped, and he felt the first ripples of her climax. He gritted his teeth as the pressure mounted and she began to rock against him, driving his shaft deeper until he wanted to shout out her name.

His overexcited cock spurted its seed, coming with her in a spasm of delight. She collapsed against his chest, the jewelry warm against his skin as she gasped for air. He eased out of her and took his time unfastening the jewels.

Sara lay against him, her body pliant, her breathing even. He stroked her hair as he removed the last piece of the necklace. She had surprised him tonight. His innocent wife was learning how to please him. His cock filled out again as he studied her naked body. Perhaps he could indulge himself and make love to her more than twice. Perhaps she'd enjoy it, too.

Sara stifled a groan as she descended from the carriage. She'd spent the morning shopping in the most fashionable shops in the city and was tired from walking. Her body still ached from the excesses of Valentin's lovemaking the night before. Despite bathing, his scent clung to her skin, and every breath reminded her of his mouth on her breasts. The physical marks of his attention helped her ignore the more spiteful of the ladies of the *ton* who chose to ignore her at the lending library and the milliner's.

She had hoped to enjoy London this time, but her peers seemed determined to overlook her very existence. Only Lady Isabelle and Evangeline Pettifer had been kind and approachable. She missed her sisters and the comforts of her provincial life more than she would've anticipated. But at least she had Valentin. She clenched her teeth. Valentin, with whom she had a bone to pick.

She ignored Bryson, the butler, and made her way into the drawing room. She pulled at the peach ribbons on her bonnet and tossed it toward the nearest chair. Her husband appeared in the doorway, his charming smile flashing out.

"Valentin, have you slept with all the women in London?"

"Only the married ones, my dear."

Valentin caught up her bonnet in one hand and gestured toward the doors that led through to the music room. Sara paused for breath and noticed the presence of another older gentleman behind him. She bit her lip and wondered if the man had heard her unfortunate remark. From the slight smile on his face, she guessed he had.

"Don't worry, my love, I'm sure he won't be shocked." Valentin murmured as he took her arm and led her toward the doors, "Not only is he Italian, but Signor Clementi has an even worse reputation with the ladies than I do."

Sara raised a hand to her cheek. "Signor Clementi?" What was the most sought-after piano teacher and well-known composer in London doing in her drawing room?

She broke away from Valentin and hurried forward. "I am honored to meet you, sir."

Signor Clementi gave her a charming smile and kissed her hand. "Your husband assures me that the honor will be all mine. I understand you play the harpsichord."

Sara glanced uncertainly back at Valentin, who simply smiled and urged her farther into the music room. She gasped as she saw the new pianoforte covered in rose petals and lit by five sets of candelabra.

"I meant to have it here when you arrived," Valentin said, "but there were some difficulties with the order."

Signor Clementi made an inelegant noise. "Ha! The fools at the workshop didn't realize who the pianoforte was for. When I found out that the request came from my old friend Valentin Sokorvsky, I took over the project myself."

Sara seated herself at the pianoforte and ran a trembling hand over the keys. She'd asked her parents to replace her harpsichord with a piano, but they had considered it too great an expense for a woman destined to marry.

"Play something for me, my lady." She started at Signor Clementi's soft voice close to her ear.

Valentin gave her a piece of sheet music, and, blindly, she moved her hands over the keys. She soon forgot who was listening and simply played, her body flowing into the melody as her fingers flew over the keyboard. When the last note faded, she looked up, determined not to show her sudden flowering of nerves, now that the music had finished.

Signor Clementi didn't smile. "I teach many society ladies, but you will not be one of them."

She winced as her fingernails dug sharply into her clasped hands. Out of the corner of her eye she sensed Valentin move an urgent step closer.

"Signor Clementi."

The musician bowed to Valentin. "Hush, my lord. I cannot teach your wife what she already knows." He turned back to Sara. "I will teach you like the true musician you are."

She looked up into Signor Clementi's eyes and let out her breath. "Thank you. I will not let you down."

"At a guinea a lesson, you'd better not," Valentin muttered as he drew Sara into his arms. She stroked his cheek, tears ready to fall from her eyes.

"Thank you. You have given me an opportunity beyond my wildest dreams."

He smiled down at her, his real smile, not the one he used to block her out, and shrugged. "It is nothing. I am glad to be of service."

When he behaved like this, all her doubts about the haste of her marriage receded. His gift was both thoughtful and loving. How could she not believe that he cared about her? She hugged him hard.

He stepped back, his social smile firmly back in place, and placed her hand on his sleeve. "Perhaps you might ring for some tea." He guided her back into the drawing room with Signor Clementi. "Now, what were you saying about me sleeping with every woman in London?"

Later that afternoon, Sara smiled at her mother-in-law and took the proffered cup of tea. The drawing room at Stratham House was large and imposing. To her surprise, the decor reflected the Regent's current interest in all things oriental. The couch was covered in green silk and had crocodile legs, and the small tea table was finished in bamboo. It was not a style that appealed to Sara's more eclectic tastes, but it suited the vast expanse of the town house.

"I appreciate your agreeing to see me, my lady."

Lady Isabelle sipped her tea. "Please call me Isabelle; we are family, after all." She grimaced. "After the way my husband

and Valentin behaved at your first dinner party, I'm surprised you consented to visit me at all."

Sara sipped at her tea. "Are they always so . . ."

"Aggressive, argumentative, and downright unpleasant? Yes, unfortunately they are. I believe they are too alike. Neither of them seems able to allow the other to have a single redeemable quality."

Mindful of her promise to Valentin, Sara picked her words carefully. "After their troubled past, I suppose some hostility was inevitable."

Isabelle sighed, and some of the tension disappeared from her shoulders. "Poor Valentin. He returns from a life of slavery to find his mother is dead and a girl barely five years older than he is has suddenly become his new mother. I'm not surprised he resented me."

Sara shifted uncomfortably in her seat. "He speaks of you with great respect."

"I know, and he has never been anything less than polite, but I hoped for so much more." She put down her cup. "I wanted to mother him, but he would barely let me near him, let alone take him into my arms and make everything better. Perhaps I was foolish to be hurt by that."

Her smile faltered. "Then, of course, the marquess tried to make Valentin attend university and behave like a privileged English gentleman. Valentin didn't want that. Even I could see that it was too late for him to accept guidance from the man he believed had abandoned him. He needed to carve his own path." Isabelle frowned at her entwined fingers. "I've tried to heal the breach over the years, but neither of them is prepared to bend an inch."

Sara thought about her own family. How would she feel if she were at odds with them? Even though her mother drove her to distraction, she couldn't imagine never speaking to her again or living in a state of such animosity.

"I would like to help."

Isabelle clasped her hands together. "I'm delighted to hear it. My eldest son, Anthony, idolizes Valentin. It would be so nice if we could be a family again."

Sara tried to hide her confusion. Valentin had indicated that his half brother resented him and coveted his title and inheritance. "How old is Anthony, my lady?"

Isabelle got up to ring the bell. "Please, call me Isabelle. He is almost nineteen. Just at an age where he needs the guidance of an older man."

"Have you asked Valentin to help?"

She sat back down. "I tried, but he insisted I discuss it with his father first. Of course, the marquess was offended that I'd even suggested bringing his sons together."

The door opened, and a tall dark-haired young man entered. His smile reminded Sara of Valentin at his most unguarded. He stopped in front of Isabelle and bowed. His eyes were a dark blue like his mother's.

"Mama, I promised I'd drop in this afternoon and meet your guest." He turned to Sara, his gaze full of interest. "I hear you've married my brother. May I wish you happy?"

She couldn't help but smile back at him as he kissed her hand. "Thank you, and please call me Sara."

Anthony looked at the door. "I think I saw Val's carriage arrive to take you home. He's probably on his way up."

The butler announced Valentin. Sara got to her feet as he bowed to Isabelle and came toward her. His long black driving coat swirled around him like a gathering storm.

"Good afternoon, Lady Stratham, Sara. Have you enjoyed your visit?"

Sara frowned at him. "Yes, I have, but I had hoped it would be longer." Valentin had made no mention of coming to collect her. Was he afraid she might spill too many of his secrets after all?

Anthony strode up to Valentin and enthusiastically shook his hand. Valentin disengaged as quickly as possible and stepped back, smoothing his sleeve as if his half brother were an over-excited puppy.

"Congratulations on your marriage, Val. Lady Sara seems very nice."

Valentin smiled at Sara. "Yes, she is. I am a lucky man." He turned back to Isabelle. "If you will forgive me, ma'am, I need to hurry Sara along. I have a very young team of horses, and they don't stand well."

Before she could blink, Sara found herself outside the mansion being helped into Valentin's open carriage. She waited for him to join her. They moved off with a jerk. Valentin stretched out his legs and regarded her from the seat opposite.

"Did we really have to leave so quickly?"

He shrugged. "I told you, I hate the place. When I first returned to England, my father insisted I live there with him and his new family. It felt as cold and foreign to me as a tomb, and very little has changed since. As soon as I could I escaped and set up home with Peter." His cool gaze met hers. "My father refused to help Peter, who had no family he remembered and no one to care for him. He would've been quite happy to see him starve on the streets."

She regarded him in silence. It was obvious that the marquess had made some grave mistakes in his treatment of his son. But why wasn't Valentin able to move on?

"Did you enjoy yourself?" His gaze roamed her bosom and the soft green skirts of her muslin gown.

"In the fifteen minutes that you allowed me? Yes, I did. Your stepmother was charming. Your half brother, Anthony, seems to be a nice young man who idolizes you."

His eyebrows rose a fraction. "Why do you sound so belligerent, sweet wife?"

"Because I know you'd prefer me not to like your family."

Valentin smiled. "They have their uses. It occurred to me that you don't know many people in town. If my stepmother offers to chaperone you, you might wish to consider it."

Sara regarded him for a full minute before venturing a reply. "She did offer. You would allow me to do that?"

He smiled. "It's not an entirely selfless gesture, Sara. It means that I can get back to work and not worry about the company you keep."

"And what kind of company would that be?" She sat up straight and locked gazes with him.

"At the dinner party you seemed very taken by Lady Pettifer. While she and her husband, Sir Richard, are good solid citizens, their acquaintance will not enhance your reputation."

Sara struggled with a rising sense of indignation. "Is that because they engage in trade?" She managed a trill of laughter. "You begin to sound like your father."

Valentin's indolent expression disappeared. "I am trying to protect your interests, my dear wife. Lady Pettifer is neither well bred nor well disposed toward me."

The carriage drew to a stop, and Sara leaned forward. "I'm not particularly well bred either. Perhaps you should treat me like an adult and allow me to choose my own friends."

He caught her wrist and pulled her close. "Lady Pettifer was a prostitute before she managed to ensnare Sir Richard. I do not wish you to associate with her."

Sara shook off his hand. "And how would you know that?"

Valentin held her gaze. "Do you really want me to answer that?"

The carriage door opened. Sara accepted the footman's arm and descended the steps. She swept into the house without waiting to see if Valentin followed. By God, he *had* slept with every woman in London. She marched up the stairs, into her bedroom, and slammed the door. At least Lady Isabelle seemed immune to his charms. She seemed to bear the same exasperated affection for Valentin as if she were truly his mother.

Sara stripped off her bonnet and cloak and patted her hair. She intended to take Lady Isabelle up on her offer to chaperone her into the highest reaches of the *ton*. She scowled into the mirror. Damn Valentin and his high-handed commands. How dare he condemn his own father for being top lofty and then act in exactly the same manner?

She opened her desk and took out a fresh piece of parchment. She intended to ask Lady Pettifer around for tea at her earliest convenience.

8

"Where on earth is she?"

Sara sighed with exasperation as she scanned the crowded hallway of the Portland Square mansion. In the crush of over-scented silk-clad bodies, she'd lost sight of Lady Isabelle and Anthony. She turned and fought her way back up the wide staircase. Perhaps Isabelle had gone ahead of her after all. Halfway up, she almost fell backward as someone stepped on the train of her dress.

On the first-floor landing, she looked in vain for the marchioness but couldn't see her amongst the sea of chattering faces, nodding plumes, and waving fans. The gold lace at the hem of her green ball gown trailed on the ground. She decided to visit the retiring room to assess the damage before she attempted to meet up with her chaperone in the main ballroom.

Delamere house was huge, the ballroom occupying a whole wing to the rear of the house. Hanging from the ceiling of the curving hallway, a chandelier burned at least five hundred candles. Its blazing light reflected the gems of the guests below to produce a blinding firestorm of ever-changing radiance. She couldn't quite understand why everyone had to arrive fashionably late and congregate on the stairways. After one last look at the glittering throng below, she made her way to the retiring room. To her relief, it was relatively clear of people.

One of the maids stationed there volunteered to stitch up Sara's hem. Sara thanked her and retreated to a quiet corner while the maid deftly sewed the narrow band of gold lace back into place. Sara opened her fan and waved it gently across her face. It was pleasant to get out of the crowds. En masse, the *ton* behaved no differently than a horde of villagers on market day in Southampton. She had no desire to rush back out there, even if it was supposed to be the most prestigious ball of the Season.

While she waited for the maid to finish her task, Sara allowed her head to fall back against the wall as she summoned the strength to move. Her erotic nights with Valentin meant she was often tired during the day. She smiled to herself, picturing his lithe, muscular body moving over her, the silken feel of his hair in her fingers. Not that she would change those hours for anything, although it would be pleasant to see him in the daylight as well.

After the maid disappeared, she noticed that the green ribbon on her slipper was untied again. Half hidden behind a Chinese silk screen, she bent to fasten it, content to listen to the delicious female gossip floating around her.

Lady Isabelle was a darling, but Sara found it difficult to make friends with the ladies of the *ton*. Most of them regarded her with suspicion, if not with outright hostility, when they discovered a mere tradesman's daughter had married one of the *ton*'s most eligible bachelors. Despite Valentin's objections, she'd made tentative overtures of friendship to Lady Pettifer, which had been warmly reciprocated. Her only other friend was Peter Howard. To her delight he'd proved to be a trusted companion after Valentin increasingly delegated his social obligations to his friend.

Sara frowned at her slipper ribbon as she knotted it for the third time. She'd thought everything would be different away from the provincial town of her birth. She'd imagined herself having more freedom in London.

Of course, when Valentin inquired as to her social prowess, she lied to him and insisted everything was fine. She sensed he didn't quite believe her. So far he'd been too busy with his business enterprises to question her further. The only place she felt safe to be herself was in his arms and in his bed. He'd given her the sexual freedom to express herself in a totally sensuous way. If only the *ton* was so accepting. Sara closed her eyes as a girlish laugh rang out.

"Have you seen Anthony Sokorvsky recently, Amy? He has turned out quite well."

"I still prefer his older brother." Amy sighed. "I can't believe that countrified nonentity managed to trap the great Valentin Sokorvsky into marriage. Her father must've bought him for her, or else she pretended she was pregnant."

The two girls began to giggle. Sara sat up, her stomach tightening. Should she confront them or leave them to their gossiping? Just as she decided to step forward, another more mature voice entered the discussion.

"Miss Antrim, may I offer you a piece of advice? I'm sure your mother would be ashamed to hear the spiteful remarks you just uttered. And let me tell you, there's nothing that makes a pretty girl look more plain than spreading rumor and gossip. Men don't care for it, and women look for confidantes they can trust."

"I'm sorry, Lady Ingham," Amy muttered. "I didn't realize there was anyone else here."

The sound of a quadrille starting up filtered through the

suddenly opened door. Sara sat rigidly until the whispering girls departed.

"Lady Sokorvsky? Are you there? I'm Lady Ingham."

Sara got to her feet and moved the screen aside. The woman who awaited her was expensively dressed, her brown hair piled high on her head in a cascade of ringlets. Sara thought they must be of a similar age until she noticed the discreetly applied cosmetics and the fine lines around her companion's eyes. Her magnificent bosom swelled over the top of an amber-colored gown.

"You are Lady Sokorvsky, aren't you?"

Sara curtsied. "I am, and you must be my rescuer." Curiosity overcame her embarrassment. "How did you know who I am?"

Lady Ingham pulled a face. "I stepped on your gown on the stairs and heard it rip. I recognized you from Val's description, and I came in here to apologize and help put things to rights."

"That was kind of you." For some reason, the casual mention of Valentin's name made Sara wary. She gestured to her skirt. "One of the maids helped me sew up the lace. I only sat down to retie my slipper."

"And heard nothing but bad about yourself."

The apparent sympathy on Lady Ingham's face almost undermined Sara's composure. She attempted a shrug.

"It's nothing I haven't heard before. Even I understand I must seem a very odd choice of wife for a peer of the realm."

Lady Ingham studied Sara. "If you will excuse my familiarity, your husband has never seemed to care too much for society's opinion."

Sara picked up her fan and reticule and stared at their reflections in the mirror. For some reason, she had no desire to discuss Valentin with a woman who looked like Lady Ingham. And the woman's apparent ease with her husband was beginning to annoy her. Next to such a luscious and glowing image of womanliness, she felt like an untried girl.

"Perhaps that's a quality I should learn to imitate. Thank you for your help, Lady Ingham." Sara smiled at her companion. "I will remember it."

Lady Ingham curtsied, her hazel eyes full of wry understanding. "You are welcome. If I see the marchioness, I will tell her you will be out shortly."

Valentin strode out of the ballroom. He's spotted his stepmother and Anthony, but there was no sign of Sara. He'd intended to surprise her with his presence. A reported fire on one of his ships had concentrated all his attention for the last few days. This evening, he'd left Peter in charge at the office and carved out some time for Sara, only with great difficulty. And now he couldn't find her.

A gloved hand squeezed his arm. Valentin turned and found Caroline Ingham smiling up at him. He bowed and kissed her fingertips, noting the sway of her breasts and the golden tint to her skin. Knowing Caroline, she'd probably been sunbathing naked again.

"Valentin, I haven't seen you in ages. Where have you been?"

"I think you know, Caroline. Gossip in London spreads faster than the plague."

She pouted, catching her full lower lip in her teeth. "Are you referring to your sudden marriage? What is that old saying, 'marry in haste repent at leisure'?"

Impatiently Valentin let his gaze stray over Caroline's shoulder in a vain attempt to locate Sara. There was still no sign of her.

"If you are looking for your wife, she is in the retiring room." Caroline said. "Would you like me to fetch her for you?"

Valentin's gaze snapped back to Caroline. "You have spoken to her?"

She smiled and laid her hand on his arm. "I was able to perform a service for her. Some of the young ladies were being catty about her origins. I stepped in and reminded them of their manners."

Valentin forced himself to relax. "That was kind of you."

Her rich laughter filled the space between them. "Oh, come now, Val, did you think I might march up to her and simply tell her I am your mistress? Credit me with some sense. The poor girl has enough to deal with at the moment without having that particular truth thrust in her face." She tapped his cheek with her fan. "Shame on you for leaving her to fend for herself. As you don't seem to care for her, she's been treated abominably by a fair section of the *ton*."

Valentin didn't smile back. "Caroline...." He wasn't sure she would take well to being publicly dumped at a ball. "We need to talk."

She cast him a demure glance from under her long dyed eyelashes. "I'll be at Madame Helene's House of Pleasure tonight if you should decide to drop in. I have an ambition to experience the massage slaves in the Egyptian room." She licked her lips. "Apparently I can be covered in honey and have the men lick me clean. Wouldn't you like to watch or help out?"

Valentin caught sight of Sara and swiftly kissed Caroline's hand. "I'm not sure I could stand all that sweetness. It can become cloying after a while. But I will certainly be in touch with you soon." He bowed. "Thank you for aiding Sara. And rest assured that I intend to make sure she never feels the lack of my company again."

He hoped Caroline got his meaning. He wasn't keen on the thought of his mistress and wife getting acquainted. Caroline was a wealthy widow who had shared his bed on and off for several years. She was an accomplished lover who enjoyed experimenting.

Valentin had introduced her to Madame Helene's, and Caroline had never looked back. Her sexual imagination almost matched his. He'd even tried to persuade himself she would make an excellent wife, but she was as incapable of fidelity as a stray cat. He was prepared to overlook such behavior in his mistress but not in his wife. His mouth twisted. If Peter were here, he would probably call Val a hypocrite for his double standards. And he'd be right.

Val returned his attention to his search for Sara and located her at the entrance to the ballroom, hands twisted together at her waist. He watched as she straightened her shoulders and passed into the press of people. No one paused to greet her or acknowledge her presence. In her olive-green and gold dress, she looked like a slender, mistrustful goddess of spring. Valentin suppressed an unheard-of urge to wrap her in his arms and protect her from the stares and subtle put-downs of society's highest.

Caroline was correct, damnit. It was his fault. He had a reputation as a notorious rake, something he'd deliberately earned and wasn't ashamed of. It hadn't occurred to him that his transgressions would be taken out on his wife, who lacked family and friends to surround and defend her.

He'd been lax in his duty, asking Peter and his father's wife to escort Sara to society functions while he connected with her only in the intimacy of their marriage bed. As they were never seen together in public, the *ton* probably imagined he didn't really care for her.

It occurred to him that despite his refusal to accept his father's offer of a home and schooling, he had never truly been alone. His family name and title were sufficiently well known to allow him to do what he damned well pleased with his life. He should've been more grateful for that protection than he had been. Sara's attempts to shield him, of all people, from the realities of her situation made him feel like a wretch.

Valentin thrust his worries about his business to the back of his mind and strode after Sara. He caught her elbow as she approached the dance floor.

"Milady, would you care to dance with me?"

Her expression lightened as she turned toward him.

"Valentin, I didn't know you were here."

He swept her a bow. "It was meant to be a surprise." The orchestra struck the first chords of a waltz, and he drew her into his arms. "I've been neglecting you recently."

Her exquisite skin flushed. "Peter said there had been trouble on board one of your ships and another fire. Have you discovered who is attempting to ruin your business?"

He executed a faultless turn at the end of the ballroom. Was she still making excuses for him? Sometimes Sara was too sharp for her own good. And what was Peter doing gossiping about their troubles?

"Nothing for you to worry about, my dear. I'm sure we'll bring the culprits to justice soon."

Sara held his gaze, her blue eyes sharp. "I'm not stupid, Valentin. These latest incidents indicate a deliberate and methodical attempt to drive your business to its knees."

He let out a breath. Perhaps it was time to share his fears with her. It might be interesting to have a new perspective on the whole situation. She was his wife, after all. He could trust her.

"You're right, my love. Perhaps you'd like to attend the next meeting to discuss what we intend to do about it?"

Sara stumbled. He smoothly corrected her balance and continued the dance.

"There is no need to be hateful, Valentin," she hissed. "I was only trying to help."

He drew her closer and pushed his thigh against hers, deliberately brushing her bodice with his waistcoat. "I meant it."

She looked up at him, surprise written on her face. "I would love to."

"Then you can. We meet tomorrow in my study." He raised an eyebrow. "Now, may I enjoy the rest of this dance with you?"

After the waltz ended, Valentin stayed at Sara's side. He took her back to Lady Isabelle and even made himself pleasant for a while. Sara studied his handsome features as he talked amiably to his stepmother and Anthony. Why was he being so nice? Why hadn't he disappeared into the card room or found an excuse to leave early, as he usually did?

"My dear, would you care to promenade with me?" Valentin said. "There are a few people I would like you to meet."

Sara laid her hand on his sleeve and walked beside him. To her surprise, he introduced her to several older couples, including the host and hostess, rather than the crowd of young bucks she'd anticipated. With Valentin at her side, people seemed more willing to acknowledge her, and she found herself enjoying the attention. Eventually he guided her toward the refreshment room and presented her with a glass of champagne.

"Valentin, why are you here?"

He studied her over the rim of his champagne glass, his violet eyes sparkling. "To enjoy my wife's company. Why else?" He lowered his gaze to her bosom. "I like that dress, by the way. It reminds me of ravishing you in a field of tall grass."

Sara's nipples hardened. For the first time that evening she managed a proper smile. "I don't think that was me."

"It will be." Ignoring the chattering guests around him, he leaned forward and kissed her lightly on the lips. "I'd be delighted to lay you down right now and make love to you until you screamed out your release." He winked at her. "You do scream, you know."

Sara studied his mouth. "There are too many people here."

He removed the champagne glass from her grasp. "You're right."

He took her hand and headed for one of the narrow corridors that led into the depths of the house. As they moved into the servants' area, voices echoed up the backstairs. Valentin pressed a finger to Sara's lips and guided her into a small book-lined room. It smelled of burned toast and dog. She imagined the room belonged to the owner of the house's secretary or land agent.

In the darkness, Valentin brushed his mouth against hers; the hint of cigars and champagne on his breath made her tremble.

"I've missed you, Sara."

She smiled against his mouth. "I haven't been anywhere."

"Ah, but you have. You've been cast adrift in a room full of pompous old ladies and insufferable bores." He kissed her, his agile tongue sliding between her lips. "I've neglected you, and yet you never breathed a word of reproach."

"I'm your wife, Valentin." The slight sting of Lady Ingham's remarks made her continue. "Isn't that what I'm supposed to do? Suffer in silence while you enjoy yourself?"

He kissed his way down from her throat to her shoulder. "I've never asked you to suffer in silence. In truth, I suspect it would be impossible for you." The amusement in his voice and the nip of his teeth made her shiver. "You are always very . . . vocal in your demands."

She pushed at his chest, and he caught her hands. "Why do you always bring the subject back to sex?"

He encircled her wrist with his fingers and brought her hand to the front of his pantaloons. "Because I am a man and we are alone. Because you've made me hard and I'm going to make you wet."

He dropped to his knees and picked up the hem of her gown in both hands. "Hold this for me."

Dazed, Sara took the heavy fabric and folded it neatly into her hands. The hard tip of Valentin's tongue nudged at the cleft of her sex. After just a few short strokes, her bud swelled to meet his questing tongue. She stifled a moan as he settled his teeth on it and gently tugged.

He pressed her legs apart, his bare hands on her skin, his gloves discarded on the floor. Still trapping her in his mouth, he slid one finger inside her and pumped in and out. Caught holding up her skirts, Sara could only endure the exquisite torment.

When he finally released her clit and added another finger inside her pussy, he looked up at her. "You're wet and swollen now. You'd take my cock easily. Are your nipples hard?"

Sara nodded, for once too intent on the pleasure he brought her to waste words.

"Good. You can let go of your skirts."

Before Sara could object, he stood up, licked his fingers, and put his gloves back on. He leaned into her, crushing her aching breasts against his chest.

"You'll dance with me now. And I'll be the only man who knows how wet and ready for sex you are." He kissed her hard, his mouth bruising and arousing. "And if you behave yourself, I might play with you a little more in the carriage on the way home. Would you like that?"

Sara stared into his eyes. A flicker of excitement stirred deep in her stomach. "Am I allowed to play with you as well?" She stroked the bulge in his pantaloons. "Perhaps I might kneel at your feet and take your cock in my mouth. Would you like that?"

His pupils widened, leaving them almost black. "Perhaps I might."

* * *

It seemed to take forever after their carriage was called for it to arrive at the steps of the grand mansion. At last a footman shut the door and left them alone in the dim interior. Sara arranged her skirts as they pulled away with a sudden jolt. Valentin sat beside her, one arm along the back of the leather seat, his long legs stretched out in front of him. The meager light caught the satin sheen of his pantaloons and emphasized the heavy bulging shadows of his groin. Sara's body responded to Valentin's nearness and softened with desire.

She took off her gloves and traced a path along the sleek satin from Valentin's knee to his cock and back again. He breathed out slowly and widened the gap between his legs as if seeking more.

"Let me loosen your laces. No one will see beneath your cloak."

Sara stood up, braced between Valentin's knees, and allowed him to release her corset and bodice. She turned in his arms and sank to the floor in a froth of petticoats. At least with him, she knew who she was and exactly what she wanted. She put her hands on his knees and pushed his legs wide. It made the front panel of his pantaloons stretch tight across his erection.

The satin felt cool against her tongue as she licked over his shaft, defining the shape and extent of his passion. His fingers closed in her hair as she undid each of the buttons. She smiled with pleasure as his cock was revealed, glad he didn't wear smallclothes under his pantaloons.

She looked up at Valentin. He watched her, his face taut with the expectation of pleasure. It pleased her she could make him look at her like that. It made her feel powerful and desirable.

"If you wish to suck my cock, please do."

She gripped him at the base, cupped her other hand beneath his balls, and weighed them in her hand. He sighed as her tongue licked the tip of his wet cock. She investigated the narrow slit and the swollen crown before making her way down his thick shaft. He tasted of life and the promise of ecstasy. Sara breathed in his unique scent and kissed her way back up.

When she took him in her mouth, he groaned, his fingers contracted painfully in her hair. She took as much as she could without choking and wrapped her fingers around the rest. Soon she established a strong rhythm that had him pushing into her mouth, driving his staff deep into her throat. His balls tightened in her hand, and he went still.

"Wait."

She released his cock and looked up. Valentin's smile was tinged with lust. She moved closer as his hard fingers dragged her bodice and corset away from her flesh. He slid his engorged cock between her exposed breasts. "I want to come here."

His hands closed on her breasts, pushing them together to surround his erection. Sara could only watch as he slid against her, his thumbs pressed to her nipples, making them ache with need. He came with a growl. His hot, wet seed trickled between her breasts, over her stomach, and down to her aroused pussy. He closed his hands around her waist, and he brought her onto his lap to straddle him.

Sara shuddered as he pushed her bodice aside, caught her nipple in his teeth, and suckled hard. Her sex rubbed against his flat stomach and the underside of his shaft, seeking relief, seeking fulfillment. Despite her wriggling, he refused to penetrate her. She almost screamed when the carriage stopped.

Valentin arranged her cloak to cover her dishabille and sat her on the opposite seat. He grinned as she raised a shaking hand to her hair.

"I'll give you a two-minute head start to get up the stairs and into our suite."

Sara stared at him. She pretended to yawn. "That's very kind of you. I'm so tired."

His mouth quirked up at one corner. "You'll not be sleeping. I'm going to find you, and when I do, I'm going to fuck you."

The carriage door opened, and Valentin leaped down to hand Sara out. He whispered in her ear. "Two minutes. Starting now."

She barely remembered to thank the butler as she passed him, her gaze intent on the stairs. When she reached the first landing, she turned and saw Valentin was already in the hall. He glanced up and mouthed the word "one." Sara quickened her pace as she went along the deserted corridor toward her suite.

She opened the door and allowed her cloak to slip from her shoulders. Only the glow from a banked fire lit the rooms. For some reason, no candles added their light. Sara paused to get her bearings and heard footsteps in the corridor behind her. Did she want to hide from Valentin? Her body craved the satisfaction he could bring her, but her mind enjoyed the idea of the chase.

As the door opened, she took off, skirted the huge bed, and headed for the dressing area that connected their two rooms. There was no light in there either. Valentin must have planned this. Sara tried to still her breathing and decide where to hide. The closet that ran between the two rooms presented the best opportunity. It was long and narrow and packed full of clothes.

She moved toward the door and felt a tug on her skirt. As quickly as she could, she wiggled out of her loosened gown and kept going. Valentin laughed. Sara slid into the closet and crouched low to the ground. She stripped off her petticoat and stuffed it behind some of her winter boots. Would her white corset show up in the darkness? Sara was reluctant to take it off and be naked.

She paused as she inhaled Valentin's distinctive scent, citrus and cigar smoke. She almost shrieked as his hand wrapped around her ankle and he flipped her onto her back. He licked her foot and then proceeded to kiss his way up to her stockinged knee. Desperately Sara tried to edge away, but Valentin had too strong a grip. He pulled her closer, his mouth grazing her inner thigh, his tongue flicking her sex. She kicked out with her other leg and caught solid muscle. His hands disappeared. Sara stifled a groan as she sensed he had gone.

She rolled onto her stomach and crawled along the other wall of the closet that exited into Valentin's bedroom. Strips of moonlight illuminated the red carpet closest to his bed. There was no sign of him. Behind her lay darkness and the prospect of Valentin's lust. Her breasts ached; her sex throbbed in time to her heartbeat and accelerated breathing. She wanted Valentin to catch her and plunge his cock inside her.

Sara headed back toward the shadowed part of the suite. She moved carefully past the large chest of drawers and straight into a wall of warm, excited male. With a triumphant growl, Valentin grabbed her wrists and rolled her onto her back. His teeth clamped on her nipple, and she arched her back as he suckled hard. He drove his thigh between her legs, rubbed her swollen sex, drove her wild. The hot drip of his seed decorated her stomach.

Her body gathered itself to come, but he withdrew into the shadows again, leaving her painfully aroused and starting to get furious. She eyed the door into the main corridor. It would serve him right if she disappeared and took her rest in one of the spare rooms.

Her heart pounded so loudly she wondered if he could hear it. She reached the door, tried the handle, and realized it was locked. In mounting frustration, she peered into the gloom. Where else could she hide? Fingers tickled her ankle, and she moved quickly away. With all her energy, she ran toward the four-poster bed and disappeared between the thick drapes. Her intention was to crawl across the bed and make for the window seat on the other side.

She cried out as Valentin caught her around the waist and

prevented her from moving anywhere. His hands ripped away her corset. He maneuvered her against one of the thick wooden posts at the corner of the bed. Before she could protest he pressed her breasts and belly against the wood, trapping her in front of him.

Her breathing was ragged now, her body on fire with the desire for completion.

"Put your arms around the post." Valentin's soft command was whispered close to her ear. "And don't move or turn around."

Sara wrapped her arms around the thick column and rested her cheek against the smooth cool surface of the wood. She felt the mattress give as Valentin moved away and then returned. He took hold of her wrists and tied them together with something silky that she realized was one of her stockings. He brought her wrists above her head and secured them against the post. She had to kneel up to be comfortable.

The corner post rested between her breasts, pressed into her crotch, stimulating her already aroused pussy. She'd wanted him all night. She wanted him now. He stripped off the rest of his clothes, and the slick heat of his cock prodded her back.

She closed her eyes as Valentin played lightly with her nipples. "You sucked my cock well in the carriage. Do you like the feel of me in your mouth?"

"Yes."

He caught her nipples between finger and thumb and tugged. "Why?"

"Because I like the way you taste and how you fill my mouth."

Valentin squeezed harder, bringing her aroused flesh to a point between pleasure and pain. She shuddered as his fingernails pressed deeper.

"If I weren't a civilized man, I'd keep you naked and have you suck me whenever I wanted." Sara swallowed hard. "I like to imagine you at my feet in my office. I'd click my fingers and you'd service me instantly. Even if other people were there." He groaned low in his throat, sending ripples of desire through her skin. "All my employees would be permanently hard."

"Perhaps it is a good thing that the world is more civilized, then."

Valentin nipped her neck hard enough to make her flinch. "Trust me, the world isn't civilized. I've seen things you wouldn't—"

He stopped speaking, his indrawn breath harsh on her flesh. His flat tone alarmed her. He dropped his hands from her breasts and licked the sting from her neck with the tip of his tongue. One of his clever fingers traced the curve of her spine and paused at her buttocks. She couldn't help widening her stance, inviting him to delve deeper. She inhaled the mingled scent of their arousal.

His low laugh stirred the hair at the nape of her neck. "What do you want, Sara?"

In the darkness, she felt bolder. A woman who could ask her lover for anything, no matter how shameful her desires. She arched her back, allowed her buttocks to press against his hard, furred belly.

"I want you to touch me."

His finger stopped an inch from her anus. "Where?" He circled the tight bud. "Here?" His thumb breached her. "I would love to fill you here."

Sara stilled at the unfamiliar invasion. "I didn't know you could." She tried to relax as he slid his thumb up to the knuckle.

"It would take time to help you become accustomed to me, but it would be well worth it." He slid his other fingers forward. They sank into the thick cream that poured from her pussy. "What do you want?"

"Your fingers, inside me," she gasped as he complied. "Ah, yes, just like that."

He held her captive, balanced between fingers and thumb on his outstretched palm. She shivered as he brought his other hand down to stroke her clitoris.

"Where would you rather be, Sara?"

His soft question surprised her as she battled the urge to come. He increased the pressure on her clit. "Would you rather be dancing with me at the ball or letting me play with your pussy?"

"I'd rather you played with me." She ground herself against his fingers, desperate to come. He stopped moving and kissed her neck.

"Let me untie your hands. If you promise to stay still, I'll bring you a present."

Despite her lack of fulfillment, Sara waited obediently in the darkness as he left her. When he returned, he lit a candelabrum and set it beside the bed, illuminating them in a golden glow.

Valentin stood in front of her, a box in his hands. He held it up to the light so that she could see the illustration on the lid. A naked woman lay on a chaise, a complacent smile on her face. At first, Sara noticed only the gold rings that pierced her nipples and navel. Then her gaze lowered to the woman's hand, which rested between her splayed legs. Sara tried to make out what the woman was doing to make herself smile.

"Does it hurt to have those rings put in?" She imagined how it might feel to have a man's mouth tugging on such sensitive flesh.

Valentin smiled, his teeth white in the semidarkness. "A little, and, yes, a man likes it, if that was going to be your next question." He drew the box away. "What do you think she has between her legs?"

Sara stared at the illustration and then at him. "I'm not sure."

"She's pleasuring herself."

"With what?"

"With a fake cock."

"Why?"

Valentin removed the lid of the box to reveal the silken interior. "Because her lover is not available or she doesn't have one. There are many reasons why a woman might choose to use a dildo, or, as the Italians so romantically call it, a diletto."

Sara watched, dry-mouthed, as he unwrapped the contents of the box.

"Hold out your hand."

He laid a heavy jade object on her palm. Sara traced the intricate carving with her fingertip as her heartbeat slowed and echoed the pulse between her legs. It was a perfectly sculptured rendition of an erect cock. Sara gauged the length as over nine inches. "Is this for me?"

Valentin sat behind her on the bed and looked over her shoulder. "Yes. I have to go to Southampton for a week. I thought you might miss me." He laid the box on the quilt and showed her a narrow leather harness. "Some women like to wear the dildo when they walk around. This contraption keeps it buried deep inside you."

Sara licked her lips. "Would you like to think of me doing that when you were away?"

Valentin dragged her face around for a kiss, his mouth hard and possessive. "No, I'd resent not seeing you too much, but it would certainly give me something to think about when I made myself come."

Sara closed her fingers around the jade, which had warmed in her hand. "Will you show me how to use it?"

In answer, he knelt behind her and lifted her onto his knees, her back to his chest, her legs spread either side of him. She could see her hazy reflection in the mirror over her dressing table. She looked relaxed and wanton, her sex open to his gaze.

He closed one hand over her breast and slid the other down to her clit. "Let's make sure you are ready."

Sara choked back a laugh. "I think I've been ready since I first saw you at the ball this evening."

Valentin squeezed her clit. "I think you've been ready since the first day I met you." He penetrated her with all four fingers. "I imagined having you like this. Every night I spent in your father's house I was hard and ready to fuck you." Christ, she was so slippery and wet, his fingers went in easily. "Give me the dildo and watch carefully."

He took her hand, interlaced her fingers with his, and lowered the smooth jade to her pussy. At first, he gently nudged her clit, making sure the thick shaft was coated with her cream. "Open your legs wider. I want you to see this."

As he helped her ease the solid bulbous head inside, he squeezed her nipple hard and bit the tendon at the side of her neck, making her writhe against him. "You see? It goes in easily. You are so wet and ready for sex." He made her take the first six inches, watched her reaction, gauged when she thought she'd taken enough by the hesitation in her fingers.

He took his hand away. "Slide it in and out like a real cock." Sara sighed as she gripped the jade and moved it back and forth in a slow, languorous rhythm. Valentin rocked his hips, allowing his painfully swollen staff to slide against her naked buttocks. He rubbed her clit in time to her strokes, watched her build toward a climax. She moved the jade faster, taking a little more with each penetration. As her body climaxed, Valentin placed his hand over hers and drove the dildo deeper, until she took all of it. She spasmed against his hands; her hips bucked in an effort to absorb the pleasure.

Grimly Valentin held on to his desperate need to come as he waited for her to stop shuddering. He grabbed several pillows from the head of the bed and bent her over them. Her buttocks rose in the air as he extracted the jade. Without a word, he caught her hips in his hands and thrust hard inside her. He had no time for finesse, just an animal need to fill her with his seed as quickly as possible.

Her soft cries echoed the harsh slap of his flesh against hers, a higher sound than his groans. He didn't want to slow down. He needed her fast and hard. When his come pumped out of him in a huge rush, he roared his lust and collapsed over her, his heart thumping fit to burst.

So much for treating his wife like a delicate lady. She seemed to encourage his sexual appetites and enjoy making him break the traditional sexual boundaries of a decent, polite society marriage contracted for the sake of children. There was no denying it, he wanted to ravish her. He wanted to fill her with his seed, keep her naked in his bed to serve him alone.

Damnation.

Valentin opened his eyes and stared into the gloom of the bed hangings. The smell of sex and the unique scent of his woman floated around him. He pulled out and let Sara roll onto her back. He watched her face. She smiled at him, her gaze softened by the glow of completion.

Valentin's cock quivered. Without a word he crawled between her open thighs and studied her. So wet now, coated in his come. He touched her clit with the tip of his tongue and heard her catch her breath.

His shaft responded by becoming half erect. He pushed her thighs wider, making a place for himself between her legs. This was no longer an amusing game. She was his. He had an absurd desire to brand her with his lovemaking so that she wouldn't even look at another man while he was away. He wanted to make her so sore that every muscle ache would remind her of his cock plunging inside her, of his body possessing her, of her desire for no one but him.

He crouched in front of her, breathing hard, his primitive desire for her at war with his civilized mind. After his experiences in Turkey, he'd made sure sex was just an exquisite game, not this gut-wrenching need to guard and conquer one woman. He'd promised himself he would never again be owned or own a slave himself. His possessive feelings for Sara came too damn close to his most closely guarded emotions. He gazed at her clit, teased it again with his tongue, felt her tremble. She brought her hand down to the back of his neck and pushed his face closer.

With a groan he lapped at her, taking the gift she'd offered him. His shaft thickened, and he knew he had to have her again. His promise to restrict himself to no more than twice a night suddenly seemed ridiculous. He'd worry about the consequences of his actions in the morning after he'd exhausted them both with the pleasures of the flesh.

9

"Are you sure I can't come with you?"

Valentin checked his pocket watch before he turned back to Sara.

"This is not a social visit. Some serious accusations have been made about the manager of our Southampton office. I don't expect our meeting to be pleasant."

Even though she could tell from the implacable set of his mouth that she was unlikely to change his mind, she couldn't resist another attempt.

"I could stay with my parents. You wouldn't even have to see me."

His smile flashed out. "Then what would be the point of you being there? And if I knew you were close by, I'd be too distracted to get the job done properly."

"Perhaps I merely want to see my family, sir, not you."

He strolled across and took her chin in his long fingers. "You wouldn't miss me in your bed?"

She felt her cheeks heat as he stared down at her. How was

he able to do this to her? He stroked her bottom lip with his thumb.

"I would miss you. Perhaps I need to try harder to engage your attention."

The clock on the mantelpiece struck ten, and someone knocked on the study door, making Sara jump. Valentin stepped back as Peter entered the room and bowed to her. She smiled at him, grateful he would remain behind to keep her company while Valentin was away.

She studied Valentin as she settled back into a chair beside his desk. Dressed for travel, he looked his usual immaculate self, his smooth hair tied at the nape of his neck, his black coat and tan breeches clinging to his muscular frame. She eased back against the cushions, aware of a lingering ache between her thighs and the chafe of her nipples against her corset. Valentin's lovemaking had reached new heights on the previous night, his appetite for her apparently insatiable.

He flicked a glance at her. "Do you need another cushion, my dear?"

"I'm fine, thank you, my lord."

Peter turned to study her, his face concerned. "Are you unwell, Sara?"

Valentin's mouth quirked up at one corner as she blushed. "I believe my wife slept badly last night. Isn't that so?"

"Valentin is right. Unfortunately his loud snoring kept me awake."

"I don't remember you being a snorer, Val. When did that happen?" Peter asked as he brought another cushion over to Sara.

"It's probably his advanced age," she said sweetly. "I've threatened to fasten a clothes-peg on his nose."

Valentin started to laugh just as his secretary, Mr. Jeremy Carter, entered the study. Mr. Carter frowned at the unusual sound as he paused by the desk and dumped a pile of books on it.

"Good afternoon, my lord. Am I the cause of your amusement, or did I simply miss something?"

Valentin got up and shook his hand. "Nothing of importance, Mr. Carter. You know you are always welcome." He gestured at Sara. "I don't believe you've met my wife. I decided it was time to involve her in our family troubles."

Sara smiled at Mr. Carter, who wore thick spectacles and lacked a single hair on his shiny, perspiring head. He smelled of mothballs and dried ink. His stooped posture reminded her of the head clerk at her father's shipping office who had given her humbugs when she was a little girl.

"I'm pleased to meet you, Mr. Carter. My husband says you are an excellent and loyal employee."

Mr. Carter's narrow lips widened into what passed for a smile as he bowed over Sara's hand. "Thank you, my lady. I endeavor to keep our financial ship afloat to the best of my abilities."

Valentin sat behind his desk and pulled the ledgers toward him.

"How badly will the latest fire affect us?"

Mr. Carter cleared his throat. "As the ship was still in the harbor, the fire was put out and the damage to the cargo was negligible." He opened the largest book and pointed to a line of fine copperplate script. "If the ship had been out at sea, things would have been worse. Wool burns quickly."

"It seems as though your idea to place more guards on the ships and in the warehouses has worked well, Peter." Valentin nodded to his friend, who sat on the edge of the desk. "It's harder for our enemies to manage their crimes."

Sara leaned forward to observe the closely written pages. Along with music, mathematics was one of her passions. It took her only a moment to realize how close the company was to bankruptcy. She also noticed that some of the earlier figures were wrong. After a series of quick calculations in her head she sat back and listened to the discussion going on around her.

It was interesting to observe Peter and Valentin in their working environment. They shed their society manners and emanated a cool business sense that reminded Sara of her father. She waited for the complicated argument about man power versus new trading routes to come to a close.

Valentin pressed his fingers to the bridge of his nose and closed his eyes, a gesture of tiredness Sara had come to recognize.

"May I make a suggestion?" Sara asked.

All the men looked at her.

"Please do." Valentin spread his hands wide in a gesture of supplication.

"It is something my father did when his business came under threat from other rivals. Have you offered to combine cargoes with your competitors?"

Peter frowned. "Why would we do that? The last thing we need is to lose their goods as well as our own. Our reputation is bad enough as it is."

"I think Sara might have a point." Valentin stood up and paced the thick blue carpet. "If we offered spare cargo space to others, it would be interesting to see which ships were attacked and which were not."

"Over time, it might help you identify whose goods always survive," Sara added.

Valentin shot her a look of approval. "If the details were handled carefully, we might be able to identify a pattern and an enemy."

"That's if it is one of our competitors," Peter said slowly.

Sara frowned. "Who else could it be?"

Valentin shut the ledger. "We're not sure. Whoever it is is trying to blacken our personal reputations as well." He smiled at Sara. "Peter and I have not exactly led exemplary lives."

"Are you speaking of your time in Turkey?" Sara tried to catch Valentin's eye. "You were children."

"We might have made enemies. Attempts have also been made to blackmail Peter. And there is my family to consider."

Sara stared hard at Valentin's composed face. "You cannot believe your family wish you harm?"

"Why not?" He faced her, a challenge in his gaze. "My return complicated my father's life. It is well known that he would rejoice in my ruin. He believes I'll come crawling back to him for financial aid." Valentin's sneer became more pronounced. "Of course, I'd rather beg on the streets, but he might consider bankrupting my company a fitting way to bring me back under his thumb."

Sara didn't know what to say. From what she had seen of Valentin's father recently, she wanted to defend him. Instinct told her Valentin would not take kindly to her intervention.

Mr. Carter cleared his throat. "If you will allow me, my lord, I will investigate the possibility of carrying our competitor's goods." He got to his feet and went to collect the heavy pile of books.

Sara laid her hand on his arm. "Mr. Carter, would you mind leaving the books here tonight?" She managed a beseeching smile. "Valentin promised to show me how well you keep the shipping company accounts to teach me how to balance my household expenses." She fluttered her eyelashes at Mr. Carter. "Apparently I keep overspending, and that makes Valentin so cross with me."

She looked up to find Valentin and Peter staring at her. Mr. Carter patted her hand.

"Of course you may keep them, my lady. I'm delighted to see you strive to practice the fine art of economy."

Peter opened the study door. "I'll bring them back to you tomorrow, Mr. Carter. I have a driving engagement with Lady Sokorvsky at ten. I can collect them then. Have a safe trip, Val."

He bowed to Valentin, winked at Sara, and ushered Mr. Carter from the room.

Valentin closed the door and leaned against it.

"What was that all about? Your household accounts are always immaculate."

Sara stood up, her attention on the ledgers. "The columns don't add up."

"What?"

Sara ignored him as he joined her at the desk. "While Mr. Carter was showing you the new entry, I checked through the earlier figures. From my calculations, someone has been back and altered the amounts."

Valentin studied the sixteen narrow columns that spread across a double sheet of paper. It took him hours to reconcile a week's worth of takings. How on earth could Sara spot a multitude of errors in six months of entries?

She gestured impatiently. He handed her a quill and a sheet of writing paper from his desk drawer. Her finger settled on a line near the top of the page.

"Do you see how some of the smaller figures have been altered? Sometimes it's as simple as a zero becoming a six, but every farthing makes a difference."

Valentin squinted at the inked-in numbers. By God, she was right. The penmanship of the second writer differed from Mr. Carter's distinctive style.

"If Mr. Carter didn't do this, how come he hasn't noticed it?"

Sara scribbled so fast on the writing paper her pen nib splashed ink on the blotter. "From the thickness of his spectacles, I assume his eyesight is very poor. It's possible he wouldn't spot the errors until he completed his yearly accounts." She looked up at Valentin. "Of course, by then it would probably be too late to find the money. Who else has access to these books?"

"They are kept in the main shipping and receiving office here in London, so, in theory, anyone could get their hands on them." Valentin shoved a curl of escaped hair back from his face. "Damnation, there's no way I can keep them locked away without causing talk. Ask Peter to deal with it tomorrow, will you?"

Sara put down her quill pen. "It will take me a while to work my way through all these books. Perhaps you could keep them here at night so that I might study them."

Valentin recapped the inkwell. "I don't expect you to have such a chore. There are many capable men out there who will be able to detect fraud."

"I can do it, Valentin." Sara held his gaze, her eyes pleading. "Do you doubt me? I oversaw my father's books until he decided it was unladylike. I would consider it a fascinating challenge."

John Harrison had mentioned Sara's talent for numbers, albeit in a dismissive manner. Like a fool, Valentin hadn't bothered to understand just how capable she was. He'd been too busy imagining her naked.

"All right. You may do it."

Sara jumped up and threw her arms around him. It was the most animation she'd shown outside of his bed. In his determination to fit her into his ideal of a society wife, he'd come close to denying her considerable abilities. He hated being judged on his appearance, and yet he seemed incapable of allowing his wife to be more than a decorative item on his arm.

"Thank you. I won't disappoint you. By the time you come back from Southampton, I should have something more definite to show you."

He kissed her cheek and felt his cock rise as her womanly scent flooded his senses. Reluctantly he set her away from him. "I have to go."

She pouted, the soft rose color of her lips a lure he found hard to resist. "I will miss you."

He laughed to cover his strange reluctance to leave her. It was an unwelcome sensation. One he'd fought hard to escape in his previous dealings with women. "Nonsense. You will be too busy enjoying the Season with my stepmother and Peter to miss me. And you have the ledgers to attend to."

Sara stood on tiptoe and kissed his mouth. Her tongue flicked over his closed lips. "I will miss you. No one else makes me feel so alive."

He stared into her blue eyes as the desire to plunge deep inside her grew along with his erection. "Use the jade for me."

"I will. I'll imagine you standing by the side of my bed watching me." She slowly licked her lips a scant inch from his own. "And I'll write my lonely fantasies in the Red Book, ready for your return."

He backed away from her until he reached the door and turned the key in the lock. She studied him with wide, amused eyes as he methodically unbuttoned his breeches.

"Sit on the edge of the desk and open your legs for me, Sara. The carriage can wait a few moments more."

Sara studied Peter's angelic face as he drove carefully through the gates of Hyde Park at the unfashionable hour of eleven in the morning. Despite her father's veiled warnings about Peter's past, Sara found it easy to confide in him. He treated her as an equal, his fashion advice was excellent, and he knew all the gossip.

He tipped his hat to a military gentleman who trotted by on a magnificent black horse. Sara admired Peter's quiet command of the reins. Valentin had a more neck-or-nothing style of driving that secretly scared her.

She drew in a deep breath of crisp air and prepared to ask the question she'd agonized over since Valentin's departure.

"Peter, yesterday Valentin mentioned you had been blackmailed."

He smiled at her and heaved a sigh. "You were so busy defending Valentin's family, I hoped that part escaped your notice."

"I don't understand why anyone would want to blackmail you."

He stopped the carriage and gave the reins to his groom. Sara waited until he handed her down and laid her fingers on the arm of his dark blue driving coat. They strolled toward the trees; brown and gold leaves crunched underfoot.

"As you know, Val and I were slaves in Turkey for several years. During that time, I picked up several unsavory habits to help me survive the hell I lived through every day."

Sara studied his face and wanted to close her eyes against the harsh desolation in his expression. "I still don't understand."

"I became addicted to opium. Even after my return to England, it took me several years to get over the cravings." His mouth twisted. "I did some stupid things to ensure I had a constant supply of the purest opiate. I stole, I lied, and I cheated everyone who tried to help me. It would be easy for someone to use those lost years of my past against me. Hell, I still don't know exactly what I did."

"Is that why my father doesn't care for you?"

"Of course, he warned you about me, didn't he?" Peter looked amused.

Sara risked a quick look at his face. "My father said you were untrustworthy and a bad influence on Valentin."

"He's right. I stole from your father and lied endlessly. If it wasn't for Val I wouldn't be here now. He stood by me when everyone else despaired. He forced me to give up the opium and take charge of my life."

Sara stared back at the carriage on the rough path. The groom's red coat shone vividly against the autumnal hues of the park, his breath misting on the freezing air. Despite her father's misgivings, Sara believed Peter. He looked like a man who had walked through the fires of hell and survived. And what of her charming husband who seemed so untouched by anything so sordid?

"Did Valentin suffer as you have?"

"Val chose more 'physical' ways to deal with our slavery. He is far stronger than I am. He still bears the scars, though. Perhaps they are buried deeper than he realizes."

Sara stood on tiptoe and kissed Peter's cold mouth. "I'm glad you survived. I'm glad you decided to live."

His gloved hand caressed her cheek, his pale blue gaze directly on hers.

"Thank you for that." His voice sounded husky.

Sara glanced around to see if anyone had noticed their intimate conversation and then continued walking. After they discussed her findings in the ledgers, she directed the conversation into more general topics until Peter relaxed again. As they turned back toward the carriage, she decided to ask him the other question that bothered her.

"If I wished to give Valentin a very particular birthday gift, would you help me?"

"Of course I would." Peter glanced down at her, his expression once more concealed beneath the shadows of his hat brim. "It must be something very unusual if you think you need my help."

Sara fought the blush that rose on her cheeks. "I would like to get my ears pierced. Do you know anyone who could do it for me?"

"Your ears?" Peter stopped and gave her his full attention.

"Any competent lady's maid could do that. It takes little skill. I could even do it for you myself."

He handed her into the carriage. Sara waited until the groom was out of earshot. She squirmed in her seat, her gloved hands locked together in her lap. "What if I wished to have other things pierced as well?"

When she received no answer, she forced herself to look up. Peter held her gaze, his eyes narrowed. For the first time she saw a flash of purely male interest in his eyes.

"Why would you think I would know about this?"

He didn't sound angry, only interested.

"Because Valentin said you enjoyed experimenting with the pleasures of the flesh, and I can't ask—"

She stopped as he lifted her hand to his mouth and kissed her uncovered wrist. "It's all right. You don't have to explain. I know a woman who can help you. She's an old acquaintance of mine and Val's from our more riotous days." He winked at her. "She can pierce anything you want."

10

Valentin walked soundlessly up the stairs as the clock struck one in the morning. His suite was swathed in darkness and had a damp, unused feel to it. No one had known when to expect him home. His original plan to return from Southampton within a week had been shattered. On his arrival he'd found that his shipping manager, Mr. Reynolds, had disappeared with a substantial sum of money pilfered from the books and all the petty cash.

He had remained in Southampton for almost a month until the office was working normally again. He'd spent most of his time visiting his customers and the banks to reassure them about his company's future financial stability. It was exhausting work, even for a man of his so-called charm and connections.

Imagining Sara and Peter enjoying themselves together in London hadn't helped his temper either. Nor had the news that despite his best efforts, Mr. Reynolds remained at large. Valentin guessed he had either shipped out of the country or been taken care of by his other employers.

He lit a candle and used it to start the fire laid ready in the grate. The whole episode left a grim taste in his mouth. He and Peter had worked damned hard to put the company together, sailed their own ships at times, dirtied their hands to prevent trouble, and even killed when absolutely necessary.

Watching his life's work seep through his fingers like precious drinking water at sea rattled his sense of control. He felt as hopeless as he had when a slave, his body subject to the sexual whims of others.

He took off his caped driving coat, glad to be free of the weight. Last time he'd been home he'd come close to telling Sara about his sexual past. He doubted she would believe how he and Peter were forced to service customer after customer until they fell exhausted into their beds. Their youth, stamina, and fair skin were a draw Madam Tezoli, the brothel owner, had exploited to the full.

His mouth quirked in an unwilling smile. Not that she had been as mercenary as some brothel owners. She prided herself on the quality of her wares. She waited until they were old enough to have an erection before selling them to anyone who could afford their exorbitant price. In the first haze of sexual excitement he'd even enjoyed some of the women. The men had always been a different matter.

He caught a glimpse of his grim-faced reflection in the shadows of the mirror. At one point he'd deliberately goaded his most obnoxious male customers to cut his face, to destroy what they lusted after, to inflict the final blow and release him from torment. He was convinced his physical beauty was a curse and not a blessing. After enduring his insults, one customer broke his jaw, and only Peter's intervention saved him from a severe beating.

He smiled without humor. Peter should have let him be. If Sara knew how many women he'd fucked, would she recoil from him or continue to welcome him into her bed?

A soft noise from Sara's bedroom made Valentin turn. He opened the interior door and crossed the short distance across the dressing room to hers. Light shone through the frame. She sighed again. A lush sound of carnal satisfaction she often made when he pleasured her. Was she with another man?

Lust and jealousy roared through Valentin as he silently pushed the door open. Sara lay on her bed; her crimson dressing gown framed her luscious skin and dark hair. A pool of soft candlelight concentrated light on the silken counterpane. The Red Book was propped open on Sara's pillow as she read what she had obviously just written. Valentin's throat went dry as he realized her left hand moved slowly between her legs.

She made the delicious sensual moan again. Val cupped his erection and squeezed hard. He'd slept alone in Southampton. The longest he'd been celibate in his adult life. He hadn't wanted any other woman. He'd spent his nights dreaming of Sara and using his own hand and vivid imagination to bring himself relief. It hadn't been enough.

He leaned against the door frame, one hand still slowly rubbing his cock. She brought her right leg up and bent it at the knee. Her left sprawled out to the side. He caught the subtle glint of jade, wet with her juices against her ivory-white thigh as she pleasured herself. She arched her back and drew both her knees higher, swept the tip of the quill down over her pussy. She laughed, deep in her throat. His blood hammered in his shaft as he watched her explorations.

Without speaking, he crossed to the bottom of the bed. He braced his hands on the bedposts and stared down at her. She didn't react to his presence, just kept pleasuring herself. He breathed in the scent of her cream, the soft, slick sound of the moving jade.

Tiredness forgotten, he struggled out of his tight-fitting coat. His waistcoat, cravat, and shirt soon followed. He kept his breeches and boots on, enjoying the painful sensation of his hungry erection pushing against the thick fabric. He crawled onto the foot of the bed and crouched in front of her.

She smiled at him, her gaze heavy with arousal, both sets of her lips parted and eager. She flicked the feathered quill over her swollen sex and brushed it back and forth, kept the jade buried deep in her channel.

Valentin leaned forward and traced her labia, warm and puffed up against the green jade they clasped so tightly. He circled her opening, enjoyed the sight of her thick cream and the hard tip of her clit. His cock pounded with his frantic heartbeat, seeking relief. He wanted to unbutton his breeches and drive into her, fuck her and fuck her until he ran out of come.

Instead he sat back and rubbed the hard ridge of his shaft with unsteady fingers. His buckskin breeches were already wet and felt coarse and constricting against his rapidly swelling flesh.

Not yet.

Not until she begged.

Instead he brushed her clit with one finger. She let the quill pen fall from her hand. He moved closer, dipped his head and inhaled her scent, licked her clit with the very tip of his tongue. She shuddered and moved the jade rod faster in and out of her channel.

Valentin lowered his head and lapped his way around the jade, enjoying the contrast between her swollen, giving flesh and the smooth hardness of the stone. Carefully he eased a finger on either side of the dildo, widening her even further, making her gasp. He knew he could make her even wider. As slaves, he and Peter had often slid both their cocks into the same woman. It was stimulating for the man, too, all that friction and hardness.

Ruthlessly he quashed that thought and concentrated on Sara. He moved his fingers within her and darted hard, stabbing licks to her clit. He slid his other hand under her buttocks and lifted her into the rhythm of the jade strokes. He allowed his longest finger to slip between her cheeks and probe her anus.

Gathering her thick cream, he eased his finger past her bud and quickly added another. He nipped at her clit as his cock tried to drill its way out of his breeches, frantic to fuck.

Not yet.

He waited until the unbearable ache blended with the anticipation and pleasure. Felt the long thickness of the jade rod and his other fingers through her internal walls. Knew she must feel it, too.

While in Southampton, he'd visited an oriental trader and found some exquisite anal plugs and rings to help Sara accept his cock. For a reckless second he wished he had them with him now. But perhaps it was better that he didn't. After a month without sex, he needed to take things slowly. He knew firsthand how agonizing a forced breaching could be. Reluctantly he withdrew his fingers and concentrated his attention on her pussy and clit.

Her breathing shortened, and he knew she was close to a climax. He pulled back, barely touching her, wanting to see her face in this most intimate moment. He drew back the folds of her dressing gown to expose her breasts and nearly lost what little sense he had left.

Her rose-red nipples glinted with gold. He stared at the rings that pierced her sensitive flesh. She flinched as he reached out a finger. With great restraint, he lightly touched the ring. She would be sore for a while. Even more sore if the ring was ripped out, as had happened to him. He still bore the scar on his chest. He traced the warm metal with his tongue and removed his fingers from her pussy.

"Does it still hurt?"

She bit her lip. "A little."

He licked her nipple as gently as he could, and she sighed.

When she healed, he intended to spend a great deal of time lavishing his attention on her breasts. God, it was possible that he'd never let her out of bed again. He cupped her chin and kissed her mouth, giving her a taste of her own pleasure. His cock throbbed. He wanted to be inside her with a primitive urge that shook him to the core.

Still kissing her, he reached down and opened his breeches. His breath hissed between his teeth as his cock sprang out, blindly seeking her. She dragged his breeches down to expose his buttocks and tight balls.

"Oh, God, Valentin, I missed you."

He groaned as her fingernails scraped his skin. Releasing her mouth, he slid back down between her legs and pushed her knees wide with his hips. She'd take his cock now and scream out her pleasure.

Sara quivered as he pushed her hand away from the jade dildo and grabbed the base of his shaft. His cock was bigger than he'd ever seen it before. He guided the massive weeping crown along the lower side of the jade—engorged red flesh to pale green, velvet heat to cream-washed stone. Her sheath swallowed him below the jade.

He waited until her flesh gave willingly and then continued his slow penetration. Sensations exploded over him, the clench of her pussy, the rock-hard resistance of the stone above him. He was trapped in an erotic vise of his own making.

"Valentin." Sara clutched his muscled shoulders, her fingernails digging deep. "Oh. God, I'm going to come."

He pressed deeper until his balls slapped against her buttocks and held still as she milked his cock with the strength of a ravaging storm. He caught her screams in his mouth, refusing to end the kiss even when she nipped and bit at his lips in the final throes of her climax.

When she finished shaking, he pulled out and removed the jade dildo. He stared down at her beautiful, wet, fuckable pussy. So much for restraint. He was beyond that now, and so was she. He held up the jade and slid two fingers inside her back passage.

"I want this in here. Will you take it for me?"

"I tried it myself when you were away."

He raised an eyebrow as he slowly penetrated her with the jade. "You must have been bored. I asked you to wait for me."

Her breathing hitched as he slid the jade deeper until it could go no farther. "I thought to prepare myself for you."

"You are always so impatient, Sara, but on this occasion I'm glad."

She licked her lips as he drew her thighs over his shoulders and plunged straight back inside. She was his now; he could no longer deny it.

He buried himself in her heat with a growl. He could feel the jade even through the clench and release of her sheath as she came.

"I'm back now, Sara. No more jade in your pussy unless I put it there. No more of your fingers, just my cock fucking you for as long and as hard as you want."

She moaned and held him tighter as he continued to thrust. His welcome was assured. For the first time in his adult life, he felt sure someone would understand and forgive him his past. He groaned as his come flooded into her and knew he had truly come home.

11

"I swear to you, my lord, I didn't alter the books."

Valentin's luxurious mahogany-paneled study was bathed in sunlight, but the atmosphere remained dark and tense. Mr. Carter took off his spectacles and rubbed at the lenses with his handkerchief as if seeking to erase the errors Valentin had revealed to him.

"I didn't think so, Mr. Carter," Valentin said quietly as he tapped his quill pen on the open page. "What I would like to know is who did?"

He sat back while Mr. Carter craned his neck over the books. "I'm not sure, my lord. The alterations are so small it's difficult to tell."

"Who has access to the ledgers apart from you?"

Mr. Carter frowned. "As you know, they are kept in the main office. Hundreds of people pass through there every day. But if you mean amongst the staff, I suppose my two assistants would have the best opportunity to alter the figures."

"And they are?"

"Alexander Long and Christopher Duncan. Both men came highly recommended to the job." He bowed at Valentin, relief clear on his face. "In fact, one of the men was recommended by your father, the marquess."

Valentin let out a slow breath. "Which one?"

"That would be Duncan. He's a Scotsman. I believe he trained at your father's Scottish estate before moving to London and seeking a new position."

Peter, also present, cleared his throat. "I can gather information about these two gentlemen for you, Valentin. Who recommended the other man?"

"I believe that was either Sir Richard Pettifer or Mr. John Harrison." Mr. Carter raised a trembling hand to push his spectacles back up his nose. "I have no complaints about either man. They have always seemed conscientious, honest, and reliable."

"No one is blaming you, Mr. Carter," Sara said from her shadowed seat in the corner.

Valentin resisted an urge to glare at her. *He* blamed Mr. Carter. The man was obviously too old to do his job properly. As if he'd read Valentin's thoughts, Mr. Carter stumbled to his feet.

"Please accept my apologies, my lord. I promise I will be more diligent in the future."

Sara raised her eyebrows at Valentin. He reluctantly tamped down on his desire to fire the man on the spot.

"It's all right, Mr. Carter. We'll get through this. May I suggest you keep the details of this meeting to yourself? We wouldn't want your assistants to get wind of our interest and disappear."

"Of course not, my lord." Mr. Carter stuffed his handkerchief in his pocket, the relief on his face unmistakable. "I will be the soul of discretion."

After Mr. Carter's departure, Valentin stared at Peter and Sara.

She smiled at him. "It was kind of you to allow Mr. Carter to keep his job."

"Damned fool. He deserves to be fired. He was negligent." Valentin shut the ledger and leaned back in his seat, propping his booted feet up on the edge of the desk. "Now I suppose you'll expect me to find some way to replace him without hurting his feelings." His voice dripped with sarcasm.

Sara failed to hide her amusement. "That would be nice of you."

"Kind, nice," Valentin growled at his wife. "What other words do you wish to damn me with today?"

Peter laughed. "I'm glad to see Sara is having such a civilizing effect on you."

She got up and smoothed the folds of her green gown.

Val frowned at her. "Where are you going?"

"I've been invited to tea at the Pettifers' this afternoon." She stuck her chin in the air and gave him a challenging smile. "Perhaps I will be able to find out more about this employee of yours."

"I thought I asked you not to pursue your acquaintance with them." Valentin sat up so abruptly his boot heels thumped on the wooden floor. "And I certainly don't want you doing any spying."

Sara kissed his cheek. "I will see you at dinner. Remember, you promised to attend the Russian ambassador's ball with me tonight."

"Why should I oblige you when you don't do a damn thing I say?" He scowled at her retreating back as she shut the door firmly behind her.

"I never thought a woman would tie you in knots, Val." Peter came to sit on the side of the desk.

"Well, you thought wrong." He lit a cigar and handed one to

Peter. "Let's just hope she remembers to be discreet in her dealings with the Pettifers. She is such an innocent."

Peter blew out a cloud of smoke. "Are you worried Sara's father might be implicated in all this mess?"

Valentin stared into his friend's calm blue eyes. "Of course I am, although I'm more convinced this has something to do with my father."

"Relax, Val. I'm sure he isn't involved." Peter reached forward and brushed his finger along Valentin's clenched jawline. When Val recoiled, Peter immediately withdrew his hand. "Sorry, force of habit." He cleared his throat. "If I told you that the time has come for you to see your father for the man he is, rather than the bogeyman of your childhood, would you listen to me?"

"I'd listen, but I still wouldn't believe such nonsense. I know exactly what my father is and exactly what he wants from me. Have you forgotten how he treated you?"

"I haven't forgotten. But I can understand why he thought it best to remove all traces of your previous life after your return to England." Peter sighed. "I was a constant reminder of your past and, in truth, I was also a liability. He only wanted the best for you."

Valentin got to his feet and went to the window. Sara's carriage was pulling away from the front door.

"You are more generous than I am. He wanted to pretend nothing had happened. He wanted me to act as if I'd never left his side and that I'd been brought up as a perfect gentleman ready and willing to inherit his pathetic title."

"But you wanted to forget, too, Val. Perhaps you are more like him than you think. When have you ever taken time to talk about those horrors we endured?" Peter extinguished his cigar in the ashtray. "You still insist that nothing that happened to you in the brothel has any bearing on your present life."

Val pressed his palm hard against the windowpane as endless

memories of aroused, heated bodies whispered through his mind. He closed his eyes against the insidious voices and the ripple of unease that shuddered through him. With a curse he swung around to confront Peter.

"I'm not a woman or a poet. I don't need to gossip about my feelings, damnit!"

"There's no need to shout, Val. I'm only trying to help."

Val glared at his friend. He might no longer welcome Peter's touch, but the bond they shared went well beyond the physical. It was the only reason he was still listening to such ridiculous drivel. He struggled to refocus his thoughts on the more urgent matters in hand.

"Will you find out all you can about Long and Duncan, then?"

Peter slid off the desk, his gaze contemplative. "I'll make sure I investigate both men equally. If there is any bad news to give you, I will give it to you in person, agreed?"

"Agreed. Now I have another appointment to go to." Valentin stubbed out his cigar. "I have to meet Caroline Ingham at Madame Helene's to discuss our future, or lack of it."

"Not the best choice of venue, Val." Peter grimaced. "She'll do her best to get you back into bed with her."

"I know." Valentin gave him a brief smile. He was quite looking forward to dealing with Caroline. "Trust me, she won't succeed. Unfortunately it was the only way I could get her to agree to meet with me at all."

Sara smiled as Evangeline Pettifer handed her a cup of tea. Her hostess seemed a little overdressed to receive a visitor at home, but Evangeline's taste tended to be more elaborate than Sara's. Evangeline attempted to keep up with every whim of fashion whether it suited her or not. Today's green-and-gold-striped satin gown in the Egyptian style was not one of her better choices.

Rain drummed against the windowpane, contributing to the gloom in the cramped drawing room. There was so much furniture crammed into the small space, Sara always worried she would inadvertently set something toppling with an unwary turn or an outflung hand.

The five clocks in the room began to chime, and Evangeline jumped. Sara set down her cup.

"You seem a little distracted, Evangeline."

Evangeline's tea cup rattled in its saucer. "Do I?" She gave an artificial laugh. "It's probably because I'm expecting my husband to arrive at any moment. We have a guest coming to stay with us."

"You should have told me it was an inconvenient time. I can always come back another day."

"Oh, no, Sara, you are always welcome." She bit her lip and glanced furtively at the door. "It's just that I'm not used to having foreigners in my house. Goodness knows what the man will eat."

"Perhaps you might ask him when he arrives," Sara suggested gently.

"I don't even know if the man speaks English!" Evangeline looked close to tears. "Sometimes it is hard to pretend that I know how a lady should act in every given situation. I wish I'd never tried to better myself."

"I can wait until he arrives, if you wish." Sara tried not to appear too eager. "I speak French, German, and some Spanish. Surely he will know one of those languages."

Evangeline dabbed at her eyes with a lace handkerchief. "That is very sweet of you, but Sir Richard was quite adamant that I should not mention our visitor to anyone. Oh, my goodness!" Her eyes widened as she stared at Sara. "You won't tell anybody, will you?"

Sara fought an urge to laugh. "Of course not." She added some sugar to her tea. It occurred to her that she might use the situation to her advantage. Evangeline was very involved in the day-to-day running of Sir Richard's shipping business.

"Valentin has an employee who speaks several languages for just such emergencies—a man I think you and Sir Richard might know, a Mr. Alex Long."

"I don't remember that name." Evangeline frowned. "And as I said, I'm sure Sir Richard wouldn't wish me to involve any of Valentin's employees."

"I believe Mr. Long was previously employed by Sir Richard. I'm certain he would be discreet."

Evangeline sighed. "If things get desperate, I'll mention Mr. Long. But I doubt Sir Richard would want to deal with an employee of Valentin's. Thank you for the thought, Sara. You are such a good friend." She stiffened as the unmistakable sound of the door knocker echoed up the stairs. "That might be them now. I suppose I'd better go and be polite."

Sara got to her feet as well. "I'm sure everything will be fine."

Evangeline surprised her with a hug. "You are a dear. Now let me see you safely to your carriage."

When they descended the stairs, the hallway was filled with boxes and servants. Evangeline paused to organize the removal of the luggage, leaving Sara free to move closer to the half-open door of Sir Richard's study.

A hearty laugh, which she easily identified as Sir Richard's, boomed out. She strained her ears to hear his companion reply but failed to identify the speaker's accent. When the door was pushed open, she moved back into the hallway with all the speed she could muster.

"Ah, Lady Sokorvsky, what a pleasure!" Sir Richard came toward her and took her hand. "Have you just arrived, or are you leaving?"

Before Sara could reply, Evangeline appeared at her elbow.

"Sara's carriage is at the door this very minute!" She pointed toward the study and whispered, "Is he in there?"

Sara couldn't miss Sir Richard's frown as he turned to address his wife.

"Yes, my dear, our guest has arrived." He gestured pointedly at Sara. "Perhaps you might see Lady Sokorvsky out and then come back to greet him?"

Evangeline at her side, Sara exited through the front door and walked down the steps. As she got into the carriage, Evangeline suddenly came to life.

"I've been so silly. I know what to feed him, Sara. He's from *Turkey!* He has to like to eat it as well, doesn't he?"

With a last wave, Sara sat back in the carriage to ponder the information she'd gathered. Sir Richard had a visitor from Turkey. Was it just a coincidence that he wanted to keep his guest a secret? At this point, Sara didn't think so. She sat back against the comfortable brocade seat and smiled. She couldn't wait to tell Valentin.

Valentin handed his hat and gloves to one of Madame Helene's discreet footmen and headed for the main salon. As he'd expected, there was very little activity during the middle of the day. He smiled as Madame herself came to greet him. She wore a gold and ruby silk gown that matched the luxurious decor of the room she walked through. He'd often wondered how such a beautiful and autocratic woman had come to own such a notorious establishment. He valued her friendship too much to pry.

When Peter had first introduced him to the pleasure house, Valentin had simply been grateful to find a place where his voracious sexual appetite could be satisfied in a mutually discreet and sensual way. He surveyed the dimly lit corridor beyond the salon, which stretched deep into the house. The rooms beyond seemed to hold the seeds of sexual excitement in their very walls.

"Valentin, it is a pleasure to see you. Are you looking for Peter?"

He smiled down at her heart-shaped face framed by thick blond curls. How old was she? Nobody knew for sure. She celebrated her birth on Bastille Day, insisting that she couldn't remember when her real birthday was. He suspected she'd lost her family during the Terror in France.

"Good afternoon, Helene."

He kissed her hand. She'd been his first lover at the House of Pleasure. They'd shared one memorable night during his first lost year after returning from Turkey. Her stamina had matched his youth and exuberance, and her technique and inventiveness had easily outstripped him. They'd agreed to part, knowing they were too similar in temperament to ever make a comfortable couple.

"I'm not looking for Peter. I arranged to meet Lady Caroline here."

Helene frowned. "I believe she is in the Egyptian room again." She studied Val, her eyes sharp. "I had hoped your marriage would help you move on from Lady Caroline."

Valentin smiled. "Are you giving me advice, Helene? That's not like you."

In truth he was surprised. In all the years he'd known her she'd never once commented on his sexual excesses or his peculiar relationship with Peter.

She didn't flinch from his gaze. "I don't like Caroline Ingham. She isn't worthy of you."

Valentin's smile disappeared. "I know. Why do you think I am here?"

"For the right reasons, I hope, my friend."

"Indeed, what other reasons are there?"

He kissed Helene's fingers and strode off toward the back of the house. He knew exactly where the Egyptian room was. He'd enjoyed playing there in previous years himself. As he walked, he pictured Sara, dressed as an Egyptian slave, and imagined clicking his fingers at her. Would she come to him when he called or toss her head and walk away?

His faint smile died as he opened the door and found Caroline instead. She lay on a stone table. The room was decorated to resemble an Egyptian temple complete with marble statues, palm trees, and a sacrificial altar. Caroline's naked body lay open to his gaze as three men dressed as slaves massaged oil into her skin. A fourth knelt between her thighs and worked his mouth over her shaven pussy.

Valentin leaned back against the door and contemplated the erotic scene. Despite Caroline's groans and sighs, his mind remained indifferent, his cock unaroused.

"Do you want me to wait until you've finished, Caroline?"

His cool question made her sit up, dislodging the hands on her breasts and the man between her legs.

"Valentin? Are you here already?" She bit her lower lip and slowly ran her fingers over her oiled breasts as she turned toward him. "Would you like to help me hurry up?"

Valentin studied his watch before pocketing it. "Perhaps you could dismiss these men. I don't have much time today."

She pouted as the men disappeared and then wrapped a silk sheet around her ample breasts. "Why do you want to talk to me?"

He waited until he had her attention before he took a slim jeweler's case out of his pocket and showed it to her. "I'm sure you know. That's why you've been avoiding me for the past few weeks."

Caroline snatched the box from his outstretched hand and opened it. She gasped at the diamond necklace within. Valentin caught her wrist as she went to take it out. "I believe it is customary when ending a relationship to soften the blow by presenting one's ex-lover with a small trinket. I hope this will suffice."

"Why do you want to end our relationship?" Caroline looked genuinely confused.

"Because I have acquired a wife."

"But why should that stop you? Everyone knows she married you for your money. Surely she won't expect you to be faithful?"

Valentin smiled. "I don't know. All I know is that I intend to be faithful to her."

Caroline's incredulous expression took on the hard sheen of anger. "That's ridiculous! You're incapable of fidelity."

Valentin got to his feet. "That remains to be seen." He bowed and headed to the door. "I wish you well, Caroline."

She struggled to her feet, tripping on the trailing sheet. "Don't expect me to take you back when you tire of that mewling lowborn slut!"

"Trust me, I won't."

He shut the door as a vial of oil hurtled toward him, followed by a howl of rage. Her shrieking increased in volume as he strolled back along the corridor. He hoped the men in the Egyptian room had the sense not to interrupt Caroline's tantrum. She could be quite destructive when she put her mind to it.

12

Sara smiled up at Valentin as he removed her cloak and handed it to the footman. The vast entrance hall of the Russian ambassador's house was packed with people. Valentin wore a dark blue double-breasted coat and embroidered gray waistcoat. Massed ranks of candles illuminated his dark hair, which was held back by a narrow purple ribbon.

He caught her gaze and raised an inquiring eyebrow. "Is there something amiss?"

"No, I was simply admiring your new coat. It is very fine, and it matches my dress."

He bent to take her hand, a lustful glint in his violet eyes. "So it does. I hadn't noticed. I was too busy admiring your breasts and wondering how soon I'll be able to suckle them."

Sara took a deep breath as her nipples tightened under his stare.

He smiled. "Look, I think they want my mouth now. Perhaps I won't wait until we get home."

"Valentin." Sara picked up her skirt and made her way toward the ballroom. "You promised to behave yourself this evening."

He pulled on her arm, moving her out of the flow of people until they stood in the shadows of the vast circular stairwell. He trapped her against the oak-paneled wall. "I am behaving badly?"

"I've been looking forward to this ball, and now all I can think about is making love with you."

Valentin tucked a lock of her curled hair behind her ear. "And why is that such a terrible thought?"

"Because sometimes it feels as if you might consume me and that one day I'll wake up and find you gone."

His expression sobered. "I have no intention of leaving you, my dear." He slid the tip of his thumb between her teeth. "Consuming you, however, is a different matter. I could easily dine on the taste of your mouth and your sex for the rest of my life. Does that alarm you?"

Sara stared at him. He hadn't denied that he wanted to possess her completely. Should she be afraid of the force of his desire for her? It was sometimes overwhelming to know that her body obeyed him without question. She'd fought so hard to escape a conventional boring marriage and instead found herself in a whirlwind of emotions she sometimes feared she couldn't control.

She drew an unsteady breath. "Why me, Valentin? Compared to all the other women you have bedded, I am such an innocent."

He kissed her softly on the mouth and drew back. "But innocence in itself is a trap, don't you think? The desire to be the first man to teach you about sex was impossible to resist." Oblivious to the other couples passing by in the massive hallway, Valentine continued to study her face. "Do you wish you hadn't met me, then?"

She touched his cheek. "Of course not." She tried to smile. "It's just that sometimes it all feels so fast and unreal. Three months ago I only knew your name, and now . . ."

"And now you are married to me and embarrassed because you enjoy what we do together in bed."

She clutched his arm, felt the hardness of muscle clench beneath the cloth. "No, I'm not embarrassed."

"Prove it. Tell me something wickedly delicious and sinful you would like to do to me."

She worried her lower lip. Was she bold enough to tell him what she really wanted?

His smile widened. "Are you afraid, little girl?"

His teasing gave her the courage she lacked. "You are incorrigible. One day, I would like to tie you to the bed and do exactly what I please with you."

A flash of excitement in his eyes was followed by a bland smile. "I'm not sure you are strong enough to tie me up." He took a step away from her. "I'm not sure I'd be willing to let you."

There was a threat behind his lighthearted words. She'd forgotten about his years as a slave.

"I'm sorry, Val, I . . ."

He caught her chin in his fingers. "Don't ever apologize to me for sharing your fantasies. There are things I might wish to share with you that perhaps you wouldn't want to indulge in either." His smile this time was perfect and put her at a distance. "That's why they are called fantasies, my dear. We shouldn't ever confuse them with reality."

He placed her gloved hand on his sleeve and drew her back into the stream of people. She wanted to scream in frustration as he smiled down at her, the perfect guest at a society ball.

"Now let's go and enjoy ourselves."

* * *

"Lady Sokorvsky, may I take up a moment of your time?"

Sara turned away from the mirror and found Lady Caroline Ingham at her elbow.

"It seems we are destined to meet in retiring rooms." Sara's light comment brought no answering smile to her companion's face. "How can I help you?"

She allowed Caroline to lead her across to the most secluded corner of the room and sat down with her. Several moments passed while her companion stared at her clasped hands. At last she raised her eyes to Sara's face.

"I don't know quite how to tell you this."

Sara gave her a tight smile. "Just let it out. I find it's usually the best way."

"Valentin came to see me today at Madame Helene's House of Pleasure."

Sara tried to maintain an interested expression whilst her stomach performed slow cartwheels.

"I thought Valentin intended to break off our relationship." Caroline glanced away from Sara. "He must have told you I've been his mistress for years. Since I met you, I've tried to keep out of his way, in an attempt to lessen his desire for me." She sighed. "It doesn't seem to have worked. He told me he wants to continue our relationship and that you were quite comfortable with that."

Sara fought a desire to scream out a denial. "And if I was?"

"If you were, I just wanted to remind you that his decision leaves you with the option of finding your own lover. I didn't want to be one of those women who laugh at the poor wife behind her back." Caroline leaned forward and patted Sara's hand. "It was bad enough when Valentin and his cronies composed a list of all the characteristics a man would want in a complacent wife." Her gaze flicked over Sara. "And then he turned up with you. I never expected him to go through with his plan and marry a woman who might not understand how society marriages work."

Caroline's expression softened. "I wanted to be sure you understand that if you don't care for Valentin and his licentious lifestyle, there are always other men who would be more to your taste."

Sara withdrew her hand and fought the impulse to make a fist. "It's kind of you to share your concerns. I'll be sure to mention it to Valentin."

Caroline smiled. "That's very brave of you, my dear. Sometimes it is better to reach an understanding in these matters rather than skulk about, don't you think?" She touched her throat where an exquisite diamond necklace glittered in the candlelight. "Valentin gave this to me today. Perhaps you should demand something similar if you agree to be an accommodating wife."

She flashed Sara a conspiratorial smile and got to her feet.

Sara followed suit, her expression composed despite the raging of her emotions. Her delight over Valentin's earlier confession disappeared. Perhaps he'd chosen to tell her that he wished to keep her forever for a reason. Was he trying to bind her so closely to him that she wouldn't complain when he bedded another woman? Did he really think she would be a complacent wife, or was Lady Caroline simply stirring the pot?

Sara snapped her fan shut and allowed Peter to escort her into the supper room. Valentin had barely left her side all evening, and most of the guests had been extremely polite to her. She'd even been promised invites to some of the more exclusive *ton* parties. It seemed Valentin's attempts to be seen with her were bearing fruit.

He seemed oblivious to her mood, his manner as charming and relaxed as ever. She hadn't realized he spoke fluent Russian as well as French. Yet another polished facet to his character she had yet to explore or understand. If it weren't for her worries over his business and Lady Caroline's pointed remarks, she would almost be enjoying herself.

Peter led her over to a vacant table where Valentin stood with Evangeline Pettifer.

"Oh, there you are, Sara!" Evangeline cried. "I was just asking Valentin if he wanted to join our little party, but he said he was waiting for you." Ignoring Valentin's frown, Evangeline linked arms with Sara and towed her toward the other side of the room. Sara looked back helplessly at Valentin, who continued to scowl.

"Did you bring your guest to the ball, Evangeline?" Sara asked as Peter and Valentin fell into step behind her.

"Indeed we did." Evangeline craned her neck to see around Sara. "I'm not sure where he's got to, though. Luckily for us, he seems quite at home amongst all these foreigners. Ah, there he is."

Sara released her arm, suddenly aware that Valentin had come to a dead stop behind her. She turned, half expecting to see him confronting his father, but the man he faced was a stranger. His coat was beige, his cream waistcoat embroidered with roses, a perfect foil for his dark skin, brown eyes, and high cheekbones. Valentin's gloved hands folded into fists as the man bowed to him.

"Valentin, what a delightful surprise."

Sara stepped closer, her gaze riveted on Valentin. His face was devoid of expression.

"Do I know you, sir?"

The man's rich laugh filled the space between them. "How could you forget me? We were once so . . . close."

Peter moved to block Valentin and inclined his head. "I remember you, Aliabad. What I don't understand is how a man of your stamp gained admittance to this ball."

"Come now, Peter, you may still call me Yusef." His heavy-lidded gaze remained fixed on Valentin. "There has never been much formality between us. And, as to what I'm doing here, I'm attached to the Turkish embassy in London." He brought a lace handkerchief to his lips and dabbed at them. "I've mended my ways and prospered in the last ten years."

Sara was close enough to Valentin to feel him shudder as he stared at Yusef. She touched his hand, and he flinched away from her.

"Buying and mistreating slaves is no longer to your liking, then?" Peter's scornful remark didn't seem to disturb Aliabad's calm.

"As I said, I've moved on." He stared at Valentin again. "Are you sure you don't remember me?" He moved closer. "Perhaps if we spent some time together, your memories might return."

Valentin inclined his head, looking every inch the aristocrat. "I doubt it. I rarely bother to revisit my past. I find the future so much more satisfying." He laid Sara's hand on his arm. "I wish you good night."

The journey back to their house held none of the usual humor and sexual promise Sara had come to expect. Valentin didn't speak a word to her, his gaze fixed on the night sky beyond the carriage window. Lady Ingham's words about Valentin's choice of wife and his decision to keep a mistress reverberated in her mind, kept her as quiet as he. How could she ask him what was wrong when it was possible he had decided to marry her for the most cynical of reasons?

She glanced at his austere profile as the carriage halted. Perhaps he would be more amenable in bed. He handed her out of the carriage and led her into the hallway. Before she could speak, he kissed her hand.

"I have work to do. Don't wait up for me."

Coldness settled over her as he walked away and firmly closed his study door behind him.

*　*　*

After a restless doze, Sara could bear it no longer. She grabbed her dressing robe and brushed her disheveled hair out of her eyes. It was past three o'clock in the morning. Valentin might be able to leave things as they were, but she realized she couldn't. Every time she closed her eyes she pictured him with Lady Ingham, or, worse, the expression of revulsion on his face when he had first met the Turkish liaison.

She found Valentin in his study. He lay full length on the leather chesterfield couch, one leg bent at the knee. His discarded coat and waistcoat, thrown carelessly over the back of the settle, provided a splash of color on the dull brown leather. A half-empty bottle of brandy sat on the floor beside him, and a cigar hung between his lips. In one hand he held a book; in the other, his erect cock.

Sara took in the slow glide of his hand over his hard flesh, the pearls of fluid gathering on the tip. "What are you reading?" She sank to the floor beside the couch. Valentin didn't stop stroking himself or take his eyes away from the book.

"A fascinating treatise on the sexual legends of the gods of India." He propped the open book on his chest and ground the remains of his cigar into an ashtray.

Sara knelt up and righted the book. The engraving showed four men entangled with two women. The women had multiple rings piercing their nipples, noses, ears, and navels. She angled her head in an effort to understand exactly what she looked at and then blushed.

"I see. The two women are servicing all four men."

Valentin squeezed the base of his shaft and pumped vigorously until his fingers were slippery with fluid.

"I tried it once. I didn't find it very entertaining."

Sara closed her fingers over Valentin's and stopped his movements. "Why didn't you come to bed and let me touch you? Am I not able to satisfy you?"

He smiled without humor as he rebuttoned his breeches. "I do this almost every night—didn't you realize? I always make myself come a few times before I go to bed with you so that I can act like a gentleman."

Sara struggled to control a flash of temper. "Have I ever asked you to do that? Do you think me too weak to withstand your true passions?"

Valentin sat up, dislodging the book from his chest. "I like sex, Sara. I like it a lot. I don't expect you to put up with my excessive demands."

The clock in the hallway struck the quarter hour, the sound echoing throughout the silent house.

"I imagine your drunken behavior has less to do with what you think of me as a lover and more with your reaction to the man we met this evening."

Valentin gave a careless shrug. "Which man might that be? We met so many."

"The gentleman connected to the Turkish delegation. Mr. Yusef Aliabad. Did you meet him when you were a slave?"

Valentin swung his legs off the couch. "That's none of your business." He caught a curl of her hair in his fingers. "And we were discussing my desire for sex, not imaginary ghosts from the past." He tugged her hair. "If you object to me finding release by myself, I can always go and find a mistress."

Sara jerked away from him, wincing as her hair caught on his fingers. "I thought you already had one."

Valentin raised an eyebrow. "Again, it's none of your damned business."

"It is my business, if your mistress offers me advice." Sara struggled to her feet; hot tears rose up her throat, but she refused to let them fall.

He had the gall to laugh. "What exactly did Lady Ingham say to you?"

So he knew whom she meant. "She told me about the list you and your companions drew up for the perfect society wife. Is that true?"

"There was a list, yes, but—"

She interrupted him. "She also recommended that I get over my fit of the sulks at your continuing to have a mistress and enjoy the freedom you offered me."

Valentin sat up straight, picked up the book, and snapped it shut. "Did you imagine she spoke for me?"

"I'm not a fool, Valentin. I know that most society marriages are entered into for business reasons or social position. Lady Ingham only pointed out that you didn't intend to change your way of life to accommodate me."

"But I didn't marry you for social advantage or gain, did I?" he said softly.

She studied him through a haze of gathering tears. "No, you married me because I threw myself in your way and you owed my father a debt."

"And you are unhappy with your choice? I have given you a title, entrée into the *ton,* and a sexual education second to none. Isn't that enough for you?"

Her fingernails bit into the palms of her hands. "I didn't marry you for those things either, Valentin."

He ran a hand through his disordered hair. "Then surely you realize that believing anything Lady Ingham says is a waste of time?"

"Perhaps that's true, but she did point out that if I was happy to allow you your little affaires, you should return the favor."

"What the hell is that supposed to mean?"

Sara enjoyed the brief satisfaction of seeing his smile disappear and his face darken. He shifted his stance, and she backed away, giving him her best curtsy.

"I'm going to bed just as a good wife should. If you want to join me, please do. Otherwise have a nice evening with your little pleasures, and remember me to Lady Ingham. Tell her I have decided to take her advice."

She darted forward, grabbed the book from his slackened grasp, and threw it straight at his unprotected head.

Pride carried her back to her bedroom. Only then did she give way to the tears she'd hidden since the disastrous ball. She climbed into bed and pulled the covers up to her chin. Above her, the silver threads on the embroidered swan crest of the Sokorvsky family glinted in the candlelight. She supposed she should be grateful Lady Ingham had taken the trouble to disabuse her of the notion that Valentin cared for her before she'd confessed her love to him.

The idea that he and his friends had drawn up a list of qualities required for a complacent wife repulsed her. That he obviously thought she qualified made her physically sick. Did he truly think she'd married him for social gain? Didn't he understand that he'd appealed to every hidden yearning deep inside her? She assumed he would realize that from her wanton behavior in his bed, or did all women respond to him like that? A thread of jealousy blossomed in her chest, and she wrapped her arms around herself.

Her romantic dreams that she was unique and special to him would soon fade if she refused to nourish false hope. She would continue to do her duty toward him, and eventually, when the ache in her heart ceased, she, too, would be practical and perhaps find another lover to appreciate her.

Her courage failed at the very idea, but she drove herself on. It was her own fault. She had begged him to marry her. He must have assumed she was desperate enough to agree to anything to get a title. A tear slid down her cheek onto her pillow. Her mother always told her to be careful what she wished for.

She must never allow Valentin to realize how much he had hurt her. Their expectations of marriage were obviously not the same, and how could they be? He was an aristocrat, and she was the daughter of a tradesman. In her world, marriage and fidelity were expected and public dalliance frowned upon. Just because Valentin encouraged her to be herself didn't mean he loved her. She swiped at another tear. He had probably been trying to show her that she could have a deeply satisfying life apart from him.

In Valentin's world, there was always another ball to attend and another opportunity to hide her hurt feelings in a crowd. There was obviously always an opportunity to find a new lover as well. Sara blew out the candle and turned onto her side. In fact, she was promised to attend a ball with Evangeline and Peter in two days' time. It would be a fitting occasion to mask her true feelings and perhaps begin her own search.

"You like it, really, Valentin. Take my cock in your mouth. You'll beg me for it soon. Get down on your knees and beg, beg like a slave should."

Valentin awoke with an oath and found himself on the floor. He tried not to retch. The foul taste of his old nightmare lingered in his mouth. Blood, sex, and pain. He'd never forget that unique combination of scents and sensations. The soft pleasure and anticipation in Yusef Aliabad's voice close to Valentin's ear—too close, too damn close.

Endless days of being aroused and kept on the edge, being desperate to find release, hating his lack of control. Fear, too, and humiliation that he hadn't been able to stop his body from reacting and wanting, even as his mind screamed out in horror. He touched the raised scar hidden under his long hair at the nape of his neck. A set of initials, forever burned into his flesh.

He hadn't minded servicing the women. They were generally easy to please and had taught him a lot about pleasure. But after the first man, he'd tried to run away. That was when

Madam Tezoli introduced him to Yusef. She'd told Valentin he needed to learn a painful lesson and that Yusef would be more than happy to provide it.

Valentin's fingers closed around the discarded bottle, and he took a swig of brandy. He hadn't seen Yusef in the flesh for twelve long years, although the bastard regularly visited his nightmares. In the two years he'd been forced to endure Yusef's touch, he'd come close to breaking. Only Peter's constant vigilance had saved his sanity and his life.

He shuddered. How in God's name had Yusef found him? And, more importantly, why? After the first second of disbelief, Valentin had fought an overbearing instinct to throttle the man with his bare hands.

With another curse, he sat up. He was in his study. Someone had been in, relaid the fire, and tidied up some of his excesses. A headache of monstrous proportions pounded behind his temples. Gingerly he reached up and encountered a small lump on his temple. He placed the empty brandy bottle carefully on the tiled hearth. His staff probably imagined he and Sara had had their first marital battle and that he'd lost.

Damn, Sara had been there. She'd thrown a book at him, and he'd been too drunk to avoid it.

He pushed his hair out of his eyes. When she'd confronted him, he'd deliberately set out to hurt her. He knew he'd achieved his aim. The look in her eyes when she'd reported the gossip from his old mistress had made him feel sick.

She'd tried to get him to confide in her and, true to form, he hit right back. He groaned, the sound reverberating in his head. Let no one suggest that the great Valentin Sokorvsky open his heart to a woman and expose his deepest fears. She'd rallied, though, and walked away from him, chin in the air. Her composure continued to astonish him.

His faint smile faded. He should tell her that the ridiculous list he'd made with his companions had gone right out of his head when he met her. Even more importantly, she needed to know that Caroline was no longer his mistress.

The clock in the hall boomed nine times. Valentin got unsteadily to his feet and looked in vain for his coat. He retied his cravat and smoothed back his hair. It was time to do something that would've been unthinkable a few months ago. He had to go upstairs, make himself presentable, and apologize to Sara.

She wasn't in her room. She wasn't awaiting him in the breakfast parlor. Refusing to succumb to anxiety, Valentin rang for her maid.

"My lady went out early this morning on a breakfast ride for an alfresco event at Strawberry Hill, my lord."

"Thank you, Sally."

Valentin nodded at the woman to leave. It seemed that Sara wasn't avoiding him after all. Who could blame her for attending to her social obligations without him? He finished his breakfast and frowned at her empty chair, suddenly uncomfortable in the silence. Damnit, he was still uneasy. It wasn't like Sara to back away from a challenge. He'd expected her to meet him over the breakfast table, flags flying, musket at the ready to carry on the battle.

He got to his feet with the intention of putting on his riding clothes and following her. Before he even reached his bedroom, he hesitated on the stairs. He'd arranged a meeting with Peter and his banker about their steady loss of business income, a meeting that couldn't wait. Theft and dishonesty had a way of spiraling out of control unless they were stamped out with ruthless efficiency.

After dressing, Valentin returned to the hall and collected his hat and driving coat from the butler. He stepped into his phaeton, picked up the reins, and deliberately turned his back on Sara's route. Damnit, she'd be home for dinner. He'd apologize then.

13

Valentin scowled at his butler. "What do you mean, her lady-ship has gone out? You were supposed to inform me when she arrived!"

"I'm sorry, my lord, but it was my afternoon off." Bryson bowed, his face impassive. "I didn't know her ladyship had re-turned to the house until I saw her leave again."

Valentin turned on his heel and headed back up the stairs. He entered Sara's bedchamber and found her maid tidying her discarded clothes. He picked up a discarded silk stocking draped over a chair. A hint of roses warmed the air and reminded him of Sara's soft skin.

"Where was your mistress going this evening?"

Sally almost dropped the pile of clothes she carried as she bobbed an awkward curtsy. "I believe my lady was attending a masked ball at Vauxhall Gardens with a party of friends." She curtsied again. "Sir."

He headed for his dressing room. Sara had avoided being alone with him for two days. He'd commanded her presence at the dinner table tonight, and it seemed that she was defying him. Did she consider enjoying herself with her friends more important than having dinner with him? He frowned at his reflection in the mirror. He sounded like a jealous husband, a novel sensation for a rake like him. Sara had a perfect right to spend her evening with whomsoever she pleased. He threw the stocking to the floor.

Damnit, she should have faced him.

In the fleeting moments she'd allowed him over the past two days, she'd played the perfect wife. Her serene smile and polite but distant expression were enough to make him grind his teeth. He was supposed to be the expert at keeping people at a distance, not her. Had she already given up on him? Was she prepared to hand him over to Caroline without a struggle? Somehow the thought enraged him.

He rummaged in his closet until he found an old black silk domino and matching mask. He would attend the masquerade and surprise her. Perhaps it would prove easier to get her attention at a public ball than in his own house. As he turned back into his bedroom, his attention was caught by a flash of color on his pillow. He walked over to the bed and retrieved the Red Book Sara had left there for him.

He flipped quickly through the pages until he found her last entry.

At the masquerade ball, I am anonymous. If I should meet a man who wishes to indulge in some illicit pleasure, perhaps I should allow him the liberties my husband finds so irresistible in others. Perhaps I might begin to understand the attraction of deceit and play the game myself. Under the cover of darkness, or in the midst of the crowds, will my lover know me and seek me out, or will another find his heart's desire?

Valentin reread the words three times. A thrill of possessive anger shook through him. He'd wanted a challenge, and here it was. Was she asking him to come and find her or offering herself to another? Were the liberties she referred to those she granted him as her husband or those she believed he sought in other women? His cock hardened in anticipation. Whatever her cryptic words meant, he would find her and show her exactly why he was the only man who held the key to her heart's desire.

Sara studied the crowded dance floor through the narrow opening of her silver mask. Vauxhall Gardens were crammed to bursting in the unexpectedly warm haze of the autumn evening. Colored lanterns illuminated the dancers and shadowed the occupants of the more secluded booths. A scent of spiced wine hung in the air. It appeared that the anonymity of a mask encouraged people to lower their standards and behave in a more outrageous fashion. She glanced back at Peter and Evangeline, who sat together in the booth finishing their supper. Her toe tapped in time to the music.

"Mysterious lady, would you like to dance?"

A tall man in a blue domino and black mask bowed in front of her. For a moment, a thrill of alarm shot through her. He reminded her of Valentin. The thought of her irritating husband was enough to make her straighten her spine and stop wondering if he cared enough to come and find her.

"That would be delightful."

He swept her into the dance, his grip firm on her waist, his full mouth curved in a slight smile. "Might I say you look enchanting in your costume?"

Sara glanced down at her beaded bodice and the multi-layered thin silk panels of her harem pants. Evangeline had given her the costume as a present. "Thank you. I doubt it is an accurate representation of what those ladies really wear, but I had to maintain a measure of dignity."

The gentleman laughed, displaying white teeth. "I believe you are right, ma'am. Although it is said that any man who dares to enter the sultan's harem is put to death. So who can truthfully say whether your costume is correct or not?"

She concentrated on her steps as her partner drew her farther onto the crowded dance floor. When the music ended, he bowed.

"Would you care for some refreshment, ma'am?"

Sara looked round for her party but had lost sight of them in the melee. Reminding herself that she was looking for an adventure, she placed her hand on his arm. "That would be delightful."

She waited in one of the ground-floor boxes that faced the dance floor while her companion went to procure the drinks. The slightly raised position of the box allowed her to look out over the jostling crowd. A masquerade ball seemed to attract all levels of society. As the evening wore on, it became more difficult to distinguish between the behavior of the highest and the lowest. She studied the row of boxes opposite hers. She had the strangest feeling she was being watched.

A worm of unease slithered in her stomach. Had she allowed her impulsive nature to lead her astray? As a married woman, perhaps it would've been better for her to confront Valentin and have the matter out before recklessly deciding to embark on the quest for a lover.

But, then, she was hardly renowned for her patience, was she? If she hadn't tumbled into marriage with Valentin so quickly, she wouldn't even be here.

"Your ratafia."

Sara turned with a start as her masked partner returned. She took the proffered glass.

"You seem a little anxious, ma'am."

His quiet upper-class voice made her feel ridiculous for her sudden unease.

"In truth, kind sir, I've never been to a masked ball before. I find myself a little overwhelmed."

"It's interesting how differently people behave when they believe they are incognito, is it not?" He set down his glass and came to sit beside her. She tensed as he took her hand. "For instance, I would never dare to touch you like this if we had met under more formal circumstances."

She allowed him to hold her ungloved hand. She waited to see if her body responded as instantly to him as it did to Valentin. His face moved closer, and his lips touched hers in a chaste salute. Sara closed her eyes. She felt nothing. It would be much easier if she were simply a passionate woman aroused by any man. How was she ever going to get over Valentin if no one matched up to him?

"Sir, sir?" A persistent voice behind Sara made her open her eyes.

"What is it, boy?" For the first time, a note of irritation entered her companion's voice.

"I've got a note for you, sir. Says it's urgent. Something about your sister."

"I don't have a sister. Are you sure it's for me?"

Sara breathed a sigh of relief as her would-be suitor vaulted the box wall and followed the boy into the crowd. Perhaps she wasn't quite as ready to indulge in an affair as she thought she was.

A hand clamped over her mouth. "Don't scream."

In her distress, Sara tried to bite instead. Her captor cursed in a foreign language before spinning her around to face him. His face was half covered by a black silk mask, but Sara had no difficulty recognizing Valentin's luscious mouth or the glint of his violet eyes through the slits of the mask. She fought a desire to throw herself at his chest. A lingering sense of outrage reminded her why she had come to the ball without him.

He removed his hand from her mouth and stared down at her. Sara gave him her brightest smile. "Valentin, what a delightful surprise. Did you come with Lady Ingham?"

His mouth tightened. "Of course not."

"Ah, you came to find another woman, then."

"I suppose you might say that." A faint smile flickered across Valentin's face.

Sara ignored the treacherous protest of her stomach. "Well, you should take yourself off in case my beau returns. He will not be pleased if I have to introduce him to my husband."

Valentin stepped away from her. He drew the curtains across the front of the box with a sharp rattle, isolating them from the colorful crowd. "He will not be coming back."

"What have you done?"

"Nothing I'm ashamed of. How about you?" He advanced toward her, his stride purposeful.

She resisted an impulse to back away. "I was having a delightful evening until you arrived."

"Really." Valentin towered over her. "Then perhaps you need to be reminded that you are my wife."

Sara raised her chin. "I thought we agreed that I wouldn't make a fuss about your lovers. Why should you be concerned about mine?"

"I agreed to nothing. You are my wife. You don't require any other lovers."

His arrogance ignited her instant ire. "Has it occurred to you that I like sex, I like it a lot, and that maybe you aren't capable of providing me with enough of it?"

His hand shot out and grabbed her arm. "Don't quote my own words back at me."

Sara pulled out of his grasp. From the hard set of his mouth, she realized she'd managed to break through his normal smiling reserve. Was she brave enough to push him further? A sense of sexual anticipation unfurled inside her.

"If I have to share you with other women, you owe me the same courtesy."

He laughed without any humor. "I don't share." He snaked his arm around her waist and pulled her close. His mouth descended and possessed hers with brutal strength. Sara kissed him back, biting at his lip, digging her nails into the soft skin at the nape of his neck. He drew back and stared at her.

"Caroline Ingham is no longer my mistress."

"Really, have you found someone else?"

His grip on her waist tightened. "I don't need anyone else. I have you."

"But you said I was incapable of fulfilling your desires." Despite her best efforts, her voice trembled. "You said I wasn't good enough."

"Sara, I was drunk, and I said a great deal of incredibly stupid and thoughtless things, but I never said you weren't good enough."

She glared at him. "You implied it."

"Then I am a fool." He brushed his thumb over her lower lip. "Perhaps we might reach a compromise."

She stared at his swollen lower lip, wanting to bite it again, to taste his blood and force him to react. His fingers slid up from her waist to caress the underside of her embroidered bodice.

"If you are determined to pursue this matter, I will show you exactly what I require in a lover. You may decide whether you want to be that woman or not."

"And what if I decide you have gone too far?"

His fingers tightened on her breast. "Then you tell me you wish to go home and I will take you. But you lose your right to complain if I take a mistress."

"And you lose your right to complain if I take a lover."

Valentin's lip curled. "Agreed."

Sara yanked his head down for another searing kiss. Her body was already aroused by his wicked suggestion of a night of unbridled sexual passion. His fingers slipped into her bodice and tugged at her nipple ring as his other hand spanned her buttocks. He was aroused, his shaft radiating heat against the thin silk of her harem pants.

Sara moaned as he bent her back over his arm and took her nipple into his mouth. In the pleasure of Valentin's skilled hands and mouth, she forgot the crowds outside the box and the man who had momentarily stirred her interest.

"Oh, it's you, Val." Even the sound of Peter's relieved voice didn't embarrass Sara. Valentin stood her in front of him; his hand still fondled her exposed nipple. Peter licked his lips, his gaze riveted on Sara's breast. "Excuse me, I was worried about Sara. I didn't realize she was with you."

"It's good of you to look out for her, Peter," Valentin said, "but she is quite safe."

"I can see that." Peter winked at Sara. "Would you like me to make sure you are not disturbed?"

"That would be kind of you. Sara and I have something to discuss before we move on to the rest of the night's entertainment."

Peter shut the door, leaving them alone. She smiled warily at Valentin. "What exactly do you wish to discuss?"

Valentin leaned against the door, his arms crossed. "Tell me why you dressed as a Turkish slave."

"The costume was a gift." Sara crossed her hands protectively over her jeweled bodice.

"From whom?"

"From Evangeline Pettifer, why?"

Valentin straightened. "You did not think it strange that she gave you a costume that might cause me some unpleasant memories?"

Sara bit her lip and ran her fingers down her silken pants. "Does it offend you?"

He circled her, his expression considering. "It was probably meant to, but I'm mature enough to ignore the slight."

"I didn't think—"

Valentin held up his hand. "I'd rather know what you were thinking when you let that man kiss you."

Sara's fingers curled into fists. She stared defiantly at Valentin. "I wanted to see if he made me feel like you do."

He stepped closer until the black silk of his domino brushed her bare arm. Despite his closeness, his voice was barely audible. "And?"

"And what?"

She shuddered as he caught her jaw in his strong fingers. "Did he arouse you? Did you think about opening more than your mouth to him?"

There it was again. A flash of danger and deep passion beneath his bland smile.

"I am your wife."

Valentin smiled. "I'm glad you remembered that, because as your husband, I have a right to . . . chastise you when you misbehave." He sat down on a chair in the center of the room and took Sara's hand. "You did say I might treat you as I really wished tonight?"

Sara barely had time to nod before he yanked on her wrist and tipped her over his lap. Her face heated as she stared down at the floor. She stiffened as cold air crept up the back of her legs. Despite her efforts to move away, Valentin held her steady, one arm clamped around her waist, pressing her into his lap.

"I've wanted to do this since the first day I met you."

He folded back her skirts and caressed her naked buttocks

with his ungloved hand. She flinched as his hand met her skin in a sharp slap. He slapped her other buttock and then returned to the first, alternating his strikes and where they fell until her skin flared with heat. She had to bite her lip to stop herself from yelping as the stinging sensation accumulated.

"Please, Valentin . . ."

He stopped. Instead of releasing her, his hand slipped between her buttocks and caressed her sex. Warmth engulfed her as he slid two long fingers inside her. She cried out as the palm of his other hand connected with her tingling buttocks, pushing her onto his encased fingers, amplifying her guilty pleasure.

Each slap added to her torment, drew her deeper into a maelstrom of feeling in which she could no longer distinguish pleasure from pain. Her sheath clenched around his fingers as she fought to come.

He removed his hand. Sara frantically tried to twist out of his hold.

"Be still, Sara. The more you fight me, the longer it will take."

Red-faced, Sara stared down at the moth-eaten carpet. If anyone peered in, how ridiculous would she look, laid over her husband's knee, her buttocks red and available to any man's gaze? God, she wanted to come.

Valentin caressed her tender flesh, his hand cool against her hot, tingling skin. "Don't kiss other men. I don't like it."

"Only if you stop kissing other women."

She bit her lip as his hand connected with her buttock with a crack, driving her past pleasure into the unknown. To distract herself from the intensity of her emotions, she counted six more slaps until his fingers touched her sex again. One finger settled over her bud, another penetrated her sheath, while his thumb breached her anus.

He held her like that, balanced on his hand, not moving. Her nipples ached to be sucked, her womb throbbed to be filled. Didn't he understand that she needed him to move?

Of course he did.

"Do you have something to say to me?"

Sara closed her eyes. "What do you want me to say?" She moaned as he withdrew his hands, leaving her stretched across his lap like a limp blanket.

"If you don't know, perhaps we should continue your chastisement." He ran one finger between her buttocks. "I like to see you like this. Spread out for my enjoyment." He rolled her onto her back. She gasped as her tender buttocks connected with his hard thighs. He dragged down her skimpy bodice, and his mouth descended on her nipple and suckled hard.

Before she could react, he turned her back onto her stomach. His hand descended, reheating her aroused skin, pooling warmth in her pussy. She wanted to come.

"Valentin, I'm sorry."

Another slap. "Sorry for what?"

"For letting another man kiss me." Another slap. "You are the only man I want to kiss me."

She tensed, waiting for the next sting, but there was nothing. Her body trembled as she waited for some sign that he had understood. His teeth bit into her right buttock, and she cried out.

"Good."

He slid her off his lap. She looked up at him, afraid to speak in case he changed his mind and put her over his knee again.

"It's time for us to leave." He held out his hand, one eyebrow raised in a challenge.

Sara took his hand. Although her body struggled with the lack of fulfillment, her mind was too wary to attempt to deal with it. She straightened her clothing and allowed him to wrap her in his cloak.

He led her straight out of the gardens into his waiting carriage. Vaguely Sara hoped that Peter would give Evangeline her apologies. She flinched as her bottom connected with the leather seat and wondered if Valentin had noticed.

He sat opposite her. His right thumb moved rhythmically over the huge bulge in his white breeches as he stared at her breasts. Sara squeezed her legs together and hoped the rocking of the carriage would push her toward relief.

"Don't make yourself come."

Sara glared at Valentin. He smiled lazily back.

"That privilege is mine tonight, remember? You agreed to put yourself in my hands."

She didn't think he would need his whole hand to help her climax. One finger would probably be sufficient. After a short while the carriage stopped outside a discreet white stuccoed town house in one of the newer neighborhoods around Mayfair. Valentin took off his mask.

"Are you ready for your adventure? This is Madame Helene's House of Pleasure, where any fantasy can become a reality."

Sara accepted his assistance out of the carriage as she studied the large building. If this was the place Caroline Ingham had mentioned, Sara was surprised. She'd expected something more seedy and run-down.

The interior of the house was as richly furnished as her own. Scarlet silk lined the walls, which were covered in paintings, depicting all kinds of amorous activity. Whoever Madame was, she obviously had bottomless funds and influential friends to run an establishment on such a grand scale.

At the top of the wide staircase, there was a large salon half filled with people. Most of the women wore masks like hers. In one corner there was a buffet and liveried servants providing drinks. Another area contained a multitude of silk floor cushions where people could sit or lie with their partners.

Sara couldn't take her gaze from a couple of acrobats in the middle of the room who wore gold paint and little else. Every balletic pose ended with the couple in a different sexual position. Sara swallowed hard as the petite female performed a perfect arabesque even as the male slid his cock deep inside her from behind.

"They're good, aren't they?"

Valentin's voice almost shocked Sara, she was so intent on the erotic tableau unfolding before her.

"Is this where you come to amuse yourself, Valentin?" She was proud of her calm voice.

"I used to 'come' here a lot." He smiled down at her. "Since I met you, I've watched more than I've participated." He guided her farther into the salon.

"I don't understand. People can join in?"

Valentin nodded at a petite blond lady on the far side of the room. "If they choose to, they can. For a vast yearly fee, of course." He drew her into a long corridor that led out of the salon. White painted doors on either side appeared to go on forever. Did the house extend into its neighbor behind? It seemed likely.

Sara paused to read the small plaque on the nearest door. She turned to him. "What does 'Little Misses' mean?"

"Why don't we go in and see?"

Sara almost stumbled as Valentin opened the door and she fell into blackness. It took a moment for her eyes to adjust to the dim lighting. Five rows of chairs, which contained several people, faced a stage that seemed to represent the hallway of a London mansion.

As she watched, two girls skipped in from the left of the stage toward a handsome footman who stood to attention outside a door. As the taller girl passed the footman, she trailed her fingers across the front of his breeches. By the time the second girl repeated the action, Sara could see his erection growing. He continued to stand in place as though nothing had happened.

Valentin sat beside her. Sara whispered in his ear, "They are not 'girls.' The blond woman is at least as old as I am."

"Shhh . . ." Valentin nipped her earlobe. "Remember, this place is for fantasies."

After a moment, the girls reappeared. This time, the shorter blond one stood on tiptoe and kissed the footman on the mouth. The dark girl cupped his groin and pressed her palm to his shaft. When the girls stepped back, the footman continued to stare straight ahead. Only the visible evidence of his arousal made him look any different to any other on-duty footman Sara had ever encountered.

"This is hardly fair on the poor man."

"Don't forget, he chose to play this part, too." Sara shivered as Valentin dipped his finger inside her low-cut bodice and toyed with her nipple.

On their third pass through, the dark-haired girl kissed the footman while the blonde unbuttoned his breeches. She draped a handkerchief over the man's cock and slid her hand inside. Sara grew warm as she watched the girl pleasure the footman through the dainty lace handkerchief. His hands fisted by his sides as she pumped hard and he came without a sound.

The dark girl took the soaked handkerchief and pressed it to her lips whilst the blonde buttoned the footman's breeches.

"Is that it?" Sara whispered as the girls disappeared again. She glanced around the room. Why hadn't anyone left?

Valentin took her hand and laid it over his groin.

"It depends."

"On what?"

"On whose fantasy this really is."

Sara gently stroked his shaft as the girls reappeared. Valentin squeezed her nipple tighter, reawakening the heat he'd built before.

When the girls paused and giggled beside the footman, he moved from his post and pinned both the girls against the wall.

Neither of them made any attempt to resist him. Sara could scarcely breathe as he picked up the smaller woman and thrust inside her. Even as he pumped away at her, his other hand disappeared down the bodice of the dark-haired girl.

Within ten vigorous thrusts, the blonde came. The footman released her, picked up the other woman, and pleasured her, too. Sara gripped Valentin's cock harder. He shifted in his seat. "Careful, love. I might need it later."

The footman pulled both women close to him and finally came, his cock jabbing between their hips as he nuzzled one woman's breasts and fingered the other's. Before Sara could protest, Valentin pressed her arm and guided her back out into the corridor. She leaned up against the wall and studied him.

"Why would anyone want to live that fantasy?"

He smiled. "It's a common one among young ladies who grew up in large households where the footmen were chosen for their good looks. I should imagine most of the women who participate are reliving a naughty fantasy they could never have carried off as a young unmarried lady."

"And the man?"

"Either he's a real servant here or he's a gentleman who's curious as to what it might be like to be considered fair game by the young ladies of the house."

Sara stared at him as his gaze dropped to her breasts. He inhaled, his nostrils flaring. "Despite your words, I think you enjoyed that. I can smell your arousal. If I touched you now, my fingers would be soaked."

"Touch me then."

"Not yet."

In frustration Sara stepped closer; her breasts brushed his waistcoat. Her hips surrounded the cradle of his erection. He gently squeezed her sensitive buttocks.

"One more room, I think, before I'll consider fucking you." He gestured down the corridor. "Is there any particular time period or scenario you require? One warning, the farther you proceed down the corridor, the darker the fantasies become."

Sara walked away from him, reading each door label as she passed. She paused beside the fifth door. " 'Roman Ritual' sounds interesting. May we go in here?"

She opened the door herself this time, anticipating the darkness of the previous room but finding instead a multitude of oil lamps. A series of chaise longues were drawn up in a circle around a fountain. Soft music floated on the perfumed air, performed by a lone musician on a balcony high above her head.

Men and women occupied the banqueting couches. All wore wreaths and variations of Roman dress. Some were dressed as slaves. No one acknowledged their arrival. Valentin touched Sara's arm and gestured toward a secluded doorway.

"If you wish to stay, we need to change."

Sara followed him into a dressing area lined with mirrors. A woman helped her don a soft white swathe of fine linen and a wreath of sweet-smelling herbs and flowers. Valentin looked at home dressed in a short white toga. He led her to one of the padded couches and laid down in one fluid motion, his head propped up on one hand.

She decided to sit on the floor cushions beside him. A slave brought them goblets of thick red wine taken from the fountain and platters of grapes, soft goat cheese, and flatbread. Sara relaxed back against the couch as Valentin smoothed his hand over her hair.

"Is this more to your liking?" he murmured as his fingers caressed her throat and drifted down toward her breast.

"It seems very civilized."

His soft chuckle feathered the fine hairs at the nape of her neck. "So it does. But nothing is ever that simple here."

Sara glanced up as a woman dressed as a slave offered Valentin more wine. When he held up his cup, the woman deliberately leaned her naked breast against his skin. Sara glared at the woman as Valentin did nothing to prevent the contact.

"Ah," he said, "here comes dessert."

A roll of drums brought Sara's attention to the center of the room, where four men dressed in nothing but loincloths deposited a large covered dish on the extensive table. They removed the domed lid to reveal a naked woman. Sara couldn't help but stare. The woman's skin was dusted with gold powder, her nipples painted silver, as were her lips.

The flute player began a new song, and the woman began to move. Her dance reminded Sara of a snake as she came up on her knees and swayed her hips in time to the sensuous beat of the drum. Still dancing, she slid off the low table and knelt before the first couch, where a bald-headed man lay.

As the music increased in volume, she cupped her breast and offered it to the man. With the encouragement of his fellow diners, the man took her nipple into his mouth and sucked hard. One of the tray bearers came up behind the woman and rubbed his cock against her buttocks before penetrating her from behind.

Sara glanced up at Valentin. His attention remained on her rather than the complicated coupling going on in front of them. His smile widened as two more people joined the press of bodies on the floor. The red-haired woman on the couch next to theirs crawled toward another of the tray bearers and slid her mouth over his cock.

It became difficult for Sara to tell which heaving body belonged to which person. One man had his head buried between one woman's legs while another sucked his cock; his fingers were busy pumping into a third woman's pussy.

She turned to Valentin. "Do you do this?"

"It can be amusing when you are young and crave sex rather than intimacy. Personally I prefer to know exactly who or what

I'm fucking." He bent to kiss her, locked his arm around her waist, and drew her tight against his side. "It's arousing, though, isn't it?"

She couldn't deny that; her body trembled with the need to explore Valentin's as soon as she could. His smile widened as he stared into her eyes. "I have just thought of the ideal room for you. Would you care to try it?"

They stepped over the writhing mass of bodies and back into the corridor. Sara's skin felt oversensitive as if the slightest touch would send her spiraling into a never-ending climax. The very air she breathed seemed to encourage her to lose her inhibitions and join in the erotic antics. She knew why Valentin craved such a place. She suddenly understood his hunger to explore every facet of his sexuality. Where safer than here, in such lush, discreet surroundings?

"Wait here a moment."

Valentin went through a second door, leaving her alone in the corridor. No sounds permeated the heavy silence, although Sara had no doubt there was noise aplenty within most of the rooms. She slid her hand beneath her tunic and stroked her swollen sex. The thought of Valentin's mouth on her made her even wetter. She stared at the cream silk walls. Did she regret that Valentin had helped her discover this hidden aspect of her sexuality?

She shook her head. Even if he walked away from her, she'd learned something valuable. He'd made her realize women could enjoy sex, too, and that she had a right to sensual satisfaction. They were lessons most women would never have the opportunity to learn. At least he'd given her that.

"I have your clothes."

He handed her the harem costume. "Let me help you put it on."

Before he could aid her, she stood on tiptoe and kissed his mouth. His arms came around her and pinned her hips firmly against his. She kissed him with all her newly discovered sensuality. He replied in kind until she drowned in the wave of desire they created together.

When he raised his head, he was smiling. "What was that for?"

"For bringing me here. For giving me this chance to explore my fantasies and understand yours."

His expression intensified. "Perhaps the other room will wait. It's time we found our own games to play."

The room he chose was furnished with gold drapes. Cream satin bed linen covered the narrow four-poster bed, which sat on a raised platform in the center. Valentin wondered if Sara realized the significance of that. He slowly removed her clothes, exposing her luscious breasts and pussy. He wanted to drive his cock inside her until she screamed out her pleasure. He wanted to lick and suck her clit until she begged for more. She allowed him to sit her on the end of the four-poster bed. He watched the agitated fall of her breasts and knew she was close to orgasm.

He stripped in front of her, taking his time, making her wait. His oversensitive cock pulsed as he released it from his breeches. Sara stared at him and made a soft sound of need. He drew his hand down over his shaft, cupped his sac, and spread his fingers.

"Is this what you want?"

Sara nodded and licked her lips. He brought the crown of his cock to her mouth and rubbed it back and forth. So glorious to be free with his wife. So liberating that she seemed to like his outrageous behavior.

"I have a game for you." He stepped back and placed her hands around the corner posts of the bed. "At Madame's there are many ways to pleasure yourself or be pleasured. There are also many levels of watching." He glanced around the well-lit room. "At the moment, we have complete privacy. If we chose, we could open some of these drapes and allow others to watch us through the mirrors and peepholes."

He watched Sara's face. She didn't seem revolted by his revelations. In truth, her breathing quickened. Valentin smiled. "If we wished, we could allow others to walk through the room and watch us." He squeezed hard on the base of his shaft. "We could even let them touch us, join us, enjoy us."

Her pupils dilated, and her lips parted. Valentin's cock throbbed in response.

"The game is called Five. Whoever comes first loses. The winner gets to decide whether we open the curtains. Do you agree?"

"Just the curtains?" Sara sounded breathy but curious.

"Yes, for this round. If we choose to continue, perhaps the stakes will rise."

He tensed as Sara considered him. Did she trust him enough to play?

She gripped the bedposts and opened her legs in a silent invitation for him to continue. He placed his hands just above hers.

"Shall we begin?"

14

"Five kisses. You may go first."

Sara blinked at Valentin as he lowered his face to hers. "On your mouth?"

"Yes, where else?"

She leaned forward and gave him five quick kisses on his closed lips.

"Now it's my turn." He took longer over the small caress, outlining her lips with his tongue, changing the pressure and angle of his mouth against hers.

He smiled at her. "This time, I get to go first. Five open-mouthed kisses."

She shivered as he slid his tongue inside her mouth, banking the fires of desire he'd brought to life earlier. His hands remained gripping the bedposts; only his mouth worked against hers in a subtle invitation to explode with lust. He sucked her tongue into his mouth, and she fought an urge to whimper. Valentin kissed like a god and never neglected to do so even when he was eager to move on to other things.

Despite his initial caution, Sara knew her acceptance of this side of his nature would open him up to her. She felt as though she'd only skimmed the surface of his volatile sexual appetite before. Something deep within her thrilled to his outrageous advances and responded in kind.

Her lips were swollen by the time he released her, her nipples tight enough to hurt. She kissed him back, recklessly pushing him onward, trying to balance her own voracious needs with her desire to beat him.

He was panting when she drew back. Wetness gleamed on the crown of his cock. Her own cream trickled down her thigh.

"It's difficult, isn't it?" he murmured. "Trying to push me over the edge without sending yourself into the abyss. We still have a long way to go. It's your turn. Five licks to each of my nipples."

Sara knew he loved to be touched like that. Would this be her opportunity to win? With the first stroke of her tongue, his nipple hardened. She licked him slowly, relishing the hard point of his flesh against the softness of her wet mouth. His hips moved toward her, and his cock brushed her stomach, leaving a trail of pearly liquid strung between them.

Valentin glanced down. "That doesn't count. It's pre-cum. You'll know if I come; you'll be soaked in it." He bent to her breast. Sara held on to the bedposts with all her strength as he took a leisurely lick of her nipple and the golden ring threaded through it. He growled deep in his throat as she shuddered. She wanted to come. His cock nudged her belly again as he laved her nipple. So easy, to drop her head and take him in her mouth, so deeply satisfying to suck him dry and have him in her power.

"Sara . . ."

She opened her eyes. Her breasts gleamed from his mouth in the soft candlelight. She was so on edge she could still feel the tug of the gold through her own heated skin. A faint sheen of sweat dappled Valentin's muscular chest as he loomed over her.

"It's my turn to start again." Valentin breathed hard. "This time I'm going to suck your breasts. Hold still."

As soon as his lips closed over her nipple, Sara knew she would lose this particular battle. The first ripple of her orgasm shuddered through her. With a soft cry she leaned forward into the enticing curve of Valentin's shoulder. She bit him hard as her climax grew and flowered through her.

When she finished shuddering, Valentin moved away. "You have lost. I choose to open the curtains."

She couldn't resist watching him as he strode across the room. His wide shoulders tapered to a narrow waist and taut buttocks. His dark swathe of hair was gathered at the nape of his neck. His front view was equally impressive, his expression arrogant, his confidence undaunted.

"Do you wish to play again, or do you concede defeat?"

Sara deliberately studied his cock. He couldn't stay this erect forever—could he? She had gained her release; surely she would be able to outlast him this time?

"I will play again."

"If you lose, I open the door." He resumed his position in front of her, his hands again grasping the bedposts. "What will you do if you win?"

"Shut everyone out and make love to you until you are too exhausted to move for the rest of the night."

He raised an eyebrow. "Bold words from a woman who takes her pleasures seriously. Do you really think you can exhaust me?"

"Isn't that what this is all about? Me proving that I'm capable of being your full sexual partner?" She tensed, waiting for his reply. What if she had destroyed the spell and he retreated behind his smiling mask of bland courtesy?

He smiled. "It is my turn to start the game. Are you ready to play?" He kissed her closed mouth five times. Part of her was relieved he'd started from the beginning again, the rest of her screamed a protest at the agonizing buildup of sensations.

By the time Valentin finished suckling her nipples, Sara realized one orgasm was obviously not enough to placate her deprived senses. Valentin seemed unperturbed by his erection, which constantly dripped pre-cum onto her flesh.

"What next?" She attempted to sound calm but knew Valentin wouldn't be fooled.

"Of course. You haven't progressed past this point in our game before, have you?" He glanced down at his cock. "Five licks on the crown of my cock for you."

"And for me?"

He smiled, confidence blazing in his beautiful eyes. "Five licks of your clit. I'll even let you go first, if you prefer it."

Eager for the opportunity to make him come before she had to endure the torment of his mouth on her sex, Sara bent her head and studied his shaft. Pearl droplets oozed from the purple slit atop his crown. His stomach muscles contracted as she licked a drop of pre-cum into her mouth with all the delicacy of a cat. She licked again, running the tip of her tongue along the slit, probing inside it, flicking the swollen flesh. He groaned low in his throat and pushed his hips toward her, pressing his cock deeper into her mouth.

When she raised her head, he was breathing hard, his pupils wide and black, obliterating almost all the violet. He managed a shaky grin. "Close, but not quite close enough."

Sara tensed as he slid his hands down the bedposts and sank to his knees in front of her. Her sex throbbed at the mere thought of being touched. Were people already watching them through the mirrors and peepholes? Could she hold on and not come?

Valentin's first delicate pass over her sensitive flesh made her shiver. His second harder stroke made her want to grab his hair and force his face against her until he made her come hard enough and long enough to satisfy them both. She barely resisted the violent urge as he licked her again and again. Each tiny flick of his tongue ratcheted up her tension and added to her insatiable need.

He licked his lips as if desperate to catch every taste of her. She wondered if she looked as depraved as she felt. She was so close to coming again, so close. Would he allow her to go first again?

"Five sucks of your clit now."

She braced herself as he slowly returned to his knees, arms still stretched out, only his mouth able to touch her. Sara inhaled as he drew her clit into his mouth. Her fingers dug into the oak bedposts as he drove her wild. Before she could stop herself, her hips came off the bed and drove into Valentin's eager mouth. She climaxed as she ground her pelvis against his teasing mouth, unable to stop even when he set his teeth on her clit and held it delicately between them.

His grin when he sat back made her furious. "You lose again. I'm going to open the door. Are you afraid to continue?" He swung the door wide.

"I'm not afraid," Sara snapped back even before she realized it was true.

He turned to look at her. "Good, because I am enjoying this."

"So am I."

They stared at each other across the small space.

"How are you able to stay so erect?"

"Practice." He winked at her as he strolled back, his stiff cock pointed at his stomach. Before he settled back into place, he released his hair from its ribbon. "Ready to play?"

Valentin eased between her spread legs. God, he was so close to coming. If things went as he hoped, Sara would have her victory now. She didn't need to know that he had no intention of letting anyone else join in their lovemaking. Her willingness to play the game no longer surprised him. The depth of her sensuality complemented his perfectly. He was amazed and humbled that he seemed to have found his sexual equal in his own wife.

"I'm ready, Valentin." She gave him five chaste kisses on his mouth and allowed him to do the same.

As the game progressed, Valentin managed to hang on to his sanity when she licked his cock, and she managed not to come when he licked her clit. She waited for his next instructions, her nipples tight and wet from his mouth, her clit swollen, her pussy running with cream. God, he could lick her all night.

"For you, five deep sucks of my cock. For me, five forays with my tongue inside you."

He crouched in front of her, careful not to let his aching shaft brush the bedclothes or her skin. Her sex lay open to him, her labia puffed and welcoming, her clit as hard and erect as his cock. He took a breath and slid his tongue deep inside. He used his chin against her flesh to further stimulate her as he mimicked the thrusting motion of his cock. She shuddered around him but didn't break.

When he sat back, his face dripped with her juices. He loved the smell and taste of her arousal.

"Now it's your turn."

He stood up and tensed as she leaned forward, slid her mouth down the length of his shaft, and slowly sucked him. He clenched his teeth as he felt his balls contract, ready to come. He endured three more lascivious slow sucks, the third so deep that the crown of his cock hit the back of her throat before he gave up the struggle. He let himself come in harsh, juddering waves.

Her smile of triumph was all the reward he needed.

"I won!"

He let go of the bedposts and went to shut the door. "Is your womanly honor satisfied?"

She gazed at him, a hint of speculation in her eyes. "Is there more to this game of Five, or have we exhausted its limits?"

Blood thundered back toward his cock as he studied her. "You wish to play again?"

"If there is more to discover. What happens after this?"

He cupped his rapidly growing erection. "The game progresses using our fingers to pleasure each other and ends up with five strokes from my cock in your pussy and five strokes of your fingers wrapped around my shaft until one of us screams for mercy."

She reached forward and stroked him. "I would like your fingers on me now."

Without a word, he slid one finger inside her pussy and rested the pad of his thumb on her clit. "I am yours to command, ma'am."

She grabbed his wrist. "More fingers, please, Valentin."

He added three more, felt her sheath clench around him. With a muffled cry, she hooked her arm around his neck and drew him down on the bed. He pumped his fingers through her thick cream as he waited for his cock to reach its full size. She came for him again as he crawled on top of her, pushing her thighs wide.

"Fingers first and then fucking. Wasn't that what you wanted?"

She didn't reply, her face fierce in concentration on her pleasure as she gripped his shoulders. His cock was ready for her now. He removed his fingers and penetrated her fast and deep, his hips slamming forward, his flesh slapping against hers. She writhed beneath him, but he kept her pinned to the mattress as he forgot finesse and simply pounded into her, determined to leave his mark, to make her his, to possess her very soul.

He shouted her name as he came. Looking down at her satisfied, replete expression, he realized with a shock that nothing would ever be the same again. He didn't believe in love, yet he knew in his soul that he loved Sara. She belonged to him now, and he'd fight and kill to keep her.

15

Sara knocked on the front door of the Pettifers' narrow-fronted town house. Evangeline had invited her to tea, so why was no one answering? It was almost a week since the unfortunate incident at the ambassador's ball, and she hadn't heard a thing from the Pettifers until today.

With a sigh, Sara walked back down the steps and surveyed the exterior of the house. All the shutters were closed, and the curtains were drawn. She glanced uncertainly down the cobbled street and wondered whether she had done the right thing in sending her carriage away for an hour.

After receiving Evangeline's frantic note, she'd rushed out of the house without informing anyone where she was going. As she shivered on the steps it occurred to her that she should've been more careful, considering the current state of affairs. If Sir Richard was involved in a plot to ruin Valentin and Peter, her presence here might make things worse.

And if she was honest with herself, she knew that if she saw Mr. Aliabad, she would have difficulty restraining her curiosity as to exactly what his relationship with Valentin had been. Reluctant to stay out in the drizzling rain, she ascended the steps to shelter under the portico.

"Sara!"

She hesitated as someone hissed her name. Looking down through the iron railings that surrounded the basement, she saw Evangeline waving at her from the kitchen door. She followed the stone steps down another level and was hustled into the deserted kitchen. The fatty scent of roast lamb filled the dingy room, but there was no sign of the live-in cook and butler.

Evangeline's brown hair lay tangled around her shoulders. She looked as if she'd been weeping. Her cheek bore the fresh imprint of a blow. Sara touched her arm.

"Are you unwell? Has something happened to Sir Richard?"

Evangeline peered around the kitchen as if she feared her husband lay in wait for her under the table. "He didn't see you, did he?"

"Sir Richard? No, I don't think so. He didn't answer the door. I left my carriage at the posting house at the corner of the square and walked across."

Evangeline sank down on a bench beside the large pine kitchen table. "Thank goodness." She lifted her tear-stained face and touched her bruised cheek. "I don't care what he does to me. I had to warn you."

Sara's recent happiness dissolved in a cloud of misgiving. Did Evangeline's tears have something to do with the unwelcome visitor from Turkey? She took a seat near her friend and handed her a clean handkerchief. After dabbing at her cheeks, Evangeline regained her composure.

"This morning, I overheard Sir Richard and Mr. Yusef Aliabad discussing your husband and his business."

Sara tried to compose her features. She didn't want Evangeline to think she was too eager to hear her news.

"It seems Mr. Aliabad believes he can further blacken Valentin's reputation and ruin him completely."

"I do not understand."

Evangeline swallowed hard. "I hate to be the one to tell you this. Mr. Aliabad insists he has evidence to suggest that Peter Howard and your husband are lovers."

"That's ridiculous!" Sara almost smiled at the notion. Evangeline shook her head.

"I'm sorry, Sara, but people often gossip about the strong bond between them. Some believe that the only reason Valentin chose to marry you was to avoid just such a scandal as this." She dabbed at her eyes with the damp handkerchief. "Just before your marriage, Peter was embroiled in a scandal with a footman, whom he'd molested. Aliabad insists that Valentin married you to divert attention away from Peter and stop the rumors about them."

Sara patted Evangeline's hand.

"I know that Peter and Valentin are close. They were slaves together. It would be unusual if they hadn't become friends after sharing such a horrific experience."

In her eagerness to defend Valentin and Peter, she tried her best to ignore Evangeline's unflattering assumptions about the reasons for her marriage.

She winced as Evangeline's nails dug into her palm.

"According to Mr. Aliabad, your husband and his partner were slaves in a Turkish brothel that catered to both men and women."

Sara remembered Valentin's intense reaction to Yusef, the way Peter jumped in to defend his friend from the other man's insinuations. If Valentin had indeed been enslaved in a brothel, his behavior toward Yusef made perfect sense. She fought a rising sense of unease. Had he ever intended to tell her the truth about his past, or did he still consider her too innocent to understand?

Evangeline squeezed Sara's hand, her eyes softly pleading.

"Mr. Aliabad claims he paid to have carnal knowledge of them both on more than one occasion."

Sara shrugged off Evangeline's obvious pity. "Even if we choose to believe such a man, what happened in the past has no bearing on the present."

"But if they are still lovers . . ."

Sara searched her memory for any signs that Peter and Valentin had been deceiving her. In truth, they were extremely close, and Peter did touch Valentin more than other men. But between her sexual demands, his work, and their social obligations, when would he find the time to engage in a dangerous and socially disastrous love affair with his best friend?

"I'm sure you meant well in telling me this, Evangeline, but . . ."

"You don't understand! There is more."

Evangeline got to her feet, her agitation obvious as she paced the cold flagstones. "Apparently Valentin contacted Mr. Aliabad and offered to meet with him and Peter at Madame Helene's on Tuesday." She stopped and studied Sara. "Do you know where that is?"

Sara nodded, her thoughts in an uproar. Why would Valentin agree to meet a man he loathed at the pleasure house he loved?

"Sir Richard was concerned that Mr. Aliabad would walk into a trap. But Yusef seems to believe Valentin is anxious to rekindle their love affair." She clasped her hands to her bosom. "Oh, Sara, if word gets out that your husband is involved with other men and was once a sex slave in a brothel, no God-fearing man will ever do business with him again."

Evangeline sat down with a rustle of silk. "I didn't hear anything else. The butler appeared with the tea, and I had to slip away." She clutched Sara's sleeve. "I don't wish you to be caught up in a horrid scandal. Sir Richard was furious when he realized I'd been listening." She touched the bruise on her cheek. "Perhaps you might consider returning to your parents."

Sara forced a smile. Did Evangeline really think she would abandon her husband so easily?

"Actually my father is due in Town tomorrow. I've already arranged to meet him at Fenton's Hotel for dinner."

Evangeline let out her breath. "I'm so pleased. I feel better now that I know you have someone to turn to." She hesitated, the handkerchief still clenched in her hand. "I'm not quite sure what Sir Richard plans to do with Yusef's information. If I find the opportunity, I will beg him to keep the whole matter private. Perhaps he can persuade Valentin to give up his business, and then he won't have to mention all the other unpleasantness."

Sara simply stared at Evangeline. How very like her social-climbing friend to believe that her status in society meant more to her than her husband's infidelity and possible incarceration or hanging for indecent acts. She couldn't imagine Valentin willingly giving up his business either.

She picked up her bonnet and placed it back on her head. "Evangeline, may I ask one more thing? Who introduced Mr. Aliabad to Sir Richard?"

"I'm not quite sure," Evangeline said, frowning. "Although it's possible it was Valentin's father. He is very well connected to the Russian embassy and all those other foreign places." She gently pushed Sara out of the half-opened kitchen door. "Promise me you will take care of yourself."

Sara caught Evangeline's hand. "Thank you for telling me."

A fresh sheen of tears filled Evangeline's eyes. "Valentin was once very important to me. I would hate for him to lose everything. I know how it feels to be down in the gutter."

Sara pondered that remark as she returned to her carriage. Was Evangeline secretly glad to see her former lover embroiled in a scandal? She scolded herself for the thought. Evangeline had acted out of kindness and despite her husband's physical threats to silence her; Sara should be more grateful.

Her thoughts circled back to a horrific image of Valentin and Peter trapped in a brothel. She knew little about the way a house of ill repute operated, but she had a vivid imagination. A man as proud as Valentin must have found it devastating to be owned and used like an object. Her fingers curled as she remembered the numerous scars on his back.

Would he welcome the news that it might have been his father who had introduced Sir Richard to Yusef? His worst fears of betrayal would be confirmed, and how would he deal with that? Sara shivered. And if Yusef was busy selling information to their chief competitor, it was no wonder they were being attacked on both a personal and a business level.

Evangeline's other insinuations about Peter and Valentin still seemed absurd. It seemed Aliabad was prepared to use any means to damage and destroy her husband and his best friend. What better way than to suggest they were lovers?

Sara took a deep breath as the carriage slowed and turned into Half Moon Street. Aliabad also claimed that they had all been lovers in the past. Could there be any truth in that? Judging from Valentin's reaction, any contact between them had scarcely been pleasurable for him. And if they had truly been slaves in a brothel, she imagined they had little choice over who bought their time.

For once, she quailed at the thought of questioning Valentin directly. His reaction was bound to be unpleasant. Her newfound confidence with him was still too precious to deliberately throw away. She smiled as the carriage drew to a halt. Perhaps she might risk asking Peter during their afternoon outing.

"Is it true, Peter?"

Under cover of the horrendous performance of the Dudsons' eldest daughter on the harpsichord, Sara repeated her question. "Were you and Valentin held captive in a brothel?"

Peter took her arm and guided her toward the back of the

magnificent drawing room. His smiling face didn't betray the tension revealed in his celestial blue eyes.

"Who told you that?"

"Evangeline Pettifer."

Peter frowned. "The Pettifers are becoming a damned nuisance. You know I can't answer your questions. You need to talk to Valentin."

With ill grace, Sara decided to try another tack. "Do you and Valentin still meet at Madame Helene's?"

Peter looked less guarded. "Occasionally, why?"

Gazing at his angelic face, Sara was reluctant to repeat the nature of Evangeline's disclosures. Peter had suffered enough without being dragged down by new gossip and innuendo.

Sara tried not to groan as Caroline Ingham appeared at her shoulder.

"Excuse me for eavesdropping, but of course Valentin and Peter still meet there," Caroline said. She gave Peter an unpleasant smile. "If I remember rightly, you demanded Valentin's presence there every Tuesday night." She patted Sara's sleeve. "I tried to warn you about Valentin's little indiscretions, but you chose not to listen. Are you regretting your decision to stand back and play the long-suffering wife? "

Sara ignored Caroline and concentrated her attention on Peter, whose frosty expression reflected the accuracy of Caroline's comments. Her newfound sense of satisfaction dissipated. Surely Valentin had an answer for all these questions? She had to believe he wanted only her. After their night together at Madame Helene's, he'd told her she was the only woman he desired, and she had believed him. But what if he wanted a man as well?

Caroline Ingham walked away, laughing. Sara took Peter's arm and returned to the drawing room. He stopped her in the doorway.

"Sara, talk to Valentin. He is the only one who can answer your questions."

She smiled at him to show she wasn't upset. She'd been too impetuous in the past. She'd tried to force Valentin to confide in her, and it hadn't worked. In truth, he'd just become more distant and cutting. Perhaps she should learn from her mistakes. The thought of asking him to explain himself this time was somehow more frightening than remaining in ignorance. For once in her life she would try to be patient.

16

Sara glanced at Valentin as he allowed the footman to refill his wineglass for the third time. Unable to find the courage to confront him, she'd managed to avoid him since her disastrous conversations with Peter and Evangeline on the previous day. He sipped his wine, his gaze shadowed and distant. He was dressed in dove gray with a black waistcoat and white cravat. She couldn't imagine him servicing customers in a brothel. Surely her father wouldn't have married her to a man like that? To her relief, Valentin seemed too preoccupied to notice her agitated state.

"Are you going out this evening?" Sara asked.

Valentin looked at her, his wineglass poised midway to his mouth. "Why, is there something I have forgotten? Some ball or musical evening you insist I attend with you?"

Sara put down her fork. "I am perfectly capable of going out by myself. Signor Clementi asked me to accompany him to the opera, and then I plan on paying a visit to my father."

"Ah, I forgot your father was in town. Give him my best, will you, and make sure to invite him for dinner tomorrow night."

"You are fond of him, aren't you?"

He raised an eyebrow. "Of course I am. He rescued me from an intolerable situation."

"You must have felt your debt was substantial in order to make you marry me."

His gaze sharpened. "I told you, your father saved my life. I consider my debt to him beyond mere money. Why do you ask about this now? Your father must have explained his reasons for agreeing to the match."

She held his gaze. "He didn't want me to marry you, but he believed he had no choice. Why did he feel like that when you say the debt was yours?"

A muscle flexed in his cheek. "What do you want me to say, Sara? That he didn't consider me a good choice for you because he knew I could never make you happy? Or would you prefer to believe that I forced him into it?"

"Why was he so reluctant, Valentin?"

He got to his feet. "Why are you insisting on an answer, Sara?"

She stood up, too, her hands curling into fists. "Because I want to understand whether I was sold or bought. Surely you have some sympathy with that?"

He went as pale as the crisp white collar of his shirt. "If you are determined to cast me as the villain of the piece, I bought you, Sara. I paid your father's debts and settled a considerable amount of money on you as well."

She stared at his unsmiling face and desperately tried to gather her composure. What had she hoped to accomplish by starting this ridiculous conversation? Her anxiety over the evening's potential events had taken over her normal calm good sense. She took a careful breath.

"I'm sorry, I'm not even sure what I want you to say."

He rubbed his hand over his jaw. "I would've lent your father money if he had asked me for it. It was his choice to offer me one of his daughters. I married you because I wanted to."

He hesitated, his gaze locked on hers. "I have never tried to make you feel like my possession. I apologize if that is how you see our marriage."

She shook her head, almost beyond speech at his halting words. How could she push him any further when he was being so kind to her? "You have always allowed me to be myself. Perhaps I haven't shown my gratitude very well."

Why did she feel as if they might never speak to each other again? Did he intend to leave her after all?

He shrugged. "There is no need. You have become everything I hoped you would be."

"I still wish to thank you." She walked across to him, laid her hand on his shoulder, and brushed her mouth against his. "Don't go out tonight."

He smiled down at her, his expression touched with sadness. "You are the one with all the plans, my dear. And I fear it is too late for you to contact Signor Clementi and spoil his evening."

Her hand dropped to her side, and she forced a smile. "You could come with me."

Valentin gave an exquisite shudder. "I'd rather not listen to any caterwauling opera singers this evening. It's more than likely I'll go out with Peter." He patted her arm. "Don't wait up for me." He leaned down to kiss her hard on the mouth. Before she could respond, he turned away.

As the door closed behind him, she resisted an urge to cry out and tell him to be careful, that she had begun to love him and that he was far too precious for her to lose. Instead she resumed her seat and sat dry-eyed until the footman began to clear the dining table around her.

What did she feel about the prospect that Valentin loved men in a physical way? She'd never seen men behaving like that. In her conversations with Peter, she sensed his sexuality was as complex as Valentin's. It hadn't made her feel uneasy or threatened. Then again, she'd never imagined the sexual depths she would explore with Valentin herself. She was sure Madame Helene's held the key.

She put down her wineglass with a thump. It was time to stop hiding and face her demons, whatever they were. At least Valentin had given her the self-confidence to do that. She'd leave the opera early and take a hackney cab to Madame Helene's. If Evangeline was right, Mr. Aliabad expected to meet Valentin and Peter there. Rather than risk Valentin's anger with her questions, perhaps she should simply find out what was going on for herself.

Valentin headed up the second flight of stairs at Madame Helene's to the rooms where she allowed only a favored number of clients. Peter had arrived early for their meeting and, according to Madame, had taken advantage of the facilities.

Valentin turned the ornate gold handle, and the door to room 206 opened silently. Valentin strolled across to a wing chair by the fireside and critically assessed the tangle of bodies on the immense bed. There were at least two men and a woman with long blond hair. He vaguely recalled the woman was called Grace. One of the men was Peter.

Valentin angled his head to one side to better appreciate the view as the blonde ground her pussy into Peter's face, her breasts jiggling with the effort. The second man was busy sucking Peter's cock. As he watched, Valentin was glad he had reduced his role in Peter's fantasies to that of occasional observer.

When they'd first returned from Turkey, Peter had craved Valentin's presence in his bed almost as much as he'd craved the opium that was slowly killing him. It had taken a while for Valentin to persuade Peter he'd rather not fuck another man. Even then, Peter had asked him to participate in many foursomes, with Val concentrating his attentions on the woman while the others attended to Peter.

Grace caught sight of him and redoubled her efforts. Valentin winked at her and helped himself from the decanter of brandy. In truth, he'd been glad to get out of any bed that contained another male. When it was just Peter, it was bearable. He understood Peter's needs and fears, and at least he could set the rules and boundaries. With another man, you never knew. Valentin's painful experiences in Turkey with Yusef had soured him on that particular sexual combination for life.

Peter groaned and rolled onto his stomach, dislodging Grace. It gave the man behind him the opportunity to slide into him. The woman grabbed Peter's hand and settled it between her legs. Valentin glanced at his pocket watch as the man's hips pumped hard against Peter's buttocks. When the man came, he bit down hard on Peter's neck. Valentin inhaled the scent of sex and perfumed skin as Peter climaxed. All he could think about was Sara.

Eventually Peter opened his eyes and smiled like a satiated big cat. "Val, if I'd known you were there, I'd have invited you to join in."

Valentin crossed his legs and sipped his brandy. "I was quite happy to watch. You made such a beautiful threesome, I'll be dreaming about you all night."

Grace smiled and kissed Peter's cheek. The man frowned, his hand clenched possessively on Peter's shoulder. Peter patted it.

"There's no need to be jealous, Reggie. Valentin prefers women these days. Or should I say, one woman in particular."

"You may say it as long as you don't mention her name."

Peter's eyebrows rose as he shrugged into a robe. "I've never heard you use that possessive tone before."

Valentin got to his feet as Reggie and Grace left the room.

"I've never been married before. Perhaps it comes with the territory." He paced the carpet as he waited for Peter to wash himself and get dressed.

Peter paused in front of the mirror, his cravat in his hand. "Sara's heard some ugly rumors about us from Evangeline Pettifer."

"Has she? She hasn't said anything to me." Valentin tried to sound nonchalant. She'd kept out of his way for most of the last two days. Was that why? A knot of unease settled low in his gut. It wasn't like Sara not to tackle any issue between them head-on. He remembered the strange conversation they'd had before she left for the theater. He frowned. "What kind of rumors?"

Peter finished tying his cravat. "Ask her yourself. I refuse to become a go-between."

"You are right, I'll ask her. But thank you for telling me anyway." He passed Peter his coat. "Are you ready to face Yusef Aliabad now?"

"Are you?" Peter returned Valentin's gaze. "I know how much you despise him. I saw what he did to you. I remember how hard you fought him."

Valentin studied the toe of his riding boot. "You didn't see the half of it. When he got me alone for our 'private sessions,' he made me beg for it." His stomach tightened at the distant echoes of his own screams. "He made me crawl on my knees and beg."

Valentin raised his head and saw the understanding on Peter's face. Would anyone else ever comprehend the hell they'd been through? Sometimes he wanted to tell Sara all of it. Then he imagined the look of passion on her face turning to disgust—or, even worse, to pity. He wasn't sure he was ready to risk that yet.

"Sara should know," Peter said, as though he'd read Valentin's thoughts. "She deserves to hear the truth. It'd be far worse if she were married to me. I'll fuck anything. At least you know you prefer women. Unfortunately my tastes remain more eclectic." He glanced down as he rearranged his cravat. "I've already told her about my opium addiction."

"And what did she say to that?"

"She kissed me and said she was glad I had chosen to live." Peter's self-mocking tone disappeared. "She's an unusual woman, Val."

Refusing to be drawn, Valentin walked to the door. "Aliabad should be here by now. Madame has allowed us the use of her private salon so that we may talk undisturbed."

They went down one of the discreetly lit back staircases. "What I don't understand is how Aliabad is mixed up in this business to ruin us," Peter said.

"Well, we agree that he is at least a part of it. His appearance at this juncture is too much of a coincidence otherwise." Valentin paused on the next landing. "He must be working with someone who knows how our business runs on a day-to-day basis. There is no way he could control a matter of this size from the wilds of Turkey. I doubt he has the brains for it either. His style has always been physical and sexual intimidation."

"What do you think he wants from us tonight, then?"

Valentin smiled. "I should imagine he will threaten to ruin us socially unless we give him money. That would be much more his style. His partner is probably hoping we'll give in to his demands and drain even more money from the business, thus hastening our demise. "

"How long has Aliabad been in the country, then?"

"According to my sources, about three weeks, so far. And our problems began long before that. He is due to sail back in three months."

Peter leaned up against the wall and crossed his arms. "I've finished checking out Mr. Carter's associates."

"And?" Valentin tried to gauge Peter's expression in the dim lighting.

"Alex Long was recommended for his post by Sir Richard Pettifer, not Mr. John Harrison, so Sara's father is not implicated in any way."

Valentin allowed himself to relax a little. "What about the other one—Duncan, wasn't it?"

Peter sighed. "Christopher Duncan used to work at your father's estate in Scotland."

Valentin didn't speak. He should've felt triumphant that his suspicions about his father had proven correct. Instead he felt numb. With Sara and Peter's help, he'd reluctantly begun to come to terms with the notion that his father bore him no ill will.

"Before you jump to conclusions, we still don't know which one it is, Val."

"When will we know?"

Peter's smile wasn't pleasant. "They are both being watched. If one of them so much as sneezes in the wrong place at the wrong time, we will know about it."

Valentin set off down the stairs again. "Good. If anything happens, tell me at once."

Peter followed him down the back stairs until they emerged outside Madame Helene's elegant suite of rooms. Valentin hesitated at the door. Could he face his old enemy without losing his temper? For everyone's sake, he hoped so.

Sara picked up her skirt and ran down the steps of the opera house. She'd managed to convince Signor Clementi that she was ill and avoided his gallant offer to escort her home. During the interval, he'd asked if she would like to perform on the pianoforte at a private concert for the Prince of Wales. Gratified beyond belief, she'd felt more overwhelmed when Signor Clementi dryly remarked that Valentin had not only given his permission but wondered why he'd been asked for it in the first place.

She felt guilty even doubting Valentin after that. But she made herself climb into a waiting hackney cab. She asked to be taken to Madame Helene's, hoping the driver would know where she meant.

He set off without asking for further directions. Relieved, Sara took her silver half mask out of her reticule and put it on. She wasn't quite sure how she would gain admittance to Madame's. Valentin had walked in as though he owned the place. Would the staff remember her, or would she have to reveal her identity?

At the discreetly lit entrance, Sara made sure her black cloak covered her evening gown before she stepped through the massive double doors. A footman dressed in a gold and scarlet uniform, lace at his throat, bowed to her. He handed her a piece of parchment and a quill pen.

"Good evening, ma'am, will you please sign your real name so that I can verify your admittance with Madame?"

Sara complied and warmed her hands before the massive fireplace until the footman returned. He gave her a practiced bow.

"Enjoy your evening, my lady."

Sara hurried past him up the stairs until she reached the grand salon at the top. The room was crowded, and despite her efforts she couldn't see Valentin or Peter. There were a great deal more men present than women, and the atmosphere seemed coarser and subtly more threatening. A hand fastened around her ankle. She looked down to see a young man dressed in a woman's nightgown grinning up at her.

"Please, fair lady, come and play with me." His voice was slurred, the stench of brandy on his breath unmistakable.

Sara tried to move away, but the man kept hold of her.

"Let me go."

His fingers crept up toward her knee. "I'm only trying to be friendly, my little dove, don't you want to play?"

As Sara tried to kick free, a footman came up behind the drunk and grabbed him under the arms.

"Let go of the lady, sir. She has business elsewhere."

The footman gripped the man's wrist and pried it away from Sara's flesh. She stepped away as the drunk was persuaded to leave.

As she turned back to the salon, she caught a glimpse of the blond-haired woman Valentin had acknowledged on their last visit. She made her way over to the buffet area and tapped the woman on the shoulder.

"Ma'am, I am looking for someone. Can you help me?"

"Of course, ma petite. I am Madame Helene. I know where everyone is." Her shrewd blue eyes searched Sara's face. "I'm not sure we've met, although I believe I have heard quite a lot about you." She took Sara's arm and walked with her to a quieter area of the salon. "You came with Valentin the other night."

Sara let out her breath. "Yes, I'm Valentin's wife. Is he here tonight? He told me he would be."

Madame Helene frowned. "I believe I saw him with Peter earlier." She surveyed the crowds. "I'm not sure exactly where they have gone, but I will find out for you."

She clicked her fingers, and a footman appeared at her side. She murmured to him. He bowed and disappeared down the long corridor beyond the salon. Sara pressed herself back against the wall as a group of men staggered past, a lone woman in their midst. Two of the men were busy kissing, their faces engrossed, hands fumbling at each other's clothes.

Sara stared after them. "Do Peter and Valentin often come here together?"

Madame Helene shot her an amused look. "Why do you ask, my lady?"

Sara said nothing. How could she ask if her husband came here to meet his male lover? She would sound naive and provincial. And Madame might think she was going to make a scene. At least there was no sign of the unpleasant Mr. Aliabad. Perhaps Evangeline had prevented Aliabad from attending the meeting, and Peter and Valentin had gone on to other things.

Madame Helene swore in very unladylike French under her breath. "My apologies, I have to go and deal with a certain gentleman who continues to ignore my requests for him to stay away from this house." She patted Sara's hand. "I will return in a moment." She headed purposefully for the front entrance, where a tall blond man gazed disdainfully around him.

"My lady?"

The footman had returned and waited at Sara's elbow.

"I've found the gentleman you seek. Would you care to follow me?"

Sara thanked him. He led her down a narrow staircase and into another wide corridor decorated in gold and cream.

"Your gentleman is in Madame Helene's private suite."

"Is he alone?"

The footman bowed. "I'm unable to tell you that, ma'am." He opened the first door for her. "May I suggest you wait in here until Madame returns to assist you?"

Sara allowed herself to be abandoned in the magnificent bedroom. Several mirrors on the walls and the ceiling reflected her worried-looking image back at her. She managed a faint smile. At least Valentin wasn't romping naked on the bed with Peter or a variety of well-endowed women. She heard the murmur of voices through the half-opened door into the dressing room. Ignoring the footman's advice to wait for Madame, Sara peered through the door. There was no one there.

She ducked back into the bedroom as someone entered from the opposite side and noisily used the chamber pot. When he returned to the other room, she waited for the click of the latch but heard nothing. If she was careful, could she listen at the opposite door? She crept across the dressing room and pushed open the door a little more. She remained on her knees, hardly daring to breathe.

Valentin stared at Aliabad across the table. "I repeat. We will not give you a penny. You can spread all the gossip and rumors you like. No one will believe you." He deliberately laid his hand over Peter's and linked their fingers. "I'm married now. As far as the polite world is concerned, I'm a reformed rake who's finally settled down and accepted his responsibilities. Who is going to listen to the ranting of a foreigner when a peer of the realm's son is implicated?"

Aliabad sneered. "I'm sure your wife would be interested to hear about your past."

"My wife is young, unsophisticated, and naive. Even if you told her what I 'supposedly' have done, she wouldn't understand." He raised one eyebrow. "Why do you think I took so long to find a wife? It was difficult to locate someone so innocent. And I've taken great care to make sure she is bound to me both sexually and legally."

He smiled then as Aliabad's eyes filled with rage. It was imperative that Aliabad believed Sara had no value to him, or she might be used against him. "Thanks in part to you, and my days spent servicing countless women in Turkey, apparently I'm irresistible in bed."

Aliabad shot to his feet. "You haven't heard the last of this. I'll give you and Peter a few days to reconsider your position, and then I'll be back."

"With your partner?" Valentin inquired. "We would love to meet the person who is attempting to bleed our business dry." He shared a glance with Peter. "He is obviously the brains behind the plan."

"I'll wager you would love to know who it is, wouldn't you?" Aliabad leaned forward, his palms flat on the table until his face was level with Valentin's. "Peer's son or not, we will ruin you." He licked his lips. "I'm looking forward to having you on your knees again, Val, begging for your life and at my mercy."

Valentin swallowed down his rage and disgust and kept his gaze locked to the other man. "Don't hold your breath." He sat back. "If I find you within five feet of me, Peter, or my family again, I will use my influence to have you deported as a spy. Good night."

Aliabad spoke in Turkish, his words a mere whisper. "This is mere bravado. You'll beg, Val. I'll see to it." He slammed out of the room, making the door shake on its hinges. Peter got up and poured them each a large glass of brandy. He clinked his glass against Valentin's.

"That seemed a little too easy."

Valentin paused as he registered the sound of the door latch turning. Had Aliabad decided to return? He grabbed Peter's head and kissed him hard on the mouth. Brandy from Peter's glass sloshed over his sleeve and soaked it. He grinned at Peter's stunned expression. That should give Aliabad something to think about. Peter's hand slid up to caress his cheek.

A soft draught of perfumed air alerted him to the fact that the door that had been opened led back into Madame's dressing room and not the corridor beyond. Something about the quality of the silent presence behind him was familiar. Valentin released Peter and slowly turned around. Sara stood framed in the inner doorway. A silver mask concealed her eyes, but her body language spoke eloquently of her shock.

Valentin smiled at her. "Didn't your nurse ever tell you that eavesdroppers never hear well of themselves?"

"Val. . . ." Peter murmured.

Sara stormed up to him and slapped him hard on the cheek. He kept smiling even as he realized his joke had fallen flat. How much had she heard? How much had she believed was the truth?

She turned and disappeared the way she'd come. Valentin fought a sudden rise of nausea. She had followed him to the pleasure house. Had she seen what she expected?

"Val. Go after her. Explain."

Peter shoved his cloak into his hands.

Valentin just stared at him.

"Val." Peter grabbed his arm. "Come on, I'll go with you."

On the stairs, Sara ran straight into Madame Helene, who took one look at her face and directed her away from the more public rooms and toward a secluded exit door in the basement.

While Madame arranged for a hackney cab, Sara stood against the wall and shook as if she had the ague. Valentin's disdainful words kept repeating themselves in her head. He'd chosen her for her stupidity. He'd used sex to enslave her.

She touched her brow as a headache settled behind her eyes. She jumped when Madame Helene handed her a handkerchief, unaware that she was crying.

"My dear, where do you wish to go?"

Sara simply stared at her. She couldn't go home.

"My father's staying at Fenton's Hotel. I'll go there."

"Are you certain you do not wish to wait for Valentin? I'm sure there is a perfectly reasonable explanation. . . ."

"Thank you, Madame, but I'd rather leave by myself."

Madame Helene kissed her cheek and waved her off from the covered entranceway, her beautiful profile marred by a frown.

Sara huddled in the corner of the carriage, her arms wrapped around herself. Valentin had kissed Peter as if he'd done it a thousand times before. Peter had looked as if he were in heaven. . . . Had she been lied to, and had her father been privy to Valentin's true nature all along? Thank God he had come to London alone. She could ask him to his face. Perhaps he could make everything right for her again.

She wept harder at the thought. She was too old to believe her father could fix the universe for her. But at least he might give her some hope. Surely Valentin hadn't meant everything he'd said? There she was, making excuses for him even now. She clenched her teeth and stared out into the rain-washed night.

Her father's expression when she knocked loudly on his door changed from annoyance to concern when he saw her bedraggled state.

"Sara? Is something amiss? Come in, girl. I intended to call on you tomorrow."

She waited while he shut the door and poked the fire to life. His coat hung over the back of a chair, and he'd removed his boots in favor of a pair of worn slippers. Despite the sudden warmth, her teeth continued to chatter as she turned to face him.

"Father, can you tell me exactly where you found Valentin and Peter in Turkey?"

He stopped prodding the fire and went still. "Why do you wish to know that?"

"Because there are rumors about Valentin's past. I wanted to ask you for the truth."

To her horror, her father sank down into one of the chairs by the fire and covered his face with his hands. Sara stepped closer.

"Papa, I need to know. Please tell me."

"God in heaven, what has he done? I should never have listened to your mother. I should have kept him away from you."

She sank to her knees in front of him. "Papa. . . ."

He still couldn't look at her. "I found them in a brothel when I was . . . delivering some goods to the owner."

"What goods did you have to deliver to a brothel?"

He lifted his head but wouldn't quite meet her eyes. "That is none of your business, young lady. I'm still your father."

She bit down hard on her lip. "They were servants there?"

"They were sex slaves." He sounded weary but determined. "Men and women paid for their sexual services."

"How do you know this?"

He met her gaze for the first time. "Because the first time I saw them, Valentin and Peter were in the midst of an orgy. I noticed them because their skin was so light and asked who they were." He shuddered. "The owner thought I wanted to buy their services and told me about their various 'skills.' "

He gripped Sara's hand. "I had to get them away from there. No Englishman should be held like a slave. After my first meeting with them, I realized Peter was addicted to opium. He was so dependent on Valentin, I couldn't just leave them there to die. They refused to sleep apart on the journey home. I didn't inquire as to what they got up to."

Sara held his gaze. "Why didn't you tell me the truth before I married Valentin? You warned me off Peter, but you didn't explain anything about Valentin's past."

She realized she was angry. Great hot waves of it rose inside her, scalding out her tears, strengthening her resolve.

"Valentin offered me an immense sum of money for your hand in marriage. I took it because I foolishly believed his promises that he had detached himself from Peter and intended to honor his marriage vows."

Sara got to her feet, her damp skirts sticking to her legs. He'd forgotten to add that he had been desperate to save his business. At least she had the answer to her question. She had been sold by her father for personal gain and bought by Valentin for what? Lust or as a smoke screen of respectability?

"Sara, if there had been another way to save my business and our family, I would've taken it." The pain in her father's voice left her numb. By what right did men believe they could treat their womenfolk like stupid sheep? She couldn't decide whom she hated most—her father for agreeing to the marriage or Valentin for using her innocence as a shield for his true nature.

She swung around as Valentin entered the room without knocking, Peter behind him.

"What do you want? If you've come to offer my father more money to keep silent about your past, you're too late. He's already confirmed the worst."

"And what is that?"

"That you lied to me. That you've used me."

Valentin's smile widened. "You were quite willing to marry me. Some might even say eager. Have you decided I'm not quite to your liking anymore?"

She glared at him, so consumed by her anger that she no longer cared she had an audience. "Do you have to make a joke out of everything, Valentin?"

He bowed. "Only when it seems my lines have already been written for me and my fate decided."

Sara's father got unsteadily to his feet. "Perhaps you should leave. I'll take care of her."

Valentin frowned and took a step toward her, his hand outstretched.

Sara backed away from both of them. "I don't want either of you to come near me." She looked at Peter. "Will you escort me home?"

Valentin's hand dropped to his side, and he nodded at his father-in-law.

"Sara is right. There's no need for either of us to cause her further distress. She will be quite safe in her own house. I've decided to leave on a business trip to Russia."

Peter cleared his throat, but after a glance from Valentin he remained quiet.

"I'll be back in a few months, after I've repaired our ailing fortunes." He looked straight at Sara, but she could detect nothing behind his bland expression. "Perhaps that will give you enough time to work out how you want to go on." He bowed again, his face a perfect mask, and walked away from her into the night.

Sara watched him leave, aware of Peter's distress and her father muttering like a mournful Greek chorus behind her. Her anger died as quickly as it had risen, leaving her cold and shaken. She had a sense of teetering on the edge of an abyss as she heard Valentin's boots clatter down the stairs.

God in heaven. What had she done?

17

"For goodness sake, Peter, why didn't Valentin explain this to me when he had the opportunity?"

Sara turned on Peter, her petticoats swirling around her. He sat at his ease on her couch sipping tea, his booted feet stretched out toward the heat of the fire. Winter was closing in on the city, its deathly cold grip evident in the frigid air and the lowering black skies.

"You didn't exactly give him a chance, did you? Val kissed me because he thought Aliabad had come back to snoop. He didn't mean anything by it." Peter shrugged. "I, of all people, know that."

Sara closed her mouth with a snap. Peter had a point. On that fateful night at Madame Helene's, she'd been too angry and betrayed to listen to anyone. Her memories were still fragmented. Her fury at her father had collided with her rage with Valentin and canceled out all common sense.

After Sara had refused to accompany him home, her distraught father had returned to Southampton alone. She wasn't quite sure how she felt about him anymore. His inadequate explanation for being in the brothel in Turkey made him less of a man in her eyes.

Peter put down his cup. "You have to understand, Sara. Val's never trusted anyone since his experiences in Turkey. He expects to be misjudged. He's made an art form out of appearing not to care."

"And I fulfilled his expectations wonderfully, didn't I?" She sank down on the rug and rested her head against Peter's knee. Valentin had been gone for six weeks. She and Peter had had this conversation endlessly. She missed every moment of Valentin's company, especially his presence in her bed. "I behaved like a fool."

"Don't be too hard on yourself. Val was a bigger one."

She managed a watery chuckle. "That makes me feel a little better, but now I need to know how to undo the damage I've caused."

Peter sighed. "It's not going to be easy. He doesn't give second chances."

"I should have trusted him more. I should've been less concerned about my hurt feelings and. . . ." She bit back the useless words. There was no point weeping over spilled milk. She had to move on and find a way to bring him back to her.

"And now Valentin's somewhere behind enemy lines in Europe. It's not as if I can follow him and beg him to come back."

"Do you want him back?"

Sara knelt up and studied Peter's tranquil expression. "Of course I do. I love him."

"So do I, Sara." He hesitated. "Does that offend you?"

She stroked his cheek. "Not since you've explained what you went through together. I'd be surprised if you didn't care for each other."

Peter's companionship over the last wretched weeks had provided her only source of comfort. He was the one person who truly understood what had made Valentin the man he was. Despite Valentin's fears that Peter would relapse into addiction, Peter had shown himself to be far stronger than that. He'd proved to Sara that he had beaten his demons far more successfully than her husband had.

He smiled at her. "Then we need to think of a way to bring him back to us. Something so shocking he'll feel obliged to return to save your reputation." She regarded him suspiciously as his mouth curved in a grin. "There is a rather unusual auction coming up at Madame Helene's next month. Madame believes it is her patriotic duty to ensure that no soldier goes into battle a virgin. She offers the ladies of the *ton* a chance to display their patriotism by deflowering any willing young men who have recently enlisted."

Sara's mouth dropped open. "Would I actually have to go through with it?"

"What goes on behind the bedroom door is up to you and the man you win. No one else needs to know." He thinned his lips and looked disapproving. "I, of course, would feel compelled to write to Valentin immediately about your shameless conduct and the implications for your social standing. If that doesn't get him on the next ship home, nothing will."

"And when he gets here, I'll just have to think of a way to make him trust me again." She bit her lip. "I have already thought of one way, but I will need your help."

Peter smiled. "You have to ask me that? Of course I'll help you."

"I want to understand how it was for you." She bit her lip. "You were both so young. . . ."

"It could've been worse, Sara." Peter shrugged. "At least Madame Tezoli waited a few years until we were old enough to have an erection instead of setting us to work when we first arrived."

Sara tasted blood in her mouth. "How can you say that so calmly? How can you make allowances for that awful woman?"

Peter met her gaze, his blue eyes clear. "Because I have to live with myself and who I am. I also have to forgive."

She continued to study him as he got to his feet.

"I have to show Valentin that what happened in the past doesn't disgust me. If I put myself in a position where I have to trust him implicitly, perhaps he'll be able to do the same for me."

Peter pretended to applaud, his vivid face now alive with mischief. "Go ahead, Sara. Shock him. I'll enjoy every damned minute of it."

18

Sara heard the sound of voices in the hallway and listlessly looked up from the book she was pretending to read. Snow fell outside her window, making it difficult to distinguish between the sky and the ground. The starkness of the winter evening suited the bitterness of her mood. She hadn't bothered to dress for dinner, having no appetite and no expected guests. To her annoyance, her visitor seemed in no hurry to depart. Was it Peter trying to lure her out into society again?

She wrapped a woolen shawl around her shoulders and walked out onto the landing. A tall man dressed in a furred Cossack hat and a long black cloak stood in the hall below talking to her butler. Even before he turned to look up at her, she knew it was Valentin.

The three months since she'd seen him had altered his appearance. He'd grown a beard. His face was thinner, his eyes shadowed as if he'd ridden through hell to reach her.

Sara brought her hand to her mouth. "What are you doing here?"

Without breaking his gaze, he took off his snow-encrusted hat and handed it to the butler. "Weren't you expecting me?" In the yellow gaslight, the dark sable lining of his cloak rippled like a live animal. "In truth, I was already on my way back from Russia when I received news of your predicament."

Her chin came up. "I didn't ask you to come."

He stripped off the heavy cloak. "No, you didn't, did you?" His gaze swept her body. "Are you ready to go out? I suspect we need to be seen together as soon as possible to dispel any rumors."

He walked into the morning room, trailing his cloak behind him. When Sara caught up with him, he was studying the invitation cards she'd left unopened on the mantelpiece. He handed her three.

"We'll attend these. I need to change and get rid of this damned beard. Be ready in half an hour."

"But I don't want to go out."

His polite tone and bland face couldn't disguise the cold fury in his eyes.

"I didn't ask you what you wanted."

He turned on his heel and headed up the stairs.

Sara remained in the center of the room, clutching the engraved cards like a fool. Did she have time to send a message to Peter to ask him to meet them at the first ball? If her plan was to work, she needed his assistance. She stared at the cloak Valentin had discarded over a chair and couldn't help but pick it up and hug it to her chest. It carried his unique scent and warmth. She buried her face in the thick folds and struggled to regain her composure.

He'd come home.

For her.

Sara wasn't surprised when Valentin appeared in the doorway that connected their rooms. She nodded at her maid to leave. He held out his hand for her hairbrush, and she seated herself at her dressing table.

He'd shaved and changed into a long black silk dressing gown. Without his beard and mustache, she could see the classic lines of his face, the sharp angles of his high cheekbones, and his magnificent violet eyes.

He began to brush her hair, his strokes smooth and even. "You must have known Peter would contact me about your activities."

His conversational tone ignored the fact they hadn't spoken to each other for three desperate months.

"What particular activities are you referring to?"

He smiled without humor. "Your adultery with two recently enlisted soldiers in the rifle brigade. I believe they were twins."

"Identical twins."

The brush stopped midstroke. "You don't deny that you fucked them?"

"Why should I? If you heard about it in the wilds of Russia, it has to be true."

He resumed brushing. "And were they worth it?"

Sara pretended to look puzzled. "Worth what?"

Valentin gave a short laugh. "Your reputation, my dear. I understand from Peter that you have been shunned by certain sections of society."

Sara shrugged. "I'll survive. You would know that better than anyone." She glanced in the mirror, hoping for a reaction. His expression remained unnervingly pleasant.

"Tonight we will begin to repair the damage. I'll appear at your side as if nothing is wrong. Soon another scandal will erupt and everyone will forget about it."

"Is it really that simple?"

Valentin put the brush down. "We'll have to see, won't we?" He slid his hand into his pocket and brought something out.

"Perhaps you would care to wear this for me this evening? It might help you concentrate on pretending to be a loving wife besotted with her handsome husband."

Sara studied the narrow gold chains, hooks, and single pearl. Her body shuddered to life as she realized he hadn't brought her anything remotely conventional.

"I think you will have to help me."

Valentin pushed her dressing gown off her shoulders. "Then you will have to stand."

He studied her naked body in the mirror. Her nipples tightened and pulled against the gold hoops inserted through them. His hands came around her waist and fastened the first of the interconnected chains in a circle low on her hips. He brought two thin chains up to her breasts and linked them through the rings in her nipples.

"The woman who sold it to me said the caress of the pearl is similar to a man's fingertip on the tip of your clit. It's meant to stimulate you, to make you think constantly of sex." He let the final piece of the chain, containing the pearl, hang down between her legs.

"Did she tell you this while she modeled the piece for you?"

Valentin didn't answer. Sara fought to contain a shiver as his hand cupped her mound and slid the thin gold between her labia and back up toward her buttocks. He knelt at her feet, his expression serious as he looped the chain under and over the length around her hips.

He found the pearl, which seemed to move on the chains. He pressed it against her clitoris and held it there with the pad of his thumb. The fine links from her nipple rings tightened and pulled gently on her aroused flesh. He adjusted the length of the chain between her buttocks and secured it at her waist.

He looked up at her like a dressmaker inquiring over the fit of a new gown. "Are you uncomfortable?"

Sara straightened and immediately felt the pearl slide against her clitoris; it warmed to her skin by the second.

"Is this how you intend to punish me?"

Valentin got to his feet, his cock clearly visible between the silk folds of his dressing gown. He made no attempt to hide it.

"It's a start, don't you think? We'll discuss how we mean to go on at the end of the evening. Stay there."

Sara had reached for her corset but obediently stood still. Valentin pushed his dressing gown to one side and pumped his shaft with his hand. She found it impossible not to watch the rough strokes of his fingers as he grew wet and engorged. Her nipples tightened, and her body responded with a gush of her own cream.

"I'd like to come against your stomach now and take you out naked and covered in my seed." He tightened his grip on his shaft. "It's amazing how territorial a man can become. Every-one would know you belonged to me then."

He grimaced as his come spurted through his fingers, his breath short. Turning to Sara, he brushed his soaked fingers over her closed mouth.

"Be ready to leave in fifteen minutes. I'll wait for you in the hall."

Valentin glanced down at the composed face of his wife as they danced. In the flesh she was even more beautiful than he had imagined in his tortured dreams. Her long dark hair, se-cured into an intricate array of curls and braids, framed her fea-tures. So classically English, yet she had such a rich sensuality beneath that perfect skin.

For the first time in his life, he was uncertain. He'd regretted his abrupt decision to leave as soon as his ship sailed. He should've stayed and fought for what he wanted, not disappeared as though his guilt was already established. In truth, he'd never stood up for himself. It had been easier to ignore unpleasantness, to hide behind an amiable smile, to allow hate and self-disgust to fester deep in his soul.

But Sara now knew the worst of him. When he arrived, he'd half expected her to order him from the house. Instead she had welcomed him, allowed him to touch her, and proved a pleasant and attentive companion all evening. Despite Peter's anxious letters, he hadn't noticed Sara receiving any major snubs from the *ton*. It was possible that his mere presence had discouraged the gossip. He was more inclined to think Peter had deliberately overestimated Sara's predicament in an attempt to entice him home. Peter didn't need to know he'd already turned back.

"Are you enjoying yourself, my dear?"

"Yes, my lord. It is a very pleasant evening."

She smiled at him again, her blue eyes wide and untroubled. He'd hoped that when she saw him she would be angry at first and then allow him to explain and persuade her that he was sorry. He'd even braced himself for her pity. Her cool reception, and the fact that she hadn't denied taking a lover, reignited all his possessive instincts.

He gritted his teeth against an impulse to take her by the shoulders and shake her until her teeth rattled.

"Why are you being so nice to me?" he asked abruptly.

"Isn't this what you wanted? A nice conventional wife who wouldn't turn a hair at your infidelities?"

Within Valentin's chest, fury and lust fought a losing battle against good manners. He stopped dancing and marched Sara off the dance floor, his grip on her arm so tight he felt all the bones in her wrist. He dived into the first deserted room he found.

"My name is Valentin, not my lord."

She raised her chin. "I am well aware of that." Her bodice rose and fell with each hurried breath. He remembered the chains attached to her nipple rings, the pearl buried in the soft folds of her sex. The silence between them seemed to shiver with sexual heat and anticipation.

"I am still your husband. You still belong to me."

"I don't belong to anyone."

He stared into her eyes. "Perhaps you need to be convinced."

He pressed her up against the wall and fell to his knees. His mouth brushed the soft satin of her dress. "Lift up your skirts."

The soft rustle of satin and petticoats sounded loud in the hush of the library.

"Open your legs."

He slid one arm behind her buttocks so that her pussy was angled toward him. The pearl rested on her clit, now surrounded by whorls of her cream. With a groan he pulled her toward his mouth; his teeth grazed the pearl and sucked it hard with her swollen bud.

Sara moaned as he licked and licked the pearl and thin gold chain. He wanted to fuck her hard up against the wall. He didn't care if anyone came into the library and saw them. God, he'd love to see how jealous any other man would be if he saw Sara coming in his arms.

She started to shudder and pulse around his wild mouth. He fought a wave of emotions that threatened to overwhelm him. With deliberate care, he got to his feet and wiped his hand across his lips. He studied her aroused face and struggled to find his customary amused expression. Fury burned through his gut. How dare she pretend not to care about his sexual past? How dare she pretend to be unaffected by him?

It occurred to him that he wanted her anger. He craved her fury so that he could persuade her to forgive him and take him back. He forced his unruly, unmanly thoughts down and gave her his most insolent smile.

"I believe I must leave you. I've promised the next dance to an old lover of mine."

He just caught Sara's hand before she slapped his face. He

kissed her hard until she stopped trying to bite him. She kicked out at him, her kid dancing slippers sliding uselessly against his shins.

"You are a bastard, Valentin Sokorvsky."

"Am I? Aren't I just behaving like a cuckolded husband?"

She glared at him, her bosom rising and falling with each panting breath.

"You walked away and left me for three months, and now you expect me to feel sorry for you?"

He straightened his cravat and stepped away from her. "I don't want your pity."

"You don't know what you want."

He held her gaze, let her see the anger in his. "Tonight I want you to beg."

Her blue eyes snapped right back at him. "We'll see who ends up begging, won't we?"

19

I sit on the floor by the fire in your bedchamber. I am naked, apart from the diamond collar around my throat. A thick gold chain attached to the collar falls between my breasts and coils against my mound. My hair is braided down my back so that I cannot hide my body or my expression from you. This is how you prefer it, and I am your slave and must obey.

Your valet passes by as he arranges your belongings. As a paid servant, and not your slave, he considers himself superior to me. Sometimes he will crouch down beside me and touch my breast or squeeze my nipple. I endure his touch because I must. Sometimes it excites me.

As I wait, I wonder how you will treat me. Sometimes you ignore me and I fall asleep by the fire alone. If I am fortunate, you will allow me to remove your clothes and make love with you. If you mood is less certain, I will have to try to anticipate your desires and provide for them as quickly as I can.

*Sometimes you let me take your cock into my mouth
and swallow your seed without even touching me. I do
not complain. I am honored to serve you. If you are unhappy, you might bring me close to pleasure and then
walk away. I am not allowed to bring myself release unless you give me permission. I like it when you watch me
come.*

*My favorite nights are when you bring me to my feet,
unbutton your breeches, and take me hard and fast
against the wall. I love the feel of your body slamming
against mine and your urgent mouth suckling my breasts.*

*Sometimes you bring Peter with you, and those are the
best nights of all . . .*

Valentin glared at the servant as he watched his carriage disappear down the road. After Valentin's dance with Lady Ingham, Peter had told him Sara had left. He had chased after her
into the hall, only to find he'd missed her and that she had
stranded him at the ball.

"The lady said to give me what?"

"This, sir." The liveried servant held out his hand. Valentine
recognized the red silk cover of the book immediately.

"Thank you."

He turned away from the open front door, seeking a quiet
corner. Peter followed him. A note fluttered to the marbled
floor. Peter picked it up and handed it to him. Valentin read it
out loud.

"I want to experience what it is like to be a pleasure slave."

In the deserted library, Valentin flicked through the closely
written pages until he found the last entry in the book. It was
dated earlier that evening. He read the words and then read
them again. All the blood in his body deserted his brain for his
cock. He gave the book to Peter.

" '. . . Sometimes you bring Peter with you, and those are the best nights of all.' What in damnation do you think that means?"

Peter looked thoughtful as he passed the book back. "I think your wife intends to give two former slaves a very interesting evening."

Valentin closed his eyes and visualized Sara naked, waiting at his feet. His shaft thickened even more. "I doubt she will be at home."

Peter turned to the door. "I should imagine she'll be at Madame Helene's. It's safer there. I'll go and order my carriage while you find our cloaks and hats."

Valentin paused outside the white painted door. A small china plaque bearing the number seven was the only ornamentation. He'd asked Peter to wait in case they had misunderstood Sara's message. He rested his palm on the smooth white surface, counted the uneven beats of his heart.

What exactly did he expect? If Sara had planned this evening to humiliate him, he knew he would never recover. But what if she wished to follow this particular fantasy to help her understand what he and Peter had gone through? By becoming what he most feared, by subjugating herself to him, was she deliberately seeking his trust?

He squared his shoulders. So what if she shredded his pride? She was worth it. He knocked on the door and went in.

For a moment, he imagined he was back in his own bedchamber. A uniformed servant laid out his favorite dressing gown on the bed and bowed to him.

His gaze strayed to the fire. Sara knelt by a chair, her head bent, the long luscious lines of her naked body glowing in the firelight. A diamond collar clasped around her slender throat caught the light as she lifted her head.

"Do you wish me to help you undress, sir?" The servant's pleasant voice intruded on Valentin's consciousness.

"No, you can leave, and don't come back unless I call you."

After the man disappeared, Valentin returned his attention to Sara. He walked across to the fire and stared down at her. A heavy gold chain ran down between her breasts and disappeared between her legs. He reached down and picked up the chain. He weighed it in his hands. It was warm from her body and the fire and wet where it had rested against her sex.

He tugged gently on the chain, and she looked up. He could see no hint of mockery or unease in her expression. Only a desire to please, which inflamed his senses. How far would she let him go? How far would she trust him when he had her at his mercy? The temptation to test her limits consumed him.

"Suck my cock."

She knelt up and unfastened his breeches with steady hands. He was already erect and more than ready for her. She wrapped one hand around the thick wide base of his shaft, cupped his balls in her palm and took the rest of him deep inside her mouth.

Valentin closed his eyes as she sucked and licked and stroked his pulsing cock. He'd taught her how to pleasure him well. He slipped his hand between their bodies and tugged on her right wrist.

"Take your hand away. I want it all in your mouth."

He was too big for her; he knew that. He waited to see what she would do. To his surprise, she took more. He shuddered as the tip of his penis slid way down her throat. He came then, in harsh, painful spurts, too deep for her not to swallow.

He opened his eyes and looked down at her. Her cheek rested on his thigh, and she was breathing hard. God, he must have nearly choked her when he came. He wrapped the chain around his hand and urged her to her feet. He pushed his hand between her thighs and found her soaking wet. His cock stirred again. He firmly rebuttoned his breeches.

* * *

Sara shivered as Valentin stared down at her. He gestured toward a chair behind her. "Sit down." She hastened to comply, her body already screaming for his attention. "Open your legs." He pushed her thighs wide and hooked her knees over the chair arms, exposing her entirely to his gaze.

She waited as he studied her, aware that his gaze made her sex throb with the desire to be touched. The satin brocade felt cool against her heated skin, encouraging her to relax against it. He crouched between her thighs, rested his hands on her knees, and slowly brought his palms up the sides of her body until he reached her breasts.

"I'm glad you still wear these." He flicked the golden rings through her nipples and licked the one set in her navel.

"I wear them for you, my lord, because they give you pleasure." She kept her eyes lowered as she spoke, aware of her nakedness, aware of his controlled strength. Did he understand that her vulnerability made him vulnerable, too? His fingers brushed her swollen bud, and she shuddered.

"Do you want me to put my mouth on you?"

"It is for you to decide, my lord. I am here to please you."

He touched the hard bud of her sex with one careful finger. "You are very wet. Have you missed me?"

"Yes." Sara stifled a moan as he flicked the tip of his finger back and forth.

"What about the twins you took to your bed? Didn't they satisfy you?"

Sara closed her eyes. How unfair of him to bring the subject up when she was at her most defenseless. She would have to be honest. He had always been able to tell when she lied.

"I won them in an auction. They were due to go off to war, and neither of them wanted to die as virgins."

His finger stopped moving. "So you were doing your patriotic duty, then?"

Sara gathered her courage. "No, I was hoping to lure you back to me. I wanted to attract your attention."

Valentin leaned forward and sucked her clit into his mouth. He suckled so fiercely that Sara almost flew out of the chair. When he drew back, he licked his lips, which were covered in her cream.

"I find I am a possessive man. Your attempt to engage my attention was successful." He stared at her exposed body. "Were they good?"

"No, they were eager, overexcited puppies. They had no idea how to please a woman."

"Until you showed them."

"I tried, but they were more interested in their own pleasure than in mine." Valentin didn't need to know that the twins had been more interested in fucking each other. Madame Helene had helped her choose exactly the right couple to bid on.

A faint smile flickered over his set features. "That must have been . . . frustrating . . . for you." He knelt up and touched the tip of her nipple with his tongue. She bit back a gasp at the heat of his mouth on her cold flesh, the grating sound of metal against his teeth as he tugged on the golden ring.

The pearl buttons of his waistcoat pressed against her stomach; his cock pushed hard against the confines of his breeches. He circled his hips, grinding cool, smooth satin into her hot, wet pussy.

"They came at least three times each before they even managed to get near me," Sara gasped as orgasm threatened.

"That must have been unpleasant. I see why you called them puppies now. Not well house-trained."

Sara stifled a smile. Valentin had always been able to make her laugh at the most inappropriate times. He slid his hand between them and fingered her pussy.

"If you really were my slave, I'd have you pierced here. I'd love to be able to lead you around naked with just a thin gold chain attached to your labia." He laughed softly as her wetness gushed over his fingers. "Damnation, you like the idea. You'd let me, wouldn't you?" He pulled back from her. "I might not be able to lead you around by your clit, but I think we should go and find Peter. He's out in the public rooms."

He got up and walked to a cherrywood armoire and opened the first two drawers. "You'll need a mask to cover your eyes and something to drape over your hips. I don't want every man in the place to know how wet and ready for sex my slave is." He frowned as he turned over several short lengths of silk. "I'll call for a servant." Sara readied herself to move, but Valentin held out his hand. "You can stay just as you are."

Sara remained seated, her legs over the arms, displaying her pussy. Her thigh muscles ached from the strain, but she knew better than to complain. The footman who answered Valentin's summons was quite young. His gaze kept straying to Sara as he listened to Valentin's request.

To Sara's surprise, Valentin didn't seem to mind the man's behavior. After the servant showed him where longer swathes of silk were kept, Sara expected him to dismiss the man, but he didn't.

She felt a tremor of excitement when he beckoned the servant over to her chair. The young man licked his lips as Valentin came and stood bedside him.

"What is your name?"

"Parrish, sir, Tom Parrish."

"Well, Mr. Parrish. Do you think she is beautiful?"

Tom gave Sara a sideways glance. "It's not really my place to say so, sir, but, yes, she is."

"Doesn't Madame Helene allow you to be intimate with the guests, then?"

"Oh, yes, sir, she tells us to do whatever the customer wants, and that includes fucking and everything, sir." He frowned down at his shoes. "I ain't been 'ere very long, but I know we ain't supposed to do nothing we don't fancy either, sir."

"And would you fancy touching this woman?"

Tom blushed. "Only if you promised not to thump me afterward, sir."

Valentin sat down on a chair opposite Sara's. "I give you my word that I won't harm you. Touch her anywhere you like."

Sara tensed as Tom turned his attention to her naked body. He reached out his hand and stroked the gold ring through her nipple.

"Does that hurt, miss?"

Sara shook her head. Valentin gave a soft laugh.

"Take it into your mouth and suck hard. She loves it."

Tom placed his hands on Sara's knees and bent down. She could see the faint beginnings of his first beard beneath his flushed cheeks. His mouth closed over her right breast, and she moaned.

Valentin spoke again. "Slide your fingers inside her while you suck. She won't mind."

Sara opened her eyes as Tom slid two fingers inside her. Valentin watched her, his expression unreadable. If she protested, would he stop Tom? She knew that as a real slave, he had had no power to stop anyone touching him if they paid for his time.

And yet how was she supposed to stop her body from reacting to another man's touch? Had Valentin found pleasure with some of his customers and hated himself for it? Tom sucked harder and pumped his fingers faster, his enthusiasm far outweighing his skill. Did Valentin want her to come or not? She was so close.

Valentin got up as Tom started to groan and push his hips against her belly.

"Open his breeches and take his cock in your hand. Help him."

Sara barely had time to wrap her fingers around Tom's shaft before he climaxed with a shuddering cry. His mouth relaxed against her nipple, his breathing uneven. He mumbled into her breast, "Thank you, miss. Thank you."

Valentin threw the man a pouch filled with coins as he left, an idiotic grin plastered on his lips, his satin breeches stained at the crotch. Sara lay back and waited for Valentin to return. He flicked a gold coin at her, which landed between her breasts, the metal cold against the flushed warmth of her skin. Humiliating heat rose in her cheeks, and she yearned to throw it back in his face.

"I didn't think a slave was paid, my lord."

"If she pleases her master, then, yes."

"It pleased you to watch another man touch me?"

His gaze hardened. "If you truly were my slave, you would not ask such impertinent questions. You would simply do as you are told."

"Should I have come for him, then, when you are my master and I didn't desire him?"

He studied her quietly, one hand in his pocket. "A slave has no choice when his body is bought and handled. A slave learns to take his pleasure when he can."

He leaned forward, removed the coin, and put it back in his pocket. She shivered as he placed a wet, scented cloth on her stomach.

"Clean off his come, but don't touch your pussy. I like you wet."

She did as he requested and obediently stood up while he wrapped the length of yellow silk around her hips. It fell almost to the floor, leaving her left leg partially exposed. She glanced down at her nipples, which were permanently erect now. Did he intend to take her into the main salon? She remembered the drunken man who had tried to touch her when she was fully dressed. What would happen, now that she was almost naked?

Valentin's tied-back hair gleamed in the soft candlelight as he bent his head to secure the silk on her left hip. His scent streamed upward, making her dizzy with desire. She wanted to feel him moving hard and fast inside her. As though in a dream, she brought her hand up to touch his cheek. He turned his head and kissed her fingers, drawing them into his warm, sinful mouth. She staggered slightly against him, and he caught her hips.

"You'll need a mask as well." He rummaged through the drawers until he found one to his liking. His gaze held a cool challenge as he picked up the chain attached to the collar around her neck. "Are you ready?"

She had to trust him. She had to believe he would never harm her. When Valentin was a slave, he would not have had any control over the person who bought his services. He had faced endless possibilities of pain and humiliation. Sara bit her lip. How had he borne the uncertainty?

"Yes, my lord."

He led her out into the silent corridor. Her bare feet made no sound on the soft red carpet. Music and the subdued murmur of conversation floated toward them from an open door at the end of the passageway. Sara drew a steadying breath as she followed Valentin into the room. To her relief, they were only a dozen people scattered about the small intimate salon. One of the men was Peter. He got to his feet and bowed as Valentin led Sara forward.

"Good evening, my dears. The performance is just about to start." To Peter's credit, he managed to keep his eyes locked on Sara's face. "Why don't we all sit down?"

Valentin sat on the nearest couch. He pushed gently on Sara's shoulder until she knelt on the carpet beside him. Peter sat at an angle to her left, shielding her from the rest of the room. In the center of the circle of chairs stood a small woman with thick black hair that flowed to her hips. She was naked, her pussy shaved, as were her legs. She smiled at the assembled onlookers.

"Bon soir, my name is Renee. Welcome." Her accent was distinctly French. She pointed at the door. "This is my partner, Gastard. We hope to entertain you."

Sara stared up at Gastard as he made his way through the chairs. He had to be at least six and a half feet tall and was built like a farm worker. Renee was at least eighteen inches shorter than he. Sara jumped as Valentin slid his hand from her shoulder and played with her nipple ring.

Gastard took off his breeches. Several of the ladies screamed and clapped.

Peter gave a soft whistle. "He's built like a horse."

"And he's not even erect yet," Valentin added as he circled Sara's tight nipple with his index finger. "It will be interesting to see how he mounts her."

Sara couldn't even imagine taking a man that big inside her, and Renee was tiny. Valentin spread his fingers until he cupped her whole breast.

Renee picked up an ornate glass bottle. "Would any of you like to massage some oil into Gastard's cock?"

"I'd rather oil you!" one of the men shouted. Renee laughed. "You may do that, too." She winked at him. "For a price."

Several gold coins and banknotes were flung into the circle. Sara watched as a young woman massaged Gastard's shaft and balls, the oil shining on her fingertips. Sara leaned into Valentin's thigh, her breast throbbing from the subtle pressure of his fingers. If all this sexual anticipation was meant to drive her wild, it was succeeding.

By the time Renee and Gastard were sufficiently oiled, a considerable sum of money had joined the coins on the carpet. Bets were placed as to whether Renee would ever be able to take Gastard's impressive cock inside her.

When the betting and the talk died down, Renee opened a black velvet case that lay on the table beside her. She picked it up and began a slow circuit of the chairs, allowing every person a view of the contents. Sara recognized the exquisite ivory pieces at once. They were similar in quality and workmanship to the dildo Valentin had given her.

Renee sat on the edge of the low padded table and spread her legs. "Which dildo shall I use to help prepare myself for Gastard?"

Sara wasn't sure that any of them were as big as Gastard. Peter moved restlessly beside her, the thick brocade of his coat sliding against her skin. He stroked her thigh and fingered the knot of silk where the fabric parted to reveal her nakedness.

Renee picked up an eight-inch dildo and measured it against Gastard's shaft. She shook her head. "Perhaps I should take him in my mouth first, just to see if I can."

Several people clapped and whistled as she fell to her knees in front of a grinning Gastard. Sara swallowed hard and licked her lips as Renee tried to wrap her hand around the thick, wide base of Gastard's cock. Her fingers didn't meet. How would it feel to take such a huge erection inside her mouth? Valentin was large enough and she'd almost choked when she sucked him.

"Do you think you could take him, Sara?" Valentin murmured. "How about you, Peter?"

"I'd certainly give it a go." Peter threw a gold coin toward Gastard.

Valentin squeezed her nipple with practiced fingers as Renee slowly drew Gastard's cock into her mouth. More money rained down on the performers as further bets were placed. Peter's hand slid under the silk at Sara's hip. His finger settled over her sex and rubbed in time to the subtle movements of Renee's throat.

Sara watched Gastard's shaft disappear inside Renee's mouth; her own body opened and creamed as if it were her there on her knees. Peter cupped her mound and dipped three fingers inside her. She tried not to moan as Gastard's hips jerked forward, pushing more of himself into Renee's willing mouth.

As Gastard roared his sexual excitement, Sara climaxed. She turned her face into Valentin's side and bit the cloth of his breeches as her pleasure rippled through her. She was suddenly aware that she was in a public place. She hoped everyone's attention had remained on Renee and not her. Valentin shortened the chain connected to her collar and made her look up at him. He kissed her mouth. Peter shuddered as he withdrew his fingers from her pussy.

By the time Sara looked back, Renee had stood up and Gastard now sat on the edge of the low padded table. A couple directly opposite Valentin and Sara had already received too much stimulation. The man tossed up the woman's petticoats and thrust inside her. The jeweled heels of her tiny slippers caught the light as she dug them into the man's satin-clad buttocks.

"She'll take him." Valentin sounded confident as Renee returned to her box of delights. He smiled down at Sara as Renee selected a much larger dildo and turned to her audience.

"Who would like to help me?" Her inviting smile lingered on Valentin and then passed to Peter, who laughingly shook his head.

A redheaded man waved a bag of coins in Renee's direction. "I'll do it!"

The room went quiet as he stepped into the small circle and went down on one knee in front of her. Gastard picked Renee up and sat her on his lap, her legs spread wide. Sara held her breath as the man slowly inserted the dildo inside Renee. She knew how that felt, the coldness and smoothness of the stone against the hot, wet suck of clenching flesh. She rubbed her hand along the hard muscle of Valentin's thigh.

He stopped her movements by placing his hand over hers. "I didn't give you permission to touch me, slave."

Sara withdrew her hand. She'd almost forgotten the part she'd chosen to play. Peter frowned at Valentin and then studied Sara. She refused to look at him for more than a second. She had to carry on. She had to trust Valentin.

Renee sighed as Gastard stroked her sex. "Thank you, kind sir, I feel more ready to attempt the impossible now." She removed the dildo and allowed Gastard to grasp her around the waist and turn her toward him. Her feet rested on his widespread thighs.

Sara bit her lip as Gastard slowly lowered Renee onto his cock. She could only imagine how he might feel pushing up inside her. Her pussy clenched, and she squeezed her thighs together to prolong the sensation. It seemed to take forever for Renee to absorb all of Gastard's flesh. When he was fully sheathed, Gastard drew Renee up again and turned her around until she faced their audience.

Renee looked blissful as Gastard very gently fingered her swollen clit.

"I told you he'd fit," Valentin whispered in Sara's ear. "If a woman really wants a man, she'll make room for him."

She had a vivid memory of taking both Valentin's cock and the jade inside her at the same time. She moved closer to him, rubbing her breast against the soft wool of his coat.

Valentin got to his feet as the watchers applauded the performers. He tossed a bag of coins into Gastard's hand. "Thank you, that was . . . most inspiring." He turned to Sara. "Peter will be joining us."

"Yes, please, my lord." Sara smiled at Peter. She definitely needed his help for this part of the evening. Was he still prepared to aid her?

Peter kissed her hand. "I'd be delighted."

Valentin led the way back to the bedroom and closed the door behind them. He leaned up against it and surveyed Sara and Peter.

"Are you sure this is what you want, Sara?"

She stared at him. To her astonishment she'd discovered she liked giving him complete sexual control over her. His supreme arrogance allowed her to be more wanton and wild than ever. It also brought her clarity of vision.

To make such a complex man trust and love her required extreme measures. How could he ever be free to love her if he couldn't live with himself and what he'd done? In his efforts to forget the past, he'd only succeeded in suppressing his emotions and reining in his voracious sexuality. Did he understand that yet? Could she and Peter free him from the shackles of the past?

She'd also gained a terrible insight as to how it might feel to be forced to surrender her body to someone she couldn't trust. Someone who might hurt her. If she hadn't gone along with this particular fantasy, she might never have realized how much Valentin and Peter had overcome.

Without answering Valentin, she sank to her knees and kissed his erect cock through his tight-fitting breeches.

"I am enjoying myself. Aren't you?"

He smiled at her as someone knocked on the door.

Sara knew Peter had arranged some surprises for the evening. She assumed this was one of them. She looked up at Valentin.

"Perhaps you should open the door."

20

The two women each wore a white toga that exposed one breast. Flowered wreaths crowned their braided hair. Sara inhaled the scent of spring as she surrendered her body into their care. As directed, she sat on the edge of the bed; Peter and Valentin sat opposite her on two gilded chairs.

One of the women smiled at Sara. "My name is Chloe. My partner is Flora. I have been sent by Madame Helene to make you even more desirable to your menfolk. Will you let me help you?"

Sara nodded, her breathing erratic, her eyes fixed on Flora, the darker woman who carried a covered tray. She tried to look behind her as Chloe took the tray and set it on the bed but could see nothing. Valentin sprawled back in his seat, his hand resting over his covered shaft. Peter sat forward, his attention riveted on the three women on the bed.

"First we will paint kohl on your eyelids."

Sara tried not to blink as Chloe leaned across her and painted a thin line of something sticky around the outer rim of her eyes. Chloe's naked breast rubbed against Sara's. She wondered if it was accidental.

"Now a red tint for your lips."

The brush was thicker this time. It stimulated her already swollen lips, sending shivers down to her belly and further tightening her breasts. A light dusting of color on her cheeks completed her face. When Chloe finished, Flora held up a hand mirror so Sara could see herself. Her eyes looked huge, her mouth scarlet and provocative against the ivory of her flushed skin.

Flora kissed her as she removed the mirror. Before Sara could react, both women drew one of her nipples into their mouths and suckled hard. Chloe produced yet another brush and a pot of rouge. Without speaking, she began to brush the thick paste on Sara's wet nipples. Peter groaned, his fingers working at the buttons on his breeches.

Sara concentrated her attention on Valentin as the soft bristles flicked over and over her taut nipple, darkening the tip to a hard crimson berry that begged to be taken into a man's mouth. He returned her brazen stare, licking his lips as though in anticipation of his expected treat.

She realized that the women wanted her to move. Chloe settled her against a mound of pillows at the head of the bed. Flora handed each of the men a red silk scarf.

"Tie one end around your slave's wrist and the other to the bed."

Both men obliged, moving slowly to compensate for their huge erections. Valentin snatched a quick savage kiss from Sara as he bound her wrist to the head of the bed. He refused to return to his chair. He settled himself at the other end of the massive bed, which easily contained all five of them. Peter followed suit and sat beside him. With her arms stretched wide, Sara's breasts jutted out at a perfect angle. The reddened tips made

Valentin want to gorge on her for hours, to suck the color off until she begged him to stop.

Released from its braid, her black hair fell to her hips, framing her pale skin and the dark curls of her mound. Valentin's cock throbbed so hard he wanted to thrust it past Sara's red lips and deep down her throat. He took his jacket and waistcoat off, loosened his cravat.

Chloe, the busty blond woman, separated Sara's legs to reveal her sex. She was already wet and swollen, her bud clearly visible above her engorged labia.

Flora flicked Sara's clit. "My lords, may I make a suggestion? She would look even more beautiful if we trimmed back the hair on her mound."

Valentin managed to nod. "Do it."

Sara bit her lip as Chloe carefully removed almost all the fine hair to reveal her plump pussy. Valentin swallowed a groan as Flora produced a thick brush with a wide bulbous handle and dipped it into another pot.

With every deliberate sweep of the brush, a fine coat of gold powder gilded Sara's pussy. Her hips moved in time to the rhythmic motion of the steady strokes. Chloe added a swirl of red to Sara's clit with a smaller brush. Valentin swallowed hard as Flora reversed the brush and slid the thick handle deep inside Sara's sheath.

She turned to Valentin. "Do you wish your servant to come?"

Valentin looked into Sara's eyes. "Not yet. She can wait."

Beside him, Peter cleared his throat. "When we were slaves, some evenings we were not allowed to come at all. If we did, we were punished."

Valentin went still. To the best of his knowledge it was the first time Peter had ever spoken to anyone else about their ordeal in Turkey. Perhaps in including Peter in her fantasy, Sara had been cleverer than he realized. If Peter could be persuaded to get over his past, he might no longer need drugs, sex, and Valentin to keep him sane.

Valentin kept his gaze on the handle of the brush as it slid in and out of his wife's channel. "On evenings like that, we'd give each other release afterward, if we could." To his astonishment, he felt almost comfortable discussing the horrors in front of the others, as well.

Peter knelt up to shrug out of his coat and waistcoat. "They thought it amusing to leave us with our hands chained behind our backs so we couldn't touch ourselves." He stole a glance at Valentin and then stared challengingly into Sara's eyes. "Sometimes we'd use our mouths on each other."

Chloe sighed and touched Peter's knee.

"I would love to have seen that, sir. You must have made a beautiful couple."

Valentin avoided Peter's gaze and continued to watch his wife. She was close to coming. He knew the signs. Without turning his head, he spoke to Peter.

"Do you think we should let our slave come, then, or should we make her suffer like we did?"

Peter stared down the bed at Sara. "Let her come."

Valentin nodded at Flora, who began to work the thick round brush handle more vigorously between Sara's legs. Chloe joined her, teasing Sara's clit between her finger and thumb.

Sara stifled a scream as her body arched and she climaxed. Peter ripped open the remaining buttons on his breeches and pumped up and down his engorged shaft, coming within seconds.

Valentin gritted his teeth as the scent of Sara's orgasm surrounded him. His cock was so eager to fuck, it hurt him to breathe.

"Say thank you, Sara," Valentin commanded.

Sara opened her eyes and whispered her thanks.

Chloe and Flora untied the shoulder knots on their Grecian

tunics, completely baring their breasts. "We will oil your slave for your pleasure and then leave her to pleasure you."

Valentin allowed Peter to untie Sara's wrists. His cock was so stiff he couldn't move off the bed. He almost envied Peter his swift release, not sure of how much more he could stand. He hadn't made love to his wife for three months, and he intended to come inside her and not before.

His mouth went dry as Sara arched like a cat under the women's skilled fingers. Soon her skin gleamed in the candlelight as she knelt up for the women to massage her buttocks and thighs.

Chloe bent forward and kissed her, one small hand cupping his wife's chin. Her pointed tongue darted out and delved into Sara's mouth. He couldn't stand any more. He unbuttoned his breeches, allowing his massive shaft some room. Chloe smiled as he crawled menacingly toward her.

"Do you wish to help, my lord?"

She held out the flask of oil, and Valentin took it from her. He dribbled some of the oil into his palm and warmed it between his hands. Peter joined him, and he passed the bottle over. He shuddered as he laid his hand on the small of Sara's back, one long finger sliding between the cleft of her buttocks.

She tried to turn away from Chloe and come toward him, but he kept her where he wanted her. "Peter, come closer. Sara's going to suck your cock for you."

Peter's shaft was already half hard as Sara approached him. Valentin kept his hand on her back and watched her take Peter into her mouth. Valentin slid his longest oil-soaked finger into Sara's back passage. As Peter began to gasp in rhythm to Sara's strokes, Valentin added his second finger.

Sara tilted her hips back toward his probing hand as he worked her tight channel. Four fingers now and still not wide enough for his cock. Valentin closed his eyes as she shivered and moaned against the thrust of his fingers.

Chloe moved behind him and massaged his chest, her nipples hard against his back.

"Valentin, God, touch me, please touch me, please," Peter whispered.

Valentin rested his left hand on Peter's thigh and pulled his breeches down farther. He knew what Peter wanted. Perhaps this was the best way for Sara to understand their complicated relationship. He positioned himself carefully between them. Sara's left hand was planted on the bed, the length of her arm aligned with Peter's right thigh. Valentin slid his cock into the palm of Peter's hand and waited until Peter's fist closed around him.

He slipped two oil-soaked fingers into Peter's arse, both his hands busy now. He watched his wife and best friend as their excitement grew. He kept the steady thrust of his fingers in tune to the movements of Sara's mouth and Peter's excited response.

His own shaft swelled and dripped fluid, lubricating his unhurried movements within Peter's tightening grasp. As Peter shouted his release, Valentin pushed him away from Sara, leaving him to the ministrations of Chloe and Flora.

Sara licked her lips as Valentin crawled across the small space toward her. His violet eyes were filled with lust. She gasped as he picked her up and brought her to the head of the bed, turning her away from him. She just had time to grab the rail before he impaled her pussy from behind. The force of his thrust pushed her hard against the padded headboard. He kept up the pace, slamming into her; his cock felt as wide as a fist, and she gloried in every strong, powerful stroke.

She came on his third thrust, her sheath clenching around his massive shaft. He growled his satisfaction but didn't slow down. He quickly brought her to a new level of awareness of what her body needed and what she could take from him.

He began to murmur in her ear as he worked her, the fingers of one hand stretched across her nipples, the other tormenting her clitoris. She struggled to hear him above the slapping noise of his flesh against hers and her involuntary cries.

"Tell me I'm better than those boys. Tell me you missed my cock."

Sara could hardly speak through the haze of her heightened desire. "I . . ." Another orgasm crashed over her, this one more intense than the last. He withdrew his shaft before she finished. She cried out, missing him instantly.

He placed his hands on the headboard on either side of her face, his mouth close to her ear.

"Tell me."

Sara closed her eyes. "I missed you. I missed all of you." She turned and licked his outstretched fingers. They smelled of her. The tip of his cock nudged her swollen labia. "They meant nothing to me. But I was desperate enough to try anything to get you back."

He remained still, his large hot body pressing her against the padded satin, his rapid heartbeat vibrating through her skin like a drum.

"Why did you want me back?"

"Because I should have trusted you. I should have allowed you to explain about your relationship with Peter, not believe what my father and others told me."

"And what if I had told you the rumors were true and that we were once lovers?"

"Then I would have believed you."

"And done what?"

"Nothing. You are my husband—I want you just the way you are."

He tensed his face so close to hers there was no room for her to breathe. "Why, Sara?"

She locked gazes with him. "If you can allow me to be my-self, why shouldn't I be allowed to do the same for you?"

He closed his eyes, his long black eyelashes pale against his skin. "It's hardly the same, is it?"

She kissed the corner of his mouth. "It is to me."

He smiled then, his face relaxing as he slid back inside her. She gloried in the hard pulse of his cock as he filled her. Within three thrusts she was flooded with his hot seed.

"Thank you, Sara," he whispered. "Thank you for your honesty."

She lay half dozing between Peter and Valentin. One man sat on either side of her. Peter wore a chain around his neck with half an ancient coin on it, which she realized matched the one Valentin used to wear. Chloe and Flora had gone away with a bag of gold coins and the pleasure of being sexually satisfied by Peter.

Valentin toyed with Sara's right nipple. Peter reached down to stroke her pussy. She flinched away from his questing fin-gers, which pushed her buttocks up against Valentin's half erect cock.

Peter smiled at her and then at Valentin. "Sara doesn't really understand how it is to be a slave. A slave is not allowed to get tired or sore from too much fucking. We were expected to be ready and willing all night long."

Valentin's long fingers closed over Sara's breast. "You are right, Peter. We were expected to pleasure anyone who wanted us."

Peter stroked his own cock, his expression distant. "You were much prized for your ability to stay erect all night. I wasn't as capable." He grimaced. "I hated it when I ran out of come. It's so bloody painful."

"But we learned to pace ourselves," Valentin said. "Even at

sixteen, it's difficult not to come too fast and too early. We learned how to pretend and how to prolong our erections."

Peter shuddered. "Or else we were beaten, had you forgotten about that?"

"How could I? I bear the scars on my back just as you do."

Valentin wondered how much Sara understood of the conversation. He was reluctant to disturb the flow of Peter's memories. He had a feeling his friend needed to release some of the poison that threatened to undermine his life and future happiness.

"You have more scars than I do, Val. They used to mistreat me to make you lose control."

Valentin managed to smile, although it was difficult. Perhaps Peter was not the only one who needed to unburden himself.

"I was more reluctant to perform than you were. I used to dream of someone scarring my face so that I was no longer so damned pretty." He relaxed his grip on Sara's breast, and she let out a soft breath. "I've never liked being forced to have sex with men." He hoped to God she was listening. It might save him having to explain his hellish past again.

Peter leaned forward and touched a faded scar under Valentin's right nipple. "Madam Tezoli did that to you with a branding iron when you continued to fight all the men." He laughed, the sound harsh in the luxurious silence of the gilded bedchamber. "I didn't mind whether it was a man or a woman. I was quite happy to service anyone if it meant avoiding a beating."

Valentin stared into his friend's haunted eyes. "And you think that makes you less of a man than me?"

"Of course."

"And I thought I was the stupid one. I so wanted to be like you."

"A coward and a whore for anyone who paid for me?"

"No, a man wise enough not to provoke people."

Peter looked startled. "We all have our limits, Val, even you."

"I begged in the end, Peter. I begged Madam Tezoli to let me die after she gave me to Yusef that first time." He brought his attention back to the far more pleasurable sensation of Sara's skin against his lips. When he opened his eyes, Peter was still looking at him. "Christ, what do you want me to say? It was years ago. We are not the same people anymore."

Peter eyed Sara, his expression thoughtful. "No, we're not. And your wife seems able and willing to accept us, scarred and damaged as we are."

Valentin gazed down at Sara. She watched him with calm, steady eyes. There was no hint of disgust or loathing for what she had heard. Perhaps she had given both him and Peter an opportunity to heal. His cock stirred and straightened against her spine. He needed to be inside her. Talking about the past always made him feel unclean. Images of some of his "customers" fought to take over his mind. He couldn't allow it.

He bent to kiss her nipple. Hell. He had accused Peter of using drugs and alcohol to keep his demons at bay. Using women had become his personal escape. Using them . . . damnit. Is that what he did? Was he any better than Peter?

Sara curled around his thigh and licked his shaft. He stroked her cheek until she looked up at him. "Sit on my cock."

She sat up and clambered onto his lap. Her breath caught when he turned her back to his chest and gripped her around the waist. Peter moved out of the way, giving her a perfect view of their entwined bodies in the candlelit mirrors.

Valentin slowly lowered her onto his erection. She closed her eyes as he hilted himself. He squeezed her nipple.

"Don't. I like to watch your face when you come."

She met his gaze in the mirror, her eyes shadowed and full of sensuous secrets. She was so sensitive, she was aware of every pulsing inch of his hot, hard cock.

"Have you enjoyed being my slave?"

"Some parts of it, my lord."

He gestured at Peter. "Has she made a good slave?"

Peter sat up. "She has certainly been . . . accommodating. I have enjoyed her touch."

Valentin toyed with one of Sara's nipple rings. "I think she enjoyed it." He tugged on the ring. "I think she enjoyed parading naked through Madame Helene's entertainment rooms."

Sara blushed, but she couldn't deny his comments. Valentin widened his legs, making Sara settle down harder and deeper on his cock. He nuzzled her ear. "You liked it when Peter made you come in front of all those people, didn't you?"

"Yes."

"You'll like it when he licks you now." He touched Peter's shoulder. "Lick her for me, but don't let her come yet."

Peter bent to his task with relish. The slick, slow sound of his tongue was loud above Sara's hurried breathing. Her channel tightened around Valentin's shaft. He gently pushed Peter away. He studied Sara's swollen clit in the mirror and then guided her fingertips to it.

"Do you feel how puffed-up and slick you are?" He pushed her fingers lower until they touched the entrance to her body. "Feel how wide you've opened for me and how wet you are."

He pressed her palm against her intimate flesh, and she writhed against him. "What do you imagine your family and friends would say if they could see you now? Naked and willing in the arms of two men?"

"They would consider me scandalous. They would be ashamed of me."

Valentin nodded at Peter, and he resumed his attentions to her pussy. His agile tongue drew her closer and closer to peaking. She almost cried with frustration when he stopped after a quick command from Valentin.

Valentin held her gaze in the mirror. "What would your father think of you?"

Through the haze of her sexual desire, her fingernails bit into his thighs. She resisted her first impulse to strike out at him and studied her wanton, disgraceful image. Valentin's large bronzed hand covered her right breast; his huge cock filled her to completion. Tension vibrated through his entire body. Peter stopped caressing her inner thigh and touched Valentin instead.

"If my father could see me now, he would consider me a fitting match for you." She spoke slowly and carefully so he could not mistake her meaning. "And I would have to agree with him. We deserve each other."

Valentin's breath left him in a shuddering rush. His shaft seemed to swell within her. "Would you mind if I took Peter's cock in my mouth and made you both come? There's room for him to kneel beside us."

Valentin sensed danger when he awoke to the betraying rattle of a manacle being clicked around his wrist. Had Yusef returned? He opened his eyes and found himself on his back, still in bed with Peter and Sara. Both his wrists were manacled and attached to the headboard. In a blind panic, he tried to strike out with his feet, only to discover his ankles were chained, too.

"Get these damned things off me."

"What are you afraid of, Val? It's only me and Sara."

Valentin clenched his fists. Peter knew damn well how he felt about being held against his will. How dare they use his greatest fear against him? What the hell were they hoping to achieve by making him angry?

Sara knelt at his side, her face calm. "Please don't fight us, Valentin, we only want to help you."

She dipped her fingers into a glass jar. He stiffened as he caught the cloying scent of orchids. Yusef had favored that scent. It reminded him of being forced to accept Yusef's cock inside him. It had taken days to scrub the smell from his skin and his mouth. He'd never succeeded in erasing it from his memories. Peter must know that.

He tensed as Sara circled his nipple with one oiled finger. His body responded to her simple caress, and his nipple puckered tight. She continued adding small circles of oil to the skin on his chest. He refused to look at her as she studied her work. She straddled him, trapping his half-erect cock between their bellies.

Even through the orchid scent, he could smell her arousal, feel the wetness of it pool against his taut stomach. She slid her hand into his hair and kissed his closed mouth. God, despite his chains, he wanted to respond to her. Her mouth moved lower, nipped at his jawline and down to his chest. He shuddered as she gently tongued his nipple. Every subtle touch made his cock grow against her pussy.

Peter massaged his feet and ankles as Sara knelt up, giving him an excellent view of her swollen wet sex. "I want you to lick me, Valentin."

He stared up at her. "Am I your slave now, then?"

"Do you want to be?"

She held his gaze as she touched herself and slid a single finger inside.

He gritted his teeth against the lush sight. "Untie me and I'll show you exactly what I want to be for you."

She moved higher up his chest until she crouched over his face. "Are you sure you don't want to lick me?"

Her cream dripped onto his lips, and he swallowed it like a man deprived of water. He tried his strength against his restraints again, and they held. Could he allow himself to enjoy Sara while bound? Could he forget the memories and trust her?

With a stifled groan he touched the tip of his tongue to her clit and helplessly began to circle it. She tasted so good, her thick cream sliding over his tongue and down his throat as he closed his lips around her swollen bud. His body jerked as he felt Peter's mouth slide over his cock. For a second the old terrors rose. He breathed in Sara's unique scent. It steadied his nerve.

He even began to enjoy the hard pull of Peter's mouth on his shaft, the roughness of his handling as compared to Sara's more gentle style. Peter slid three fingers inside his arse and increased the storm of emotions to fever pitch. Val groaned as Sara shimmied lower over his face and drove his tongue deep into her sheath. Peter increased the speed of his sucking until Valentin knew he was as close to coming as Sara was.

Sara moved away from his face and changed places with Peter. She positioned herself above his straining cock. She stared at him, her eyes heavy with desire and a hint of anxiety.

"I want you inside me, Valentin. Do you believe we won't hurt you?"

He realized then, as they both waited for his reply, that the night had taught them all about trusting each other. Sara had given both him and Peter fresh new erotic memories to replace the degradation they'd experienced. She'd even allowed him to admit to himself that Peter's touch didn't horrify him.

Valentin smiled. "I want you both." He gasped as Sara took him to the hilt in one urgent downward thrust of her hips. He turned his head, blindly seeking the swell of Peter's cock and filled his mouth with it. He timed his sucks to the rhythm Sara set as they built to a ferocious climax.

His body shuddered against his bonds as they both came, Sara's sheath milking his cock as he milked Peter's. He relished the aching joy of his release deep within Sara and the unexpectedly erotic joy of receiving Peter's hot come down his throat. He closed his eyes as he came. More satisfied than he had ever been before in his life.

* * *

Sara took off the manacles and again curled up between Valentin and Peter. Valentin stroked her hair as Peter curved a hand over her hip. She had brought them together. She hoped she had brought them peace.

Valentin nudged Peter. "Sara, don't go to sleep, we haven't shown you our most requested performance yet."

She frowned at him. "What could possibly be better than what we just shared?"

"You'll see."

Peter rolled onto his back, his cock already thick and eager. "I'll take the bottom position."

Valentin picked Sara up and sat her facing him, astride Peter's lap. He helped her kneel so that Peter could slide his cock into her pussy. She gasped as Peter wrapped an arm around her waist and gently pulled her back until she lay stretched out against the length of his body. Peter spread his legs wide and planted his feet flat on the mattress, taking Sara's legs with him.

His chest hair prickled along her back as she squirmed against him. His left hand cupped her breast. It felt strange to be so exposed.

"You look beautiful, Sara."

Valentin kissed her clit and then wrapped his hand around his cock. He carefully slid two fingers inside her sheath to widen her. She felt Peter shudder as Valentin's fingers grazed his already embedded cock. He scissored his fingers until she couldn't stop moaning his name.

He drew his fingers out and licked them before grasping the thick base of his cock. The crown of his thick shaft was wet and slid easily in on top of Peter's. When his balls touched her and Peter's buttocks, Valentin stopped and held still, his weight balanced on his outstretched arms.

"Touch yourself, Sara, feel us both. Feel how wide we've made you."

She moaned as she brought her hand down and circled their

cocks. She was stretched so wide, it was almost too much to bear. Valentin moved her fingers to her bud, trapping her hand between their bodies as he began to move. Peter matched each of his downward thrusts with an upward one. Sara screamed as she came in hard, clenched pulses.

Both men held still until she stopped shuddering and then resumed their remorseless advance and retreat until her whole body writhed mindlessly between them. Her skin grew slippery with their sweat, and she moaned in time to each devastating thrust. Valentin climaxed at the same time as Peter, driving her to another shattering orgasm. She imagined their mingled seed flooding her womb and making her dripping wet.

With a groan, Valentin rolled off Sara and lay beside her, his fingers lightly stroking her breast as Peter slid out of her. With a sigh, she turned toward Valentin. He cradled her head on her shoulder and allowed his hand to rest on Peter's hip. Too exhausted to speak, Sara simply inhaled their combined scents, more sheltered and content than she ever had imagined possible.

With the last piece of energy Valentin possessed, he blew out the candles beside the bed, leaving the room in half darkness.

"Peter."

A sleepy murmur answered him.

"If after tonight's adventure, Sara has twins, I promise we'll name one of them after you."

Sara's sleepy giggle made Valentin smile. He breathed in the scent of the people he loved. For the first time in many years, he fell asleep without fearing his dreams.

21

Valentin sat back and listened as Sara practiced the piano in the music room above his study. His body still ached from the excesses of the previous night, but he didn't regret a thing. For the first time in his life, it seemed he had found a way to be at peace with his past. Sara had given him that.

Peter had tried to help him understand the complexity of his feelings about Turkey, but Valentin hadn't wanted to hear his friend's advice. He'd been too busy trying to solve Peter's problems while ignoring his own. Wasn't that always the way? It had taken facing his worst fears to make him realize he needed help.

He had never imagined he would be content with one woman and maybe even the occasional presence of another man in his bed. Sara connected his past and present and held out hope for his future. What more could a man ask for?

His smile died as he went back to work. In his absence, his business worries had not improved. Peter's hard work had prevented any more losses, but they still needed to regain their previous standing. He'd managed to bring back enough money from his contracts in Russia to keep them afloat for another few months but no amount of money could compensate for the gradual loss of trust and general unease he sensed in his customers.

It seemed Aliabad and his partner had been content to wait until Valentin's return to try to complete their plan to ruin him. It only confirmed his suspicions that it was deeply personal. He stared at the scribble of figures on his blotter. He was tired of waiting for them to come to him. Perhaps it was time to force their hand.

As soon as Peter discovered which of his clerks was feeding information to Aliabad's still unknown partner, Valentin would have to act quickly. After her last visit with Evangeline, Sara was convinced it was Sir Richard Pettifer, but Valentin wanted to be sure. He rubbed his hand over his chin. Damnation, did he really want to find out that his father was in league to ruin him?

When his study door was flung open, he looked up with a welcoming smile, expecting it to be Sara. He got slowly to his feet when his father strode into the room.

"Have you seen Anthony?"

Valentin sketched a bow. "Good morning, Father, yes, I am quite well. How is my dear stepmother?"

The marquess slammed his gloves and hat on the desk. "I don't have time for pleasantries. Anthony didn't come home last night."

"He's not a child. Perhaps he went out drinking with his friends and hasn't come to his senses yet?" Valentin glanced at the clock. "It is only ten in the morning."

His father's mouth tightened into a thin line. "Something is wrong. His horse returned to the stable yard last night without him. I fear foul play."

Valentin sat down again and managed a polite smile. "Did you come here to accuse me of murdering your favorite child?"

The marquess stopped his pacing to glare at Valentin. "Of course not!"

He looked old, his face haggard in the early morning light. He visibly gathered his temper. "I thought that as his brother, you might be able to find him more easily than I can."

Valentin crossed one leg over the other.

"How strange, you usually tell me to keep away from him in case I corrupt him with my notions of working for a living."

The sick feeling in Valentin's stomach persisted. If his father was involved in a plot to kill him, this would make an excellent ploy to get Valentin out searching for his little brother and a perfect opportunity for him to walk into a trap.

"Good God, man, do you have to let our past contaminate every conversation we have? Can't you get over it?"

"Can I? Can I forget that you abandoned me to a band of pirates who sold me to a brothel?"

His father flinched as if he had struck him.

Valentin let out a slow breath. Sara would be furious with him if he ruined this opportunity to help his father.

"I apologize, sir. That was uncalled for. I truly wish to move on."

"Valentin. I know we don't always see eye to eye, but . . ." His father hesitated and then faced him. "For god's sake, I lost you and ruined your life. It was hard enough to deal with that and the fact that you believe I abandoned you. I don't think I can bear to let it happen again."

Valentin held his father's anguished gaze. He'd never really admitted to himself that his father might have suffered, too. As a young, arrogant, deeply scarred man, it had been far easier to blame his father than to try to understand his stumbling attempts to make things right again.

"I will certainly do all in my power to ascertain Anthony's whereabouts." He walked around the desk and handed his father his hat and gloves. "I'll send him home as soon as I find him, preferably groveling on his knees for worrying you so."

His father gave a bark of laughter. "I'd just be grateful to see the young pup." He shook Valentin's hand, his expression more hopeful. "Thank you, Valentin. I appreciate it more than I can say."

After he left, Valentin made his way upstairs. He paused at the door of the music room to admire Sara's graceful hands on the keyboard and the way her body swayed in time to the music. Her intensity reminded him of her lovemaking. He truly had chosen a woman who wasn't afraid of embracing and expressing her deepest passions. After she played the last chord, she sat back with a satisfied sigh.

"My father was here." He waited until she gave him her full attention and then walked farther into the room. "Anthony has gone missing."

She swiveled in her seat to stare at him. "Anthony?"

"It might be a false alarm, but the timing strikes me as interesting. One day after I return to London, something happens to a member of my family. Is this a plot set up by my father to lure me out in the open and make me vulnerable? Or has Anthony been taken by someone else who wishes to use him as a bargaining counter."

"What did you say to your father?"

Valentin smiled at her anxious expression. "I told him not to worry and to go home. He is right about one thing; whatever has happened to Anthony, I'm in a far better position to find him than my father is."

Sara got to her feet, her expression resolute. "I wish to help. Tell me what I can do."

He kissed her cheek. "Unfortunately there's nothing we can

do at the moment. I'll get Peter to send out word of Anthony's disappearance. If nothing comes of that, I suspect we'll receive a message fairly soon from whoever is holding him."

"Do you think it has something to do with Aliabad?"

"It bears his despicable stamp, don't you think? Kidnapping a young, defenseless boy who many say bears a striking resemblance to me?"

Sara's face paled, and she clutched Valentin's waistcoat. "We can't leave him with that man. We can't."

Valentin's smile was not pleasant. "Don't worry, love. We won't."

Peter paced the drawing room carpet as he repeated his news to Sara. The clock on the mantelpiece struck four as the meager winter light outside faded into blackness.

"There's no sign of Anthony in all his usual haunts. None of his friends have seen him since last night. He insisted he was too drunk to ride his horse and decided to walk home by himself from White's."

Valentin reappeared, a piece of crumpled paper in his hand. "He's definitely not at home. A street urchin just left this in Bryson's hand at the front door." He unfolded the paper and began to read. "If you wish to see your brother again, bring ten thousand pounds to Madame Helene's tonight at midnight." He looked up at Sara and Peter. "Well, that's clear enough."

"Ten thousand pounds would ruin us, Val." Peter continued his pacing. "If we withdraw such a large sum from the bank or start insisting on payments in full, our customers will panic."

Sara glanced from Peter's tense face to Valentin's cool one. "We don't have ten thousand pounds in the bank anyway." She anticipated Valentin's unasked question. "Your books are unreliable. From my calculations, Mr. Carter has allowed thousands to be bled from the accounts over the past few years."

Peter frowned. "In all the commotion over Anthony, I forgot to mention that Alexander Long was seen entering Sir Richard Pettifer's house last night."

"Despite the fact that Evangeline insisted Sir Richard had no contact with him at all." Sara glanced up at Valentin. "At least that leaves your father in the clear. We can assume his cry for help for Anthony was genuine."

Valentin said nothing, but she sensed a slight relaxation in his posture. She hesitated. "As to the money, there is a thousand pounds settled on me by my grandmother at your bank, Valentin. You are welcome to use those funds."

Valentin sat down by the fire. "That's very kind of you, my dear, but I have absolutely no intention of paying out any money to anyone."

"Of course you don't, Valentin," Sara said. "All we have to do is alert the Turkish authorities and let them handle it."

"Oh, no, I'm don't think we need to involve them." Valentin's tranquil expression belied the cold fury in his eyes. "If Aliabad has Anthony, I'm going to deal with him myself."

Dressed in some of Peter's old clothes, Sara felt more secure than in her skirts. She smoothed her hands over the soft buckskin. Breeches gave her a freedom she had never considered before. Despite their hazardous endeavor, both Valentin and Peter seemed to approve of the sight of her legs. She promised herself that when the threat passed, she would enjoy wearing breeches for her menfolk again.

She followed Valentin into the unlit basement of the house directly behind Madame Helene's. Soft rain fell from a leaden gray sky, making the streets shine in the moonlight. Apparently Madame allowed only a select few of her clients to hold a key to the secret entrance. Valentin, of course, was one.

He touched her arm. "Remember, I'll concentrate on Aliabad while you and Peter try to get Anthony out."

Sara kissed his cheek. "I'll do my best. You will be careful, won't you?"

She felt rather than saw his smile. "Of course. I have no wish to find myself in Aliabad's hands again."

"Are we expecting Mr. Aliabad's partner to show up?"

"If we assume it's Sir Richard Pettifer and not my father, then yes." He opened another door into the corridor and waited until they followed him out. "In fact, I've made sure that Sir Richard is aware of Aliabad's plans tonight, just in case he was kept in the dark. Aliabad has a tendency to betray his associates." He squeezed Sara's hand. "Take your time getting to Madame Helene's apartment. Find out how many men Aliabad has brought with him and where they are stationed. Try to discover what's happened to Madame herself. She'll not tolerate an ugly scandal here—she'll want to help."

After a swift handshake with Peter and a kiss on her cheek, he disappeared into the gloom. With all the courage she could muster, she turned to Peter.

"Shall we go and find Madame first? I'm sure she'll be delighted to see us."

Peter withdrew a knife from his pocket. "As you please, my lady."

Valentin didn't bother to conceal his arrival at Madame's private apartments. A thickset man stepped out of the shadows and proceeded to search him for weapons. He found the pistol Valentin had in his coat pocket but only one of his knives. He passed into the dressing room and onward into the bedroom, deliberately leaving the door ajar.

Valentin came to an abrupt halt as his gaze fastened on Anthony. The scene was gruesomely familiar. Anthony was stripped to the waist, his manacled wrists suspended over his head, the chain attached to the massive four-poster bed. His narrow frame, achingly like Valentin's at that young age, trembled with the effort to keep his head upright. A bloodied whip lay on the cream satin bedcovers near Aliabad's hand.

A cold rage filled Valentin, squeezing his breath so hard he wanted to scream with the pressure. He tore his gaze away from Anthony to find Aliabad watching him.

"He has a look of you, doesn't he?" Aliabad stepped close to Anthony and ruffled his hair. "Although he's not as willing as you were."

"Your memory fails you. I was never willing. I had to be drunk or drugged out of my senses when I knew you were expected. It was the only way they could make me come anywhere near you."

At the sound of Valentin's voice, Anthony's head jerked up.

Valentin strolled closer. Faint whip marks covered his brother's skin. He stank of sweat, fear, sex, and the faint hint of Aliabad's favorite orchid scent.

"Valentin. . . ." Anthony whispered.

He yelped when Aliabad yanked on the chain that suspended his wrists.

"Eventually you came to me and for me willingly, Valentin. You know that."

"I came for you because there was nothing else I could do. I let you rape me and torture me because I was too young to fight back."

Aliabad laughed. "If that makes you feel better, believe it. But we both know what really happened, don't we? And if you don't give me the money I asked for, the whole of London will know how much you liked being fucked by a man."

Valentin shrugged. "As I said before, no one will believe you." He pointed at Anthony. "That's why you became desperate enough to kidnap my half brother." He managed a sneer. "Did you really believe I would waste ten thousand pounds on him?" Anthony's face fell as if Valentin had struck him. "My father dotes on the boy. Don't you think I would rejoice to see him forced into the position I was in?"

For a moment, Aliabad looked uncertain. "I don't believe you."

"If Anthony disappears, my father would never recover. It would certainly pay him back for leaving me with the Turks."

"You forget, I heard that when your ship was boarded, your father fought like a man possessed to keep you. He barely escaped with his life."

Valentin hadn't known that. The whole horrific episode was a blur until he'd found himself trapped in the brothel with Peter. He went across to the fireplace and warmed his hands.

"You still haven't told me exactly what you want." He rested his shoulder against the high mantelpiece, deliberately displaying himself for Aliabad. "If you want my brother, take him. If you want the money, we can negotiate. But you can't have both."

Aliabad moved closer. "You have the money?"

"I have some money." He looked around the room. "Does your business partner know what you've done?"

Sara and Peter crept along the corridor toward Madame Helene's private rooms. The sound of breaking china made them duck into a doorway. A large man came out of Madame's bedroom and walked toward the last door at the end of the passageway.

The man's gruff voice, telling someone to be quiet, floated back to Sara. She nudged Peter. "We have to stop him going back to his post, and we need to see who he is talking to. I wager it is Madame Helene."

Peter balanced in his hand the thick cudgel he'd retrieved from one of Madame's footmen. "Come on, then. You distract him while I knock him out."

Sara took off her white footman's wig and let her hair flow down her back. She walked slowly down the corridor and bumped right into the man. Pretending to hiccup, she grabbed his right arm and hung on as though she'd lost her balance.

"I beg your pardon, sir. I appear to be lost." She licked her lips as she stared into his brutal face. "Are you one of the performers?" She ran her hand over his chest. "Would you like to come back upstairs with me?"

Beyond the man, she could see Madame Helene, her blue eyes furious above her gagged mouth. She'd obviously just kicked over a table and smashed a china vase. Sara gasped as the man's face went blank and he toppled over, sending her to the floor beneath him. By the time she struggled free of his unresisting bulk, Peter had freed Madame Helene.

Madame helped Sara bind and gag the man before he recovered his senses.

"Thank you, my friends. I am delighted to be free." Madame glanced at Sara, her pronounced French accent the only sign of her discomposure. "The Turkish gentleman said he was waiting for Valentin. He had Valentin's brother with him." She rubbed her wrists. "I was unable to warn anyone. It all happened so quickly."

"It's all right, Madame," Sara said. "We know what has occurred."

"Do you need my help?"

"Not unless things get out of hand. Valentin believes he can save his brother without resorting to violence."

"Perhaps I should contact the marquess as well."

Peter nodded. "That is an excellent idea, ma'am."

Assisted by Peter, Madame Helene got to her feet. The felled man groaned and stirred on the ground. She glared at him and kicked him hard in the ribs.

"That is for fondling my breasts when you tied me up." She smoothed her skirt and headed for the corridor.

"I'll make sure I have men close by to help if you need them. Just ring the bell or shout. Someone will answer you."

Sara watched her glide down the passageway as if nothing were wrong. Just after Madame turned the corner, a masked figure dressed in a black coat appeared from the opposite direction and turned quickly into the nearest doorway. Sara ducked down behind a chair and closed the door.

"I think Mr. Aliabad's partner has just arrived! He's gone into Madame's suite of rooms."

Peter crawled over to sit beside her. "Then we'll wait a little while and then follow along behind." He patted Sara's knee. "Between the three of us, we should be able to subdue them."

Valentin tensed as Aliabad walked across to Anthony and tugged on his hair until the boy had to look up. He bent and kissed Anthony on the mouth, his gaze still locked with Valentin's.

Before Valentin could react, the door behind Aliabad opened quietly. If the small masked and cloaked figure was Sir Richard Pettifer, Valentin reckoned he was going mad. Keeping Aliabad's attention on him, he stroked a hand down over his stomach and cupped himself.

"What would you do to have me in Anthony's place? Would you leave my business partner and family in peace if I agreed to come back to Turkey with you?"

Aliabad kept his gaze on Valentin's groin. "As my slave?"

Valentin raised an eyebrow. "Of course." He circled the tip of his cock with his thumb. "I begin to find England too straight-laced for my needs."

Aliabad stepped away from Anthony, his expression triumphant. Before he could speak, another voice interrupted him.

"Why wasn't I informed of this meeting, Yusef?" Evangeline Pettifer threw back the hood of her cloak and ripped off her mask. "Are you trying to double-cross me?"

"He double-crosses everyone, don't you know that?" Valentin bowed. "If you have been foolish enough to involve yourself in his schemes, I can only feel sorry for you."

Evangeline turned on him, a pistol in her hand. "The scheme, as you call it, is mine! You deserve to be ruined, Valentin. I will not allow you to make a new deal with Aliabad. He has already made one with me."

A bead of sweat slid down Aliabad's forehead. "My lady, I was just toying with him. I had no intention of agreeing to his ridiculous demands." He smiled, one wary eye on the gun.

"Then why did you kidnap the boy?" Evangeline pointed at Anthony. "I never agreed to that."

"Because unlike you, Evangeline, Aliabad's not really interested in the money and my business. He simply wants me back in his power. He probably thought that stealing Anthony would make me jealous and eager to exchange myself for him."

Valentin stooped, threw some more wood on the fire, and palmed the knife hidden inside his boot. Evangeline watched him carefully, the heavy pistol held steady between her two gloved hands.

"Why do you hate me so much, Evangeline?" If he could just keep her talking, perhaps Peter and Sara would have time to come to his aid.

She glared right back at him. "Because you don't deserve to be happy."

"Are you jealous because I married Sara?" He frowned as though puzzled. "I believe the attempts to ruin our business started well before that."

"You know why I hate you, Valentin."

"Because I'm a better businessman than Sir Richard?"

Evangeline made an impatient gesture. "Sir Richard is a fool. I run his business and I'm just as capable as you are."

"Are you annoyed with me because I am a man and you

aren't?" Valentin laughed. "That's scarcely my fault. I'm not God. I didn't make the rules that say men are more capable than women."

"But you benefit from them."

"Of course I do. But so do other men. Why me, Evangeline? Why pick on me?"

Her mouth tightened. "You used me to get your business started, Valentin, and then you discarded me like a piece of trash."

Valentin straightened away from the mantelpiece. "I slept with you once ten years ago. You wanted me to marry you. I refused."

"You waited until I'd sorted out your books before discarding me, though, didn't you?"

He felt weary, sick of his old self and his youthful mistakes. How many times was his past going to rise up and taint his future?

"You were sleeping with several men at the time. Why should I have believed you were particularly interested in me? From what I heard, you made the same offer to all the men you fucked."

Her grip on the pistol wavered. "Admit that we could've been successful together, admit that at least."

Valentin sighed. "I don't know. At that time we were too much alike, too hungry and desperate and grasping." He gazed into her eyes. "Can we not end this farce? If I apologize for my lack of thought and admit that you are an extraordinary woman, will you let me be?"

"No, you deserve to pay. I want to see your business ruined, your personal life a subject of scorn, and your wife left to fend for herself on the streets just like I was."

Valentin took a step forward. "Sara has done nothing to you. In truth, she has defied me to be your friend. How can you wish such a fate for her?"

With a practiced hand, Evangeline cocked the gun and pointed it straight at Valentin. "She loves you. Even knowing what kind of a man you are, she loves you. I tried to turn her against you." Her voice rose to a shriek. "I can't bear the thought of her having your children when I can't have any. It should've been me!"

The pistol went off, and Valentin dived to the floor, aware of a sharp sting on his left shoulder. He clamped his hand over the blood that seeped through his coat. By the time the smoke cleared and the roar in his ears subsided, the room seemed to have filled with people. Sara ran to his side, her face a white frozen mask.

"Valentin, are you all right? I heard a shot."

He gripped her upper arm. It took all his strength to speak without his teeth chattering. "I'm fine; go and help Anthony, he needs you."

"Valentin . . ."

"Sara, help Anthony. He won't want any of the men touching him at this moment."

She met his gaze, her eyes filled with horrified understanding.

Valentin concentrated on his breathing while he watched Sara untie his ashen-faced brother. Peter had restrained Aliabad, and Madame Helene's bodyguard held a weeping Evangeline in his grasp.

He tried to stand as another wave of dizziness shuddered through him. Giving up the effort, he fumbled his way across to Evangeline and knelt beside her.

"I never wished to harm you."

She looked at him, her face stained with tears. "But you did. I carried your child, Valentin."

He suddenly found it hard to breathe.

"I made sure I got rid of it, but I've never been able to conceive again. Sir Richard is disappointed in me. He married me to have children. Despite all my efforts to achieve respectability, I'll never have anything to show for it."

Valentin turned away. What could he say? The chances of the child being his were remote. Even in those wild desperate days, he'd always been careful where he left his seed. But if she truly believed it, did it explain her overwhelming desire to destroy him?

"Valentin, you *are* hurt! Peter and I came in just as Evangeline shot at you." Sara touched his face with fingers that shook.

He closed his hand over hers, desperate to feel her warmth. "The bullet grazed my shoulder. I'm sure I'll be fine."

She smiled then, her generous mouth trembling. "I thought she'd killed you." Her gaze faltered as she watched Evangeline being led away. "Was Evangeline truly Aliabad's partner?"

"Apparently so. We knew there had to be someone with intelligence behind Aliabad."

"But why?"

He squeezed her fingers, amazed that he sounded so calm. "I'll explain later. Perhaps we should get Anthony home and decide what to do with Aliabad."

Peter dragged Aliabad into the center of the room. "We could kill him. It would be my pleasure."

Valentin studied his nemesis, who now looked more like a frightened elderly man than a real threat. "I think there are better ways to make him pay." He turned to Madame Helene. "Do you still have that contact down at the dockyard naval office?"

"Yes, I do. In fact, I believe Captain Jackson is upstairs at this very moment. Would you like me to fetch him?"

Aliabad paled. "What are you going to do with me? I am on the ambassador's staff. I will be missed."

Valentin smiled. "I'm not going to do anything. I believe we can safely leave that to Captain Jackson. He's in charge of the Royal Navy press gangs in this area. They are always looking for fit, honest men to sail the seven seas."

Before Aliabad could speak, Peter deftly gagged him and gave him into the hands of Madame Helene's bodyguard. Valentin managed to find a chair to sit in, glad of something solid behind his back. He half closed his eyes as a wave of pain rocked his shoulder.

"Peter, can you take Anthony home?"

"It's all right, Val. The marquess is coming for him." Peter surveyed the rapidly emptying room. "Sara, will you come and help me explain what has happened to Val's father?"

Sara glanced at Val and Anthony. "Of course I will."

It was a struggle to speak into the silence Sara left behind when she closed the door. Val watched as Anthony came closer. Someone had given him a clean shirt. His face looked older, his eyes full of relief. He knelt down and took Valentin's hand in a painful grip.

"Thank you, Val."

"For what? If it wasn't for me, you would never have ended up here in the first place." He tried to sound amused, but it became harder and harder to pull the mask back over his face.

Anthony swallowed. "I won't tell Father anything you wouldn't want him to hear."

Inwardly Valentin groaned. Of course, Anthony had probably received a highly salacious account of his years in Turkey. He decided to be blunt.

"Did Aliabad fuck you?"

Anthony's long eyelashes swept down to conceal his expression. "I survived, Val. I'll forget."

For a heartbeat, they shared an all too intimate glance. Valentin realized his younger brother would never be as innocent again.

"Christ, I'm sorry." He hesitated. "If you need to talk to someone . . ."

Anthony got clumsily to his feet. "I attended a public school.

It's not the first time I've been humiliated by another male, but thanks for the offer."

Voices sounded beyond the closed door. Anthony stiffened and turned back to Val.

"Don't tell Father what happened to me." Val met his brother's determined gaze. "He really doesn't need to know."

"I won't say a thing, but he's not stupid. He might ask you himself."

Anthony shrugged and then grimaced in pain. "Then I'll lie. Just don't . . . tell him."

Val swallowed an unheard-of instinct to take his brother in his arms and hold him until he cried.

"I give you my word."

Anthony nodded. "Thank you, Valentin."

The door opened to admit the marquess, his face as pale and drawn as Val's. He started toward Anthony.

"Are you unharmed?"

Anthony stepped back, his expression remote. "I'm fine."

The marquess glared at Valentin. "This is all your doing. Why didn't you tell me Anthony's ordeal was solely because of you?"

Val briefly closed his eyes. "Because I wanted to sort it out by myself, sir."

"That's so typical of you. How dare you trifle with my son's life?"

"You asked for my help, and may I remind you that he's also my brother."

Anthony walked across and put his hand on Val's uninjured shoulder. His fingers shook as they dug into Val's flesh. "Val *saved* my life. It doesn't really matter how I ended up here. Can't you even be a little bit grateful, Father? He is your son, too."

"Christ, do you think I don't know that?"

The marquess sank down into a chair and covered his face.

His shoulders started to shake. Anthony glanced uncertainly down at Val, who kept his gaze fixed on his father. A single tear glinted on the marquess's fingers.

Val struggled to his feet. "I can only apologize unreservedly for putting you through such hell, sir. I hope in time you will forgive me. Now if you will excuse me, I have to get this trifling wound tended to." He frowned as Anthony, who seemed to have declared himself Val's unwanted champion, started to open his mouth. "He's right. It is my fault. Now go home and hug your mother. I'll wager she'll be so delighted to see you again she won't let you out of her sight for weeks."

He ignored Anthony's outstretched hand and stumbled into Madame's dressing room. Sara and Peter were waiting for him, their expressions neutral. He managed to smile at Peter.

"Perhaps you could help my family get home."

Peter nodded "I'll escort them up to their carriage. I'll also make sure Anthony knows he can talk to me about anything."

After the room cleared, Sara came to sit by Valentin on the love seat. He looked pale, his eyes half closed, and his mouth tight with pain. He sat with his head against the back of the couch, his legs spread out before him. Madame had already sent for the discreet doctor who conveniently lived across the square.

Valentin opened one eye.

"You're still here, then."

She touched his cheek. "Yes, I am."

With a sigh he rested his head on her shoulder. "Don't leave me."

"I don't intend to." She stroked his disordered hair away from his face. "I love you Valentin, I love you just as you are."

He opened his eyes and studied her. "God knows why, but I believe you."

She smiled down at him, hoping he could see the love shining in her eyes. "You've let me be myself, Valentin. Why shouldn't I do the same for you?"

His slow smile was beautiful to see. "You've always struck me as a woman of remarkably good sense, Sara. Now let me kiss you before that damnable doctor arrives to torment me."

She bent her head to kiss him, knowing in her heart that an outright declaration of love from such a complex man might be a long time coming. But like knew like. He completed her. She kissed him again before becoming aware of a discreet coughing sound from the doorway.

Madame Helene stood there with a tall, thin man carrying a large black leather bag.

Valentin sat back. "Ah, doctor. I was just about to tell my wife how much I loved her." He winked at Sara. "But then, as I intend to tell her that every day for the rest of our lives, perhaps she'll forgive the interruption."

Sara simply stared at him as a tear trickled down her face.

He brushed the tear away, his face close to hers, and the emotion in his eyes almost unbearable to see. "I love you, Sara Sokorvsky," he whispered. "I always will."

Kate Pearce turns up the heat as she returns to Regency England with her House of Pleasure series. . . .

A WICKED PROPOSITION . . .

Forced to wed at a young age, Abigail Beecham is tired of living in a sexless marriage. She longs to succumb to the delicious pleasures of pure carnal lust that she has only read about. And if her husband can't satisfy her erotic needs, she's ready to find a man who can. . . .

A WILD PAST . . .

Peter Howard is accustomed to unusual sexual requests. His ten years as a slave in a Turkish brothel left him skilled in sensual delights. But there is little that actually arouses him—until he meets Abigail. Now he longs to tease and torment her until she cries out with pleasure. Maybe then he'll finally experience that exquisite feeling of bliss he so desperately desires. . . .

Please turn the page for an exciting sneak peek of

SIMPLY SINFUL

the second book in Kate Pearce's House of Pleasure series
now on sale!

PROLOGUE

Beecham Hall, Henham, Essex
April 16th, 1817

My dearest James,
    Thank you for the beautiful hothouse flowers and fruit you sent from London to celebrate our wedding anniversary. It was very thoughtful of you.
    You ask if there is anything else you can do for me. I hesitate to write this, but as I see you so rarely it is the only way I can be sure that you will respond to me. There is something you can do. I want you to come home and give me a child.
With fondest love,
Abigail
Lady James Beecham

1

―――――――

"Am I really so pathetic?" Peter Howard murmured.

He turned to his companion and discovered she was attempting to hide a smile. He mock-frowned at her as he refilled his champagne glass from the bottle that sat between them.

"I do not think you pathetic, my friend." Madame Helene toasted him with her glass and then bent to kiss the cheek of the naked young man who lounged at her feet. "Why do you say such a thing?"

Peter gestured at the crowd of revelers in the large public salon behind them. The gold and scarlet décor provided a perfect foil for the more daring members of the *ton*, many of whom were in a state of undress and engaged in riotous sexual pursuits not often seen in public. Madame's exclusive House of Pleasure offered every erotic experience a man or woman might dream of.

"You rule over an excellent establishment, Helene, but there is nothing here that excites me anymore."

Helene put down her glass and began to stroke the young man's long black hair. "What do you crave then? If you can imagine it, I am sure I can provide it."

"I'm not sure I know what I want." Peter noticed a disruption at the far end of the salon where Lord James "Beau" Beecham and his disreputable companions were seated. "Perhaps it is because all my erstwhile drinking companions are settling down. The Harcourt twins are both married and so is Valentin."

Of course, he was still welcome in Sara and Valentin's bed but somehow it no longer seemed enough. He frowned as the noise in the salon increased and looked over his shoulder. Beau Beecham stood on the table now, his hands cupping the breasts of a half-naked inebriated duchess. His cronies shouted crude suggestions as he deftly removed the lady's corset.

When Peter turned back, Joseph, Helene's latest conquest, was trying to crawl onto the chaise lounge between them. Even the sight of Joseph's well-muscled buttocks and erect cock failed to arouse Peter's interest.

"Perhaps I am getting old," Peter said, as Helene ran the tip of her index finger around the crown of Joseph's erection. Her blond hair fell in soft ringlets around her face. Her gown was so sheer that her pert and youthful body looked naked in the candlelight. Peter had no idea of her true age, and he wasn't fool enough to ask.

Joseph moaned as Helene's long nail flicked over his engorged flesh.

"You are not old, *mon ami.*"

"Jaded, then."

Peter drank more champagne. In his thirty-five years he'd probably had more sexual partners than anyone at Madame Helene's. Not all of them by choice. Being enslaved in a Turkish brothel for seven long years had ensured that his sexual expertise was limitless and that he never wanted to be owned or forced by anyone again.

Helene bent her head to lick Joseph's cock, her small pointed tongue as dainty as a kitten's. When she straightened, her lips glistened with pre-cum.

"Jaded, you?" She regarded Peter closely, one hand lazily working Joseph's cock. "Maybe you just want different things."

Peter grimaced. "Like a wife and a family? Who would have me? I'm employed in trade and have no aristocratic blood to make me eligible. The only reason I have an entrée into the *ton* is because of Valentin's high-and-mighty connections."

Lord Valentin Sokorvsky was not only heir to a marquis, he was Peter's best friend and occasional lover. They had been slaves together until their release at the age of eighteen. Their strong bond had helped Peter survive the brutal, sadistic world of the brothel and supported him through the difficult years of his return to the almost-forgotten land of his birth.

Valentin had found a woman who loved and accepted him and his scarred past. Peter had no reason to believe he would find another such paragon. He wasn't even sure if that was what he truly wanted. He'd always enjoyed sex in all its forms, craved it even, but now he found it impossible to decide what he needed.

Helene pushed Joseph away as he tried to suckle at her breast. He slid to the floor in an untidy heap and pouted. She leaned forward to touch Peter's arm. "Do you wish to talk to me privately?"

Peter glanced down at Joseph, who had wrapped a hand around his cock and was busy pumping himself to completion. Joseph would pay for that act of disobedience. Helene preferred to control the sexual outpourings of her chosen lovers.

"No, I think I'll go home and drown my sorrows in a bottle of brandy. I'm sure I'll feel better tomorrow."

Helene stood up and grasped his wrist. "Peter . . ."

He studied the narrow fingers that encircled his wrist like a dainty manacle. "Helene, let me go."

Her grip tightened, and he fought off a now-familiar chok-ing sensation.

"Why? What are you afraid of?"

"That I have become nothing more than a pity fuck for my friends and that that is all I will ever have in my life."

Damnation. He hadn't meant to speak the truth. Strange that after all this time his composure could be shaken so easily. Helene let go of his wrist and stepped back.

He drew in a deep, steadying breath and forced a smile. "Please accept my apologies. I must be drunker than I real-ized."

She nodded, her expression as carefully blank as his own. "Of course. I will accompany you down to the front hall. I need to show my face around the salons again this evening to make sure everything is running smoothly."

Joseph grunted as his cum spurted through his fingers. He-lene swept past him without a glance in a swirl of diaphanous draperies. She snapped her fingers and one of the footmen ap-peared. She pointed at Joseph.

"Please make sure that this 'gentleman' is sent home. And make sure his name is added to the list of those who are no longer welcome here."

"That was rather harsh, Helene." Peter strolled at her side as she began her tour of the large, noisy salon. "He seemed very young." They stopped at the magnificent buffet. Helene picked a fat purple grape and popped it into her mouth.

"Joseph is an ignorant fool. He is too intent on gaining his own pleasure to have any regard for mine." She sighed. "His stamina is remarkable. I thought to train him, but it seems he is simply too selfish to learn."

Peter realized he was almost smiling again. Helene had a gift for understanding men and their less-than-complicated na-tures. "Is that how you see your role? To teach the young males of the *ton* how to bring a woman pleasure?"

She raised an eyebrow. "It is not my primary purpose. But it is a useful one, *non*? Society should be grateful to me rather than pretending I don't exist outside of these doors."

His gaze wandered over the ornate room, the expensive fittings and fixtures, the lavish buffet.

"Is it enough for you, Helene? Is this what you want?"

He frowned. What was wrong with him tonight? When had he ever cared to think of the future? As a slave he had simply endured. But since Valentin's marriage two years ago, he had started to change, started to want something more.

Helene shrugged, the gesture French and totally feminine. "I have built this place with my own hands. It is enough for now."

He nodded as they continued around the perimeter of the room. Like recognized like. In her past were secrets that resonated with Peter. He could understand her deep need to make herself financially secure. She never spoke of her youth, yet he knew she had suffered as much as he and Valentin. She touched his cheek.

"You know that you are welcome to share my bed tonight, if you prefer not to go home."

He swung around to face her, his good humor evaporating. "Did you hear what I said earlier? I refuse to end up in anyone's bed just because they feel sorry for me."

She pouted, her blue eyes filled with amusement. "Actually, I was feeling sorry for myself. With Joseph gone, I have no one to fuck."

He started to laugh. She had a reputation as a voracious lover. He'd never had any desire to find out if the rumor that she could wear out three strong men in a night and still manage a fourth for breakfast was true. He kissed her hand.

"It's an intriguing offer, but I must decline. I have few friends in this world and you are one of them. I'd hate to lose years of friendship over a night of ill-judged passion."

She glanced around the packed salon. "Oh well, I suppose

I'll just have to find someone else. Joseph was black haired so I'll try for a blonde or a redhead."

"Do you collect their scalps as well?"

Helene rapped his knuckles with her fan and headed toward the noisiest corner of the room. "Of course not. I wouldn't have room to display them all." She pressed Peter's arm and pointed at the man who stood on the table in front of them. "What about him?"

"Beau Beecham? I'm surprised you haven't had him already. He seems to have fucked every other woman in town."

Peter studied the tall, commanding figure of Lord James Beecham, the heir presumptive of the childless Duke of Hertford. He wore a dark brown coat that almost matched his eyes and thick curling hair. A black waistcoat, buff breeches and shining top boots completed his immaculate dress.

Helene glanced up at Peter. "You do not like him?"

"I hardly know him. But he has a reputation as a rake and a gambler."

"*Mon Dieu*, he is a devil indeed."

Peter shrugged. "I suppose he is no worse than any other pampered sprig of the nobility."

"But still, you do not like him."

"He treats women despicably and yet they still flock around him like mindless sheep." He groaned. "Dammit, I *am* beginning to sound like a Methodist preacher."

"It is not like you to judge a man so quickly, Peter," Helene murmured. "I know of his reputation but, in truth, he rarely entertains a woman here."

Lord Beecham jumped down from the table and came toward them, a smile on his handsome face.

"Madame Helene, what a pleasure. And may I say that you are looking particularly beautiful tonight?"

Peter pretended to yawn behind his hand before taking out

his pocket watch and studying it. Something about Lord Beecham always set his teeth on edge. Not, God forbid, that he was jealous of the man; his reaction was far more instinctive than that.

"And Mr. Howard, how are you this fine evening?"

"I'm well, my lord." Peter pointedly took Helene's hand and kissed it. "Don't worry about seeing me downstairs. I can find my own way out. Why don't you stay and see if Lord Beecham can manage to come up with something more original to say to you?"

To his surprise, Lord Beecham laughed. "I fear I have drunk too much wine to be original. I'll stick with the tried and tested compliments in case I make an even bigger fool of myself."

Helene smiled at them both. "Why don't we all sit down and share a bottle of wine?"

Peter tried to catch her eye as she towed him inexorably toward a vacant couch. He sat with extremely bad grace. Did Helene expect him to act as her chaperone while she decided whether she intended to offer the insufferable Lord Beecham a space in her bed? Or was it simply some absurd feminine resolve that he and Lord Beecham should be friends? He started to rise.

"Madame, I need to go."

He winced as she kicked him sharply in the ankle. "I'm sure you can spare me a few more minutes of your valuable time, Peter."

He smiled, showing his teeth. "Unlike most of your guests, dear Helene, I have to be at my desk in the morning and it is already past midnight."

"Ah, that's right. You are Valentin Sokorvsky's business partner, aren't you?" Lord Beecham sat forward. Having anticipated an aristocrat's usual distaste for the idea of a man engaging in trade, Peter found he could do nothing but nod.

"Valentin told me to come and talk to you about investing in one of your next cargoes."

Peter faked a smile. "Unfortunately, Lord Sokorvsky is away in Southampton at the moment. I'm sure he will be delighted to attend to you on his return." Helene kicked him again. "Of course, if you are unwilling to wait, I will be in our offices for the next few days."

He handed over his business card. Lord Beecham studied it and then placed it carefully in his pocket.

"You might wonder why I am particularly interested in your company when there are so many other ventures to choose from."

His sudden descent into sobriety intrigued Peter. Lord Beecham either sobered up faster than any man Peter had ever encountered or he had deliberately pretended to be drunker than he was.

"I wish to investigate trade routes to the West Indies. I am particularly interested in companies that do not engage in the traffic of human life."

For the first time, Peter looked directly into the other man's dark eyes. Good God, Lord Beecham seemed sincere. Peter and Valentin had vowed never to trade slaves. Their own experiences would never allow such misery to sit well on their consciences.

He replied automatically, his gaze still locked with the other man's. "You are correct. It is our policy not to deal with the slave traders or their associates."

Lord Beecham nodded as he offered Peter a cigarillo.

"Would it inconvenience you if I called on you tomorrow with my man of business?"

"Not at all." Peter accepted the cigarillo and allowed Lord Beecham to light it for him from his own. "I will be available from noon onward." As Lord Beecham bent toward him, Peter inhaled his spicy cinnamon cologne and a pleasing masculine scent. He blew out a cloud of smoke as the other man continued to watch him.

"Is there something else I can do for you, my lord?"

Lord Beecham sat back, his smile undimmed by Peter's less-than-enthusiastic tone. "A game of cards, perhaps?"

Peter glanced over his shoulder at Lord Beecham's companions, who were still busy fucking the enthusiastic duchess. "Won't you miss your turn?"

He wanted to go home. He wanted to escape the noise, the raw smell of sex and the drunken laughter. Sometimes, if he closed his eyes, he could almost imagine he was back in the brothel. It was hard to remember that everyone at Madame Helene's paid an exorbitant membership fee to be allowed to behave like this.

Lord Beecham continued to study him. "I have no desire to fuck her. In truth, I would much rather play with you."

"Why?" Peter was beyond politeness now.

"Because I have heard you have the luck of the devil at piquet and I would like to see if I can beat you." He shrugged. "Of course, if you are too tired . . ."

Helene clapped her hands. "Peter, you must win Lord Beecham for me." She blew a kiss at Lord Beecham. "If Peter succeeds in beating you, I'll expect to see you in my bed tonight."

To Peter's surprise, Lord Beecham didn't look as delighted as Helene might have expected. Perhaps he too had heard the rumors about what she did to her lovers. Peter thrust his hand into his pocket and brought out a gold coin.

"I'll play for you, Helene. Lord Beecham looks as if he might benefit from your erotic tuition."

He hid a smile. Perhaps he could keep Helene happy and make it another condition of winning that Lord Beecham promised never to approach him again.

Helene beckoned to a footman, who brought over a new pack of cards. Lord Beecham broke the seal and started to sort out the pack.

"I must go and circulate, but please let me know what happens." Helene kissed Peter's cheek and left him facing his adversary. "I will also make certain that your friends don't bother you again, Lord Beecham."

Peter hoped she had seen the promise of retribution in his eyes. Her hasty departure indicated that she had. Lord Beecham glanced after her.

"She is a fascinating woman."

"She is indeed."

Lord Beecham shuffled the pack, his attention fixed on the play of the cards through his long fingers. "Have you bedded her?"

"I haven't had that pleasure."

"I hear she is a demanding bed partner."

Peter raised an eyebrow. "As I said, I wouldn't know. But I'm sure you will soon have your answers, if you survive the night, that is."

Lord Beecham stared at him, a challenge in his dark eyes. "You are so certain you will win then?"

"I very rarely lose."

"But if you lose, will you take my place in Madame's bed?"

"No. You will have to think of something else to claim as your prize." Peter held up a sovereign and tossed the coin in the air. "Call."

Lord Beecham called heads and won, which gave him the slight advantage and the right to deal. Peter accepted the cards he was dealt and settled back to review his hand.

By the time the first hand was played out, he discovered that Lord Beecham was an extremely capable and intelligent opponent. Not as good as he was, but certainly no amateur.

As they continued to play, their end of the salon emptied and the footman doused most of the candles, leaving them in a narrow pool of light. Brandy appeared at Peter's elbow, and he worked his way steadily through the bottle. A clock chimed three in the hallway and he groaned. He had to be at his desk at eight sharp for an important meeting.

His remaining cards blurred in front of his eyes. What the hell was he doing? And why had it seemed so important to beat this particular man? His attention drifted to the silent, intent figure opposite him. Lord Beecham had discarded his coat and cravat and played his cards with the desperate skill and attention of a man risking his entire fortune. Was he really so anxious to avoid Helene's bed?

"It is your turn, Mr. Howard."

Jolted from his thoughts, Peter threw out a card at random. He couldn't miss the flash of triumph on his opponent's face.

"Mr. Howard, I believe I have beaten you."

As Lord Beecham tallied the points, Peter resisted a childish desire to grab the parchment and check the numbers himself. He knew it had to be close but still couldn't quite grasp that he had lost.

There was no sign of Madame Helene. Peter suspected she had found another willing lover and already retired to her suite. He pushed his blond hair back from his face.

"Perhaps I should've asked you exactly what you wanted from me before we started the game."

For the first time since they started playing, Lord Beecham smiled. "It's quite simple. I want more of your time."

"And what exactly does that mean?"

"There is another proposition I wish to discuss with you in private. I require an hour of your time tomorrow night and your guarantee that you will hear me out."

Peter stood up and gestured at the deserted salon. "We are alone. Tell me now and have done with it."

Lord Beecham remained sprawled in his chair, his long muscled legs stretched out in front of him. He tilted his head back until he could see Peter's face. His smile was slow and satisfied.

"I would prefer to talk to you tomorrow when we are both sober."

Peter nodded abruptly. Despite his concerns he was too tired to argue. "I'll be here at ten."

Known only to a select few, these inscrutable men are bound by dangerous desires and enigmatic pasts. They are the Sinners Club. . . .

COLD CALCULATION

Within the circles of British intelligence, Benedict, Lord Keyes, is known for his cold brilliance and strict military demeanor. Yet this icy exterior masks a man of smoldering passion and scorching sexuality who will do anything to keep his past a secret. . . .

SULTRY SATISFACTION

Miss Malinda Keyes refuses to be intimidated by Lord Keyes. In fact, she enjoys a good battle, especially one of erotic wiles and carnal cunning. Determined to expose his lordship's past, she will use every wanton weapon in her arsenal to tease and tempt this sinner into the ultimate sensual surrender. . . .

Please read on for an exciting sneak peek of

Kate Pearce's

TEMPTING A SINNER

coming in August 2014!

1

County of Lincolnshire, 1827

Benedict, Lord Keyes, drew his horse to a halt in front of the dilapidated gates of Alford Park, his ancestral home, and considered his options. He wasn't quite sure why he was here, but the unsigned letter from a well-wisher had sparked his interest. In his profession, once he was on the trail of something, he never gave up until he'd achieved his goal, or caught his man. Or in this case—possibly his woman.

As he turned into the overgrown drive, he noticed smoke belching out of one of the lopsided Elizabethan chimneys. So his source had been correct about one thing. The ramshackle house was definitely inhabited. He doubted his father had forsaken his mansion in Mayfair and decided to take up residence in the county of Lincolnshire. There was no political advantage to be gained here, or anyone to bully. But if his mother's latest missive was correct, and not merely a ploy to force him home, the current Marquis of Alford was suffering from a mysterious ailment that kept him tied to his bed.

From what he remembered of the family history drummed into him as a boy, this decaying manor house had once been the seat of his family's power when trade was with Europe and wool was king. In truth, it resembled a castle rather than a house, ready to repel marauders with its stone towers and partially filled-in moat. The locale was desolate now, and from his observations as he rode north, the population scarce.

The faint sounds of a barking dog reached him from inside the house. He straightened in the saddle and checked that his pistol was primed and ready. This might be his home, but it always paid to be careful. The noise increased in volume as he made his way along the main façade of the timber-and-stone house toward the stables at the rear.

A window swung open above him. He swiveled in the saddle toward the sound, bringing his hand up as the sun struck the multifaceted panes and reflected right back in his eyes. The *crack* of a rifle shot came a second later. Still blinded by the sun, he could do nothing to stop the shock of pain and the blackness of unconsciousness slamming into him and sending him pitching forward onto the ground.

"Oh my goodness, Mally! You've *killed* him!"

Malinda lowered the shotgun and took a deep, steadying breath. Despite the fact that she was trembling like a willow tree, she'd enjoyed aiming at the man coming down the drive as if he owned the place. Even though, officially, he and his family did.

"I aimed at his shoulder, not his heart, Doris. I've merely incapacitated him." She handed the gun over to Jim, the stable hand, and observed the man on the ground. "He'll get up in a moment, I'm sure of it."

She advanced a step, her sister on her heels.

"He's not moving. What have you done?" Doris whispered.

Malinda walked right up to the apparently unconscious figure and used the tip of her riding boot to roll him onto his back.

Even in repose, he was still a handsome devil. Blood stained the upper left side of his immaculately fitted blue coat and was spreading rapidly. His hat had fallen off to reveal the thick corn blond of his hair.

"He's alive. Otherwise he wouldn't be bleeding."

"You're so callous!" Doris moaned and fell to her knees beside the unconscious man. She drew out her lace handkerchief and dabbed ineffectually at his shoulder. "Perhaps he hit his head when he fell."

"That's very likely." Malinda looked behind her at the small audience now gathered by the side door into the hall. "The window distracted him perfectly, Gwen. Will you take the horse around to the stables and ask Mr. McFadden to take care of it but keep it hidden?"

"Yes, Malinda." Unlike her sister, her cousin, Gwen, showed no signs of squeamishness as she stepped over the unconscious man and took hold of the horse's slack reins. "Do you want me to help carry him inside when I come back?"

"No. Jim and Malcolm can take him upstairs before he wakes. You can meet me there." Malinda glanced back at the two men. "Bring him up to the crimson bedchamber, please." She raised her voice. "And remember, if anyone asks if we've seen him, we have not."

Doris moaned again, but she didn't say anything. That was all Malinda could hope for at this particular moment. She knew her sister didn't like her plans for Lord Keyes, but when challenged had been unable to come up with anything better. Justice would be served and Benedict, Lord Keyes, would pay for his sins and the sins of his father whether he liked it or not.

By the time the men carried Keyes up to the already prepared crimson bedchamber, he was stirring. She instructed them to lay him on the large, four-poster bed, and dismissed them to their usual duties. As soon as the door closed behind Jim, she lifted the red velvet bedcovers, withdrew an iron shackle, and locked it securely around Keyes's right ankle. She hoped it would hold him. The chain was old and looked rather rusty in places. It was the best she could manage without going into the village and asking the blacksmith to make her something he would probably wonder why she needed.

She checked his pockets and retrieved a pocketknife, a dagger, his purse, and a very handsome and very lethal pistol.

As soon as his eyes fluttered open and fixed on hers, she raised the pistol. He blinked at her very slowly and licked his lips. "Where am I?"

"You fell from your horse."

His right hand came up to his left shoulder and he groaned. "There's no need to point a gun at me. I'm scarcely in a position to hurt you."

"So you say."

His head fell back onto the pillow and she wondered if he'd swooned again. Without opening his eyes, he murmured, "I promise not to hurt you if you do me a favor in return."

"You're scarcely in a position to bargain, sir, are you?"

"Oh, this is quite an easy favor."

"I doubt it." Malinda tightened her grip on the pistol, but her captive made no effort to reclaim his weapon.

His blue eyes opened, and she tensed. "Am I considered dangerous?"

"Quite possibly."

His brow creased. "What am I supposed to have done?"

"That's a question for your conscience, sir. None of us are without sin."

"But I'm trying to understand why I'm bleeding, and why you're holding me at gunpoint. Have we met before?"

Oh, she wanted to shoot him now. "What do you think?"

"That's the problem." His smile was charming. "I can't seem to think of anything at all."

She scowled at him. "Don't try your tricks on me."

His hand moved gingerly up toward his head. "I'm not." He winced. "Damnation, this is ridiculous. I can't even remember who I am."

Malinda stared at him for a long moment, but he closed his eyes and appeared to lose consciousness again. The door behind her opened. Gwen came in carrying a basin of water and Malinda's medicinal supplies.

"How is our patient?"

Malinda waved at Gwen to speak softly. "He says he doesn't know who he is."

Gwen came to stand alongside her and stared down at the quiet face. "He *did* hit his head. Perhaps he really doesn't remember anything." She glanced at Melinda. "Does that make our task easier or harder?"

"It depends on whether he's lying or not." Malinda rolled up her sleeves. "Let's attend to his wound and make sure he doesn't die before we have a chance to confront him with his misdeeds."

"How are we going to get him out of that coat?" Gwen stroked the sleeve. "It is beautifully made, and clings to him like a second skin."

Malinda smiled and produced the knife she'd just taken from Lord Keyes. "I think we're going to have to cut him out of *everything*, don't you?"

"The poor man will be quite naked."

"And thus unable to run away."

Malinda slit his right sleeve and soon had him out of his shirt, waistcoat, and coat. She was gentle as she moved across to his left side and eased the blood-soaked garments away from his skin. He stirred in his sleep, but didn't awaken. She paused to examine the wound that marred the perfection of his upper arm. From what she could see, the bullet hadn't lodged in his flesh, but had passed through, not hitting the bone, and exited through the muscle at the rear. She would have to make sure no strands of fabric remained in the wound, but otherwise it looked as if he would survive.

"I told you I was a good shot."

"I never doubted it," Gwen said. "After all, you practiced enough."

"As I said, I didn't want to kill him, merely *incapacitate* him a little."

"Then I think you succeeded in your aim—unless he really doesn't know who he is."

Malinda concentrated on washing out the wound and patting some basilicum powder onto the skin. She accepted the bandage Gwen offered her and slowly wound it around Keyes's upper arm and shoulder. Now that his injury had been satisfactorily attended to, she couldn't help but notice how well he'd grown into his frame and how little weight he carried around his middle. He reminded her of one of the king's racehorses, all fine bone and fast thoroughbred mettle.

"Should we take off his boots and breeches?"

Malinda tore her gaze away from the interesting contours of Keyes's abdomen. "Yes, we should."

Gwen paused as she noticed the shackle around Keyes's ankle. "Is that really necessary at this point?"

Malinda's sense of well-being dissipated. "Trust me. He's as slippery as an adder and twice as dangerous." She turned to Gwen. "Don't let his good looks and pleasant manners deceive you. This man is a survivor. He and his loathsome family will stop anyone or anything that gets in their way."

Gwen touched her hand. "It's all right, Malinda, I won't let you down."

She tried to smile at her favorite cousin. "Then don't let your guard slip for a moment. I'll sit by him until he wakes up, and see if his 'memory' has returned. If it has, he should have no difficulty recognizing me this time."

"Are you sure?" Gwen picked up the bowl of water and the bloodstained cloths.

Malinda smoothed down the unbecoming folds of her oldest brown dress. Had she changed that much? If she had, it was Keyes and his damned family who'd caused it. At some level she'd imagined that the moment he locked gazes with her he'd remember her, he'd remember it all. . . .

"Malinda?"

She shook off the old memories and concentrated on the present. She held Lord Keyes captive in his own family home. This time, the odds were in her favor, and she intended to win.

Keyes came awake into a haze of pain and darkness and immediately knew he wasn't safe and that someone was watching him. Had he been captured again? He inhaled the scent of lavender and his confusion increased. A soft hand touched his forehead and then withdrew to be replaced by the blessed coldness of a wet cloth. He sighed and attempted to open his eyes. Something was very wrong, and he didn't know what it was. Instinct told him to remain silent, but he couldn't remember why.

"Where am I?"

"You're quite safe."

He knew that sultry, low-pitched voice, but when had he last heard it? Yesterday, today, ten years ago?

"Where am I?" He repeated his question.

"In bed. You fell from your horse and damaged your shoulder and head. Are you in pain?"

He choked back a laugh. Was he in pain? How could she even ask him that when he was shivering and whimpering like a child?

"I have laudanum to give you."

Thank God. He hated the stuff, but he was beyond that now as agony sliced through his shoulder. He moved restlessly against his pillows, eager to dissipate the pain, but it just made it worse. The woman raised his head so that he could drink the laudanum from a spoon. He took it gratefully, murmuring his thanks, and allowed her to settle him back on his pillows.

Heat flared through his fingers and burned down his spine and he moaned as sweat gathered on his brow. Her hands on him again, stripping back the covers and pressing cold, dripping sponges against his burning skin. He no longer had a sense of time, only that he had to survive this agony because if he died now, he'd die not knowing who he was, or how he'd ended up in this place, and that was simply unacceptable.

The voices changed, and he could no longer sense if that was due to his fever, or that more than one woman was caring for him. Only one of them was distinct; she held him to life, her voice a puzzle he needed to solve.

He woke into darkness, the soft glow of candlelight and the crackle of a wood-burning fire. With some difficulty, he turned his head on his pillow, and spotted a small, dark-haired woman sitting beside the bed. She was reading something, her shoulder turned to the light, and her spectacles perched at the end of her nose. He must have made a sound because she looked up, a smile breaking out on her pleasant face. "You are awake! Are you thirsty, sir?"

Without waiting for him to answer, she came over, picked up the mug beside his bed, and offered it to him. He managed to grasp the cup with his right hand. To his chagrin, it proved impossible to gather the strength to raise it to his lips. With a soft sound, the woman helped him, wrapping one arm around his shoulders and her hand around his and the cup.

"There you are, sir. Drink as much as you need."

He discovered he was extremely thirsty and gulped down the entire cup. She refilled it and he drank more until, with a sigh, he sank back onto his pillows. "Thank you."

His voice sounded rusty with misuse. How long had he lain in this unfamiliar bed? "How long have I been here?"

"About a week. You fell from your horse and developed a fever from your injuries." His helper put the cup down and fussed with his bedcovers and pillows.

"But why—?"

She smiled at him and hurried toward the door. "I must tell the others that you are feeling better!"

With that, she escaped, leaving him to the comforting crackle of the fire. He looked around the room, noticing the closed red velvet curtains and the matching hangings on the four-poster bed. It was obviously a fairly wealthy household: The ceilings were high, and the furniture ornate. There was also a sense of disuse—as if time had stood still and the trappings of a previous generation's grandeur had never been replaced. Something nagged at his brain, something familiar, but the thought vanished before he could latch on to it.

Tentatively, he sat up, wincing as his fingers grazed the goose egg on the side of his head just above his ear. He'd definitely fallen from his horse. His fingers found the edge of a bandage, and he inhaled sharply and studied his shoulder and upper left arm. He recognized the hot, tearing sensation of a bullet wound beneath the bandages.

But why had he been shot?

He took another look around the room. He wasn't on the Continent. He had a vague sense that England was no longer overtly at war with France, so this wasn't the result of a battle. The woman who'd tended him had also been English. Anxiety tightened his gut. He attempted to swing his legs out of the bed only to realize he couldn't. With all his remaining strength he threw back the heavy covers and discovered he was completely naked apart from the shackle on his right leg.

With a groan, he fell back against the mound of pillows. He didn't even have the energy to test the strength of the metal. A soft *click* announced the opening of the door and the return of the woman who'd helped him drink the water.

"Oh, dear, sir, you must be cold!" She drew the covers back over him. "Please try not to set back your recovery with such foolish tricks."

"Where am I?"

She looked at him, her gaze attentive. "Don't you know?"

"Ma'am, at this point in my existence, I don't remember anything."

She cocked her head to one side. "Not even your name?"

He considered that. "No."

"You did bang your head quite badly." She was all sympathy. "My cousin is going to bring you up some nice broth."

"But—"

"Ah, here she is now."

The door opened again, and he stopped speaking as a tall, auburn-haired woman entered carrying a tray. She bore herself like a queen and had a certain air of authority that made him think she was the mistress of the house, and potentially the one who'd planned to keep him chained to his bed. Or was it her bed?

She placed the tray carefully on the table and smiled at the other woman. "Go and have your dinner, Gwen, dear. Jim is outside the door if I need him."

He waited until she finally looked at him, her gaze as searching as his own.

"Do you remember me, sir?"

Another wisp of thought, this time even fainter. "I assume you are the woman who shot me?"

She slowly blinked at him. "What else was I to do?"

"Ask my name and business like any other civilized human being?"

"Ah, but I'm not civilized, and I wasn't expecting visitors." She raised her chin. "I have a right to be wary. The last man who came here tried to force me out of my home."

"Did I look that threatening?"

"Sir, you had a loaded pistol in your hand. I couldn't take the chance that you might be an enemy."

There was no apology in her tone, which might have amused him if he hadn't been her intended victim. She leaned forward and offered him a spoon of gruel, the lavender scent of her soap enfolding him. She wore a thin gold band on her finger, and he wondered where her husband was and whether he was aware of his wife's machinations. It seemed unlikely. He was too hungry not to eat and sipped gratefully at the fragrant broth until he'd emptied the bowl. "Thank you."

She took the bowl away and sat back to study him. "Are you quite certain you don't know who I am?"

He focused his gaze on her interesting face. She'd never be called beautiful. She was all sharp angles, pale porcelain skin, and ruthless determination. "There is something familiar about you, but I just can't remember what it is."

Her lips thinned. "And what is your name?"

"I can't remember that either."

"Why should I believe you?"

His strength deserted him. "You don't have to believe anything. You have me at a disadvantage, chained to my bed. Was that *necessary*?"

"You were delirious, sir. We were worried that you might hurt one of us, or try to get up and wander about before you were well enough."

"And now?"

She rose from her seat. "You're getting better. Isn't that enough?"

"Which is no answer at all." He closed his eyes. "Good night, ma'am. Thank you for your care. I promise not to try to escape tonight."

"That's very good of you, but Jim will be here just in case. Good night, sir."

"Do you know my name?"

She paused at the door and looked back at him. "Does that distress you? Not knowing who you are, and what you've done?"

"Yes." He forced the word out.

"One would think it might be a blessing."

She swept through the door. He distinctly heard the sound of a key in the lock and the low murmur of voices before her footsteps died away.

He closed his eyes, flooded by a terrible wave of helplessness, and cursed in several languages he didn't even know he knew. *Distressed?* He was bloody terrified and she knew it. He took several deep breaths and forced himself to calm down. She knew who he was; he'd wager money on it. Now he just had to find a way to make her tell him.